You Have the Right to Remain Puzzled

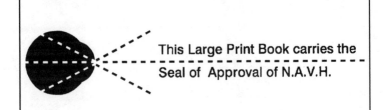

This Large Print Book carries the
Seal of Approval of N.A.V.H.

YOU HAVE THE RIGHT TO REMAIN PUZZLED

A Puzzle Lady Mystery

PARNELL HALL

THORNDIKE PRESS

An imprint of Thomson Gale, a part of The Thomson Corporation

Detroit • New York • San Francisco • New Haven, Conn. • Waterville, Maine • London

Thorndike Press® Large Print Mystery.

The text of this Large Print edition is unabridged.

Other aspects of the book may vary from the original edition.

Set in 16 pt. Plantin.

LIBRARY OF CONGRESS CATALOGING-IN-PUBLICATION DATA

Hall, Parnell.
    You have the right to remain puzzled : a Puzzle Lady mystery / By Parnell Hall.
      p. cm. — (Thorndike press large print mystery)
    ISBN-13: 978-0-7862-9326-1 (hardcover : alk. paper)
    ISBN-10: 0-7862-9326-8 (hardcover : alk. paper) 1. Felton, Cora (Fictitious character) — Fiction. 2. Women detectives — Fiction. 3. Crossword puzzle makers — Fiction. 4. Older women — Fiction. 5. Large type books. I. Title.
PS3558.A37327Y68 2007
813'.54—dc22
                                                                    2006037574

Published in 2007 by arrangement with The Bantam Dell Publishing Group, a division of Random House, Inc.

Printed in the United States of America on permanent paper
10 9 8 7 6 5 4 3 2 1

For Manny,
who makes it look easy

DEAD MAN WALKING

I would like to acknowledge the versatile Manny Nosowsky, who provided the puzzles that appear in this book. In *Stalking the Puzzle Lady,* Manny played the part of the killer. Here he slips into the role of the victim, creating the dead man's puzzles. Lesser constructors might have quaked at the task. Manny laughed in the face of danger. I can't thank him enough.

1

"The wedding's off!"

Sherry Carter punctuated the remark by slamming the door of the red Toyota in which she had just skidded to a stop at the top of the gravel driveway.

Cora Felton, relaxing in a lawn chair, looked up from her Agatha Christie novel and nodded sagely. "Good tactic. I called several of my weddings off before going through with them." She took a drag on her cigarette. Her brow furrowed, as if the nicotine had given her sudden powers of concentration. "At least two or three. Melvin, I called off more than once. I suppose that should have told me something."

Sherry was in no mood for her aunt's rambling reminiscences. "Cora, we're talking about me."

"Of course, dear. I heard you. You're not going to marry Aaron. I quite agree. Aaron's a worthless cad, and you're better off without him. Particularly after what he's done. What *has* he done, by the way?"

"Don't humor me. I hate it when you humor me."

"What can I do that you *don't* hate?"

"Oh, who gives a damn!"

Sherry stormed into the house.

Cora sighed, heaved herself out of the chair. It was late morning, and Cora was clad in her Wicked Witch of the West dress. Her favorite loose, comfortable, lounge-around-home smock, it bore cigarette burns, liquor stains from her less-than-sober past, plus the telltale signs of some none-too-accurately ingested, scrumptiously caloric treats, covering all the essential food groups, such as hot fudge, marshmallow, whipped cream, guacamole, onion dip, ice cream, butter, and maple syrup, in any and all combinations.

Sherry had given up trying to get her aunt to throw away the dress, but strongly cautioned her against wearing it in public, lest unflattering photos should wind up in the tabloid press. Cora had her reputation to uphold. Her benevolent, grandmotherly face graced a nationally syndicated crossword puzzle column. She also did TV ads as the Puzzle Lady, hawking breakfast cereal to schoolchildren. If any kids actually ate it, the joke was on them, since Cora couldn't do a crossword puzzle to save her life. Sherry constructed the puzzles. Cora was much happier poking her nose into mysteries. Real mysteries, involving real crimes. Cora was good at solving crimes.

Not matrimonial affairs.

Cora glanced around the yard, hollered, "Buddy!"

The toy poodle, snoozing in the shade of his favorite elm, stood up, shook himself awake, and trotted toward the house. Cora opened the door and Buddy bounded in.

Sherry wasn't in the living room or the kitchen. Cora pounded down the hall to the office, where her niece was on-line.

"EBay?" Cora asked.

Sherry didn't answer.

"When I break an engagement, I always buy something. To make myself feel better. The expense is directly proportional to the nearness of the wedding and the thickness of the skull of the unintended. Is that the right word? *Unintended?* Or is it *disintended?* Come on, you're good with words. Help me out."

"Cora. I'm not in the mood."

"I noticed." Cora brushed cigarette ash off the sleeve of her smock. "If you weren't so self-absorbed, you might ask why I'm not dressed at eleven in the morning. I haven't been having an easy time myself. If I were drinking, I'd be drunk." She frowned. "That sounds stupid, but you know what I mean."

"Cora, have you heard a word I said?"

"Yeah. You're not getting married, yada, yada, yada. You think you got troubles. I got this nut Benny Southstreet accusing me of swiping his puzzle. Which is pretty funny, since I wouldn't know *how* to steal his puzzle. Which means he's actually accusing *you* of stealing his puzzle. I would think you'd care."

"Damn it, Cora! I just broke up with Aaron!"

"Why? What did Aaron do?"

"You wouldn't understand."

"Right, right. Because I know nothing about men. And I've only been married I don't know how many times. I always think of Melvin as my fifth. But when you count the broken engagements . . . There's a fine line between the ones that were broken before they said *I do* or right after. Of course, legally —"

"Will you *shut up!*"

Sherry turned from the computer to face her aunt. Her eyes were filled with tears.

"Sherry, what happened?"

There came the sound of tires on gravel.

"If that's Aaron, I'm not here," Sherry said.

"Your car's here."

"It's *your* car."

"Weren't you just out in it?"

"I don't want to see him!"

"I got it, I got it."

Cora looked out the living room window.

Dennis Pride, Sherry's abusive ex-husband, was on his way up the walk.

Cora uttered a brief comment, indicating she was not thoroughly pleased with the young man's presence, then slammed out the door to intercept him.

Dennis's hair, though parted and greased back, was long. A little shampoo and he would fit right in with the members of his former rock group, Tune Freaks. Cora suspected Dennis of playing with them on the sly.

Cora blocked his path. "Sherry's not here."

"Her car's here."

"That's what I told her. She still insists she's not here. Probably because *you're* here. Why don't you leave? Then when I tell her you're not here, I'll be telling the truth."

Dennis scowled. "It isn't funny."

"No, it isn't. Your ex-wife is getting married. You're about the last person she needs to see right now."

"I have to talk to her."

"She doesn't have to talk to you. And she's got a restraining order to prove it. Get out of here, or I'll call the cops."

A VW Beetle drove up the driveway. A young woman got out. She was the type college boys would describe as *comfortable* or *pleasingly plump.*

Those qualities were not on exhibit now. Brenda was visibly upset. "Damn it, Dennis! I thought you'd learned your lesson."

Dennis wheeled away angrily and almost lost his balance. Cora wondered if he'd been drinking.

Brenda assumed he had. "Dennis, you're drunk. You must be to come here. She's your ex-wife, Dennis. Your *first* ex-wife. I'll be your second if you keep this up. Is that what you want, Dennis? Is that what you'd like? I don't want to keep you if you want to go. What do you want to do?"

"Just shut up, will you!"

"Oh, nice! That's the way to talk to your wife!"

Sherry Carter stormed out the front door. "Great. The two of you together. Brenda, you're my best friend and I love you, but if you can't control your husband I'm going to lose it. Just because your marriage isn't working is no reason to ruin mine."

"Exactly," Dennis agreed.

"Not to *you,* damn it. My upcoming marriage. My pending marriage. My marriage that may not come off if you won't leave me alone."

"Then you *do* still have feelings for Dennis," Brenda charged.

Sherry took a deep breath. Her eyes blazed. "Yes, I have feelings for Dennis. And, believe me, they aren't love. I am so angry I am about to explode. I'm yelling at Cora. I'm yelling at Aaron. I'm yelling at you. I don't want to yell at you. I just want to be left alone."

A car rattled up the driveway.

"Oh, what is this — Times Square?" Sherry exclaimed.

A young woman in a beige business suit climbed out. Her blond hair was piled up on her head. Her earrings were simple gold studs. Her subtle makeup set off a fashion model face.

Becky Baldwin looked around at the gathering on the lawn. "Did I come at a bad time?"

Sherry, Brenda, and Dennis glared at her.

Only Cora Felton smiled. "Join the fun, Becky. We were just discussing the wedding plans. Or lack of them. I'm sure you'll get a kick out of it."

"Actually, I came to see you." Becky looked Cora up and down. "But if you're not well . . ."

"I'm just fine, thank you," Cora said. "What could you possibly want?"

"Whatever it is, could you take it somewhere else," Dennis snarled. "We're having a serious conversation."

"We're having nothing of the kind," Sherry said. "The sooner these people leave, the better. Stick around, Becky. I want to talk to you anyway."

"Oh? What about?"

"Here he comes now," Cora said, pointing to the Honda skidding up the driveway.

Aaron Grant vaulted out of the car, snagging the pocket of his sports jacket on the door. The young reporter didn't notice. He glared at Dennis, set his lips in a firm line.

Sherry Carter threw her hands up in the air.

Cora waved Aaron over. "Come on in, Aaron. It's a fraternity stunt. We're trying to see how many cars we can fit in the driveway."

Aaron was in no mood to joke. Aside from Cora, that made it unanimous.

"Sherry," Aaron said.

Sherry turned her back.

"She doesn't want to talk to you," Dennis said.

Aaron wheeled, pointed his finger. "You keep out of this!"

"Says who?" Dennis challenged.

Brenda grabbed his arm. "Dennis!"

He brushed her off like a fly. "Wanna make something out of it, paperboy?"

"Sherry's a big girl. If she wants you here, fine. If she doesn't, I suggest you leave."

"Oh, now you're telling me what Sherry wants?"

"No, she can speak for herself. Sherry, you want this 'gentleman' here?"

"That's right," Sherry said. "Throw it all on me."

"Well, if you won't say what you want . . ."

"Are you enjoying this, Sherry?" Brenda asked. "Having them fight over you?"

"Yeah, Bren, it's a real blast."

Cora raised her eyebrows at Becky Baldwin. "Before World War III breaks out, you wanna tell me what's up?"

Becky swung into conciliatory mode. She put her hand on Cora's shoulder, led her aside. "I came in person because I wanted to warn you."

Cora's eyes narrowed. "Warn me about what?"

Becky took a breath. "Benny Southstreet."

"That twerp!"

"Just a friendly hint. In legal proceedings,

it's generally unwise to refer to the opposing party as a twerp."

"Opposing party?"

"Benny has retained my services."

"What!?"

"He's accusing you of plagiarism. He's suing you for damages."

"You're *suing* me?" Cora said incredulously.

"*I'm* not suing you, Cora. Benny is."

"And you're *helping* him?"

"He retained me."

"But you're *my* attorney. There's a conflict of interest."

"I'm not your attorney at the moment."

"But you have been in the past."

"That's no bar to my present employment."

"What about your conscience? Do you have to take every case that comes along?"

"My portfolio's a little thin. I happen to need the work."

"You can't need it that bad."

"It's a small town, Cora. I have two clients. One's Benny. The other's a speeder who hopes to avoid getting points on her license. I don't see her as a cash cow."

"So you wanna get rich suing me? Whaddya get? A third of whatever you bilk me out of?"

"You must have insurance."

"I have homeowner's insurance. I'm not sure it covers plagiarism."

"Maybe not, but Granville Grains has deep pockets."

Cora's eyes widened. "How in the world can you sue them?"

"You're the Puzzle Lady. They use your image to sell their cereal. If that image is built on an unfounded premise, they're guilty of false advertising."

"Oh, for Christ's sake!"

"This is a no-brainer, Cora. Did you steal a crossword puzzle from this guy?"

"You're asking me to incriminate myself?"

"Off the record."

"Off the record, on the record, I can't begin to tell you how I didn't."

"So, what's the big deal? Guy says you did, you say you didn't, he can't prove it, end of case."

"Does your client know what you think of his chances?"

"I didn't say his chances are bad. I just said he can't prove anything. That doesn't mean Granville Grains won't pay him off to make him go away."

"And you wonder why there are lawyer jokes," Cora grumbled.

There came the sound of more tires on

gravel. Cora looked up to see two police cars swinging into the drive.

"Ah! Excellent!" Cora clapped her hands together, strode back to the unhappy throng. "Dennis! Good news! The cops are here. I hope they have a tape measure. What is it, a hundred yards you're supposed to keep away from Sherry? I think you might be a little close."

Dennis's face twisted in rage. "Damn it, Sherry! You called the cops?"

"Don't be silly," Brenda said. "How could she call? She's been right here the whole time."

"*He* wasn't!" Dennis stabbed an accusing finger at Aaron. "He called 'em from his car!"

Aaron stuck out his chin. "I don't need anybody's help to deal with you."

Dennis sneered. "Like hell! Big man! Called for backup!"

Two cops came up the drive. Dan Finley, an impressionable young officer, and actually a Puzzle Lady fan. And Dale Harper, the Bakerhaven chief of police.

Cora knew both men well. She had cooperated with the police on several occasions, though *cooperated* was perhaps the wrong word.

The two officers seemed somewhat taken

aback by the crowd on the lawn.

Cora pressed forward. "Hi, Chief. Hi, Dan. Good to see you." She jerked her thumb at Dennis. "Unless you're blocking this son of a bitch's car. He was just leaving."

Chief Harper didn't crack a smile. In fact, he looked rather unhappy. "Cora Felton," he began.

"My, my, how formal," Cora said.

Chief Harper pulled a piece of paper from his pocket. "I have a warrant for your arrest."

Dan Finley took out his handcuffs, snapped one around Cora's wrist. "Sorry. Just doing my job. Cora Felton, you are under arrest for the murder of Benny Southstreet."

Cora's mouth fell open. "What!?"

"You have the right to remain silent. Should you give up the right to remain silent —"

Cora gave up the right to remain silent. Neighbors down the road could attest to the fact, as well as to the colorful metaphors and similes and malapropisms with which she congratulated the officers on their chosen profession, and suggested truly ingenious uses they might find for their warrant.

2

One week earlier.

"Congratulations!" Harvey Beerbaum was beaming. The portly cruciverbalist could not have been more pleased had he just won the American Crossword Puzzle Tournament.

Cora Felton, emerging from Cushman's Bake Shop with a skim latte and a cranberry scone, stopped and frowned. "Congratulations on what?"

"The wedding, of course."

Cora suppressed a smile. Harvey Beerbaum was a whiz with words, but amazingly gauche at social graces. "Sherry's not my daughter, she's my niece. I'm not sure I deserve congratulations."

"Well, you deserve something. It's a momentous occasion."

"It's not *my* occasion. Sherry's the one getting married, not me."

"That's hardly my fault," Harvey observed, then blushed furiously.

Cora figured that was probably true. While Harvey had never actually proposed marriage to her, in his tentative, roundabout, thoroughly exasperating manner, he had certainly indicated his eagerness to do so, given the slightest encouragement. Cora was fairly sure she'd never offered any. Particularly since she'd given up drinking.

Seeing his veiled hint had once again failed to get a rise out of Cora, Harvey ventured, "Have they set the date?"

"No, they haven't."

"Oh? How come?"

"He hasn't asked her yet."

Harvey blinked. "But . . ."

"But what?"

"I heard they were engaged."

"Oh, they are. He just doesn't know it yet. That's not important. I've married men who didn't know it till they reached the altar."

Harvey looked positively scandalized.

Cora took a slurp of her latte.

"Ah, I'm keeping you from your coffee," Harvey said.

"No, actually I'm keeping you from yours."

Harvey's eyes flicked toward the bakery. Cora could read his mind. Having failed once again to satisfy his heart, he was looking to satisfy his stomach. Harvey murmured his excuses, and went into the bakeshop.

Cora saluted his departure with her latte, and congratulated herself on her powers of deception. In point of fact, Sherry and Aaron hadn't set the date because Sherry was having last-minute jitters. That was no big deal. Cora had *always* had last-minute jitters when contemplating matrimony. There were so many points to consider. Was the gentleman one considered espousing even marginally better than the specimen one had just divested oneself of? Was the loss of alimony of the outgoing more than offset by the income of the incoming?

Cora smiled at the remembrance of the old turn of phrase, which had occurred to her in between some sequence of husbands or other in one of her more sober moments. The term *incoming,* neat enough in itself, also conjured up the image of a nuclear attack. Cora furrowed her brow, trying to recollect which of her husbands had deserved the comparison to an ICBM. Henry, surely, though he'd had other flaws. As had they all.

"Miss Felton."

Roused from her musing, Cora looked up to find a woman with a stroller, one of the

24

gaggle of young mothers who hung out in the bakeshop to swap stories of Junior's latest whatever. Cora always regretted not having children. Not enough to *have* children, but still. She enjoyed the idea of someone else having children.

The mother in question had short-cut blond hair, a thin, attractively anemic-looking face, and anxious eyes of a greenish-blue variety.

The child in question was in that gray area between not-capable-of-taking-that-first-step and rushing-headlong-across-the-busy-street. It was dressed in a neutral tan playsuit, offering no useful clue as to its gender. Cora had trouble telling the difference, which was one reason why she had always begged off babysitting. One of many reasons.

Cora was mentally loading up phrases like *your baby* in case the mother didn't offer an appellation, or the name was equally androgynous, like *Pat* or *Shelly.* She was also wracking her brain for the least clue as to the woman's identity. Cora had seen her many times. Surely, one of the other young moms had addressed her by name. If so, Cora couldn't recall it.

Cora dug into her vast vat of knowledge for some mode of address that would not frighten the woman.

"Yes?"

That frightened her. "Oh, dear," the woman said. "You have your coffee. I'm intruding."

"Don't be silly," Cora said. "You have your coffee too. At least I'm not trying to push a stroller."

The young mother had a Styrofoam coffee cup in one hand, a paper bag in the other. "Yes, but you're not intruding on me. Oh, dear, I mean . . . I'm not sure what I mean."

The bench outside Cushman's window was unoccupied.

"Why don't you sit down and tell me briefly what the trouble is?"

As if on cue, the baby began to bawl at the top of its lungs. The young mother looked mortified. "Oh, dear. Stop it, Darlene."

Ah. There was a silver lining to the ear-piercing cloud. Darlene. Cora filed the information away. The baby was a girl. Either that, or destined for a rather rocky childhood.

The young woman balanced her coffee on the windowsill. Took a muffin out of the paper bag, tore off a piece, and handed it to the screaming infant. "Here, Darlene. Have some nice blueberry muffin."

Have some nice years of therapy, Cora

thought, when the spoiled brat grows up and life kicks her in the teeth.

Darlene batted the piece of muffin away, and did a wonderful impression of an untuned steam calliope.

"Nice kid," Cora said.

Darlene's mother flushed, held out a pacifier. Darlene looked like she might have hurled the thing in the street had her mother stuck it firmly in her mouth.

Cora bent down, said, "What seems to be the trouble?"

Darlene instantly stopped crying, and tried to snatch off Cora's glasses.

"Not so fast, young lady." Cora waggled her finger in front of the baby's face, then smiled at the mother. "You were saying?"

The woman stared at her. "How did you do that?"

Cora shrugged. "She probably recognized me from TV." At the woman's expression, she added, "I'm kidding. Anyway, before she starts up again, what *do* you want?"

"It seems so stupid. . . ."

"I'll be the judge of that."

"All right. I have to talk to someone. I feel so terrible."

"Why?"

"Deceiving my husband."

Cora practically rubbed her hands together. This was more like it. Instead of feigning interest, she found herself feigning indifference. "Go on."

"He's such a good man. A good husband and father and provider."

"What's his name?"

"Oh, I'm sorry. His name is Chuck. Chuck Dillinger. And I'm Mimi."

"What does Chuck do?"

"He's a lawyer. A malpractice attorney."

"Chuck sues doctors."

"No, he defends them."

"Oh? Is that profitable?"

"Very."

"There's that many lousy doctors?"

"It's not a case of bad doctors. It's a case where, despite the best possible medical attention —"

Cora put up her hand. "Save it for the judge. The point is, Chuck has a lot of clients."

"His firm does. They're on a yearly retainer."

"From a doctor?"

"No. An insurance company."

"Figures."

"Insurance companies get zapped with huge malpractice suits. If Chuck can win even one, he justifies his employment."

"I take it he has no problem doing that."

"Absolutely. Chuck's very clever."

"So he does well?"

"For the firm, sure. He'll do a lot better when he makes partner."

These details were fascinating, but not salacious. "You mentioned deceiving him," Cora prompted.

"Yes. I feel so awful. . . ."

"Of course you do. Why don't you tell me how it happened?" Cora tried not to sound too eager.

"Chuck works in the City. Commutes every day. I drop him off at the train station. Pick him up at night."

"And the rest of the day you're alone."

"Yes. Except for Darlene."

"I think I get the picture."

"It just seems so bad. Him taking the train. And leaving me the car to get around. I didn't mean to lie to him. But I was weak. I couldn't bring myself to tell."

"Why are you telling him now?"

"I have to. I have no choice."

"I think I can help you."

"You can?"

"I don't know. But I'll give it a shot." Cora was all sympathetic encouragement. "It's not the end of the world, you know. You're young. You're foolish. You made a mistake. You'd like to put it behind you and move on.

Unfortunately, the young man in question is a jerk. He doesn't want to let you go, and he's blackmailing you. If you break it off, he'll tell your husband. You're terrified the whole thing will come out, but there's no help for it. And if the secret's going to break, the only chance to save your marriage is if you tell it first."

The woman's face twisted in revulsion. "That's *terrible!*"

"Yes, it is. But it doesn't have to end that way. I've had certain experience in these matters. If you'd like me to have a talk with the young gentleman, I'd be happy to do so." Cora smiled. "He just might change his point of view."

The young mother stooped down and tied the cap onto Darlene's head, as if to keep the baby from hearing the sordid details of Mommy's life. "That's not what I want at all."

"It's not a question of what you want, it's a question of what you can get away with. When your lover's a creep — and, believe me, most of them are creeps —"

The woman shot to her feet. "Damn it!" she cried. "I am not having an affair!"

The Reverend Kimble, heading into the bakeshop, stopped in mid-stride and his mouth fell open. He cleared his throat in embarrassment and said, "Hello, Cora. Hello, Mimi."

Mimi blushed furiously, and readjusted the baby's hat.

"Hey, Rev," Cora said. "You gonna be in later? I need to see you about a wedding."

The reverend was now thoroughly flustered. "You're getting married?"

"Not me. Sherry. Never mind, Rev. I'll drop by the church. Go get your caffeine."

The reverend went into the shop.

Cora wheeled on Mimi. "What do you mean you're *not* having an affair?"

"I'm not. What a terrible thing to say! How am I ever going to face the reverend?"

"Oh, he'll get over it." Cora wasn't sure *she* would. She wondered what the penalty was for killing a young mother. "So what the hell are you upset about?"

"The car."

"What about the car?"

"I backed into a light pole. In the mall. One of the ones with cement around the bottom. I missed the taillight, but I dented the fender. Squashed it, really. Had to be banged out. Repainted. You know how expensive that is? I'm still paying it off. Anyway, the dent was on the driver's side. I angled the car in our driveway, so Chuck wouldn't see it when I drove him to the station. Then I went straight to a garage. And you know how much they charged for just one little dent? If I told him right away it wouldn't have been so bad, but the longer I wait the worse it gets. And now he's gonna find out."

"Why?" Cora demanded.

"The car's due for inspection. Chuck always takes it in. The body shop did good work, but it's not like it doesn't show. The inspector will ask Chuck about the accident."

"No, he won't," Cora said irritably. "All they care about is that you pass the emissions test, and pay an exorbitant price for a few irrelevant parts. They couldn't care less about your damn dent."

"No. I have to tell him."

"Okay, so tell him. You don't need me."

"Yes, I do. It's important. I want to make it special. Let Chuck know I care. You said you'd help me. And it would be so easy for you."

Cora scowled. "What would be so easy for me?"

Mimi smiled. "To make a little crossword puzzle. Just for Chuck."

3

Dan Finley was holding down the police station when Cora Felton came in. Apparently, it wasn't that tough a job. The young officer was playing solitaire.

"Red seven on black eight," Cora kibitzed.

"Hi, Miss Felton. What's up?"

"I was gonna ask you the same thing. Isn't anybody killing anybody anymore?"

Dan grinned. "Not at the moment. Things are slow."

"Where's the chief?"

"In his office."

"Working?"

"Most likely taking a nap. But you didn't hear it from me."

Cora stuck her head in Dale Harper's private office, found the chief on the phone. She mouthed, "Sorry," and started to close the door, but he waved her in.

Cora flopped into a chair, hoping the chief was involved in some high-level intrigue. He was writing on a legal pad, which looked promising.

"Uh-huh. Uh-huh," the chief said. "And a pint of sour cream."

Cora figured that probably wasn't life or death.

Harper hung up the phone. "So, whaddya want?"

"What makes you think I want something?"

"You're not smoking."

"Oh?"

"When I want something, you're lighting up, looking around for an ashtray, telling me if you can't smoke in here you'll take it outside. When you want something, you're polite."

"Gee, Chief. Are you accusing me of being manipulative?"

"Heaven forbid." Chief Harper leaned back in his chair, sipped his coffee. A crumpled muffin paper was on the desk. Most likely from a blueberry ginger, his latest muffin of choice. "So what do you need help with? Sherry's wedding?"

"How come everybody knows about that? It hasn't been announced yet."

"This is a small town. If you have to learn something by reading the paper, it means you haven't been paying attention."

"That will be bad news for the groom. He kind of depends on people reading the paper."

"I wouldn't worry about it. I doubt if the *Gazette*'s circulation's changed much in twenty years. So what's up? This just a social call?"

"I'm bored. Nobody's tried to kill anybody recently. Not that I wish anyone ill. Still, if someone had to die, it wouldn't hurt if it was in your jurisdiction."

"So you could solve it for me?"

"Not at all, Chief. But it would give me something to think about. Aside from this damn wedding."

Chief Harper's eyes narrowed. "Damn wedding? You're not happy about the match?"

"Of course I'm happy about the match. They're perfect for each other. If they'd get over their petty jealousies. Which is no sure thing. Aaron's hung up on her ex-husband. Sherry keeps looking over her shoulder at Becky Baldwin."

"Can you blame them?"

"Of course I blame them. They're young. They're in love. They should be oblivious to such things while caught in the throes of animal passion." Cora found Chief Harper blushing furiously. "Or so I'm told."

"Where are they going to live?"

"They haven't worked that out yet."

"You're kidding."

"Actually, *I* haven't worked it out yet. Aaron's moving in with Sherry. He practically has anyway. Which is not a problem, until it becomes official. As soon as it does, I'm the spinster aunt in the guest room."

"I don't think anyone would call you a spinster aunt."

"I'm glad to hear it. The point is, I can't see me staying there after they're married. No one's asked me to move out. I just don't know where I'd go. My apartment's sublet. I'd have to get it back. I'm not sure how hard it is to boot people in that situation. They've been there a couple of years. They think they got license. I don't know how to evict them. I might have to marry a real estate lawyer."

"I'm glad you can joke about it."

"Who's joking? I've married men for less. And a lawyer ought to have some money." Cora dug in her floppy drawstring purse, pulled out a pack of cigarettes.

"You can't smoke in here."

"Yeah, but you're not going to give me what I want. So what's the difference?"

"You're not making much sense."

"No, I'm not. If I hadn't given up drinking, I'd get drunk. If I hadn't given up men . . . Well, never mind. I haven't given up men. There's just none on the horizon." Cora sighed. "You know how desperate I am? I thought one of the women at the bakeshop was having an affair, and I offered to help her."

"You offered to help her have an affair?"

"No. I offered to deal with the black-mailer."

"You really shouldn't be telling me this."

"It's all right. There's no blackmailer. There's no affair. She just ran into a tree."

"What?"

"Not a tree. A pole." Cora waggled her hand. "It doesn't matter. Anyway, I said I'd help her before I knew what it was all about. Now I'm stuck with breaking it to her husband that she dented the car."

"That doesn't sound hard."

"It's a snooze, that's what it is. Come on, Chief. Don't you have something you need to know? I'd be happy to dig it out. I'm going stir-crazy."

Chief Harper picked up the phone and pressed the intercom.

Dan Finley answered in the other room. "Yeah, Chief?"

"Dan, you got the file on the Wilbur case?"

"Excuse me?"

"Yeah. The Wilbur file. Could you bring that in here?"

"Are you kidding me?"

"Thanks, Dan." Chief Harper hung up the phone.

"What's the Wilbur case?" Cora demanded.

"You wanna look into something, this is it."

Dan Finley came in the door. "You sure you want the Wilbur case?"

"Don't oversell it, Dan. Your skepticism is noted."

"What's the case?" Cora asked.

"Unsolved robbery. Been kicking around for a year now."

"It's still open?"

"In a manner of speaking."

"I don't understand."

"The thing that keeps this case open, instead of sinking into the depths of the great unsolved, every month or two Mr. Wilbur comes in and refiles the complaint."

"Can he do that?"

"I have no idea. But short of arresting him or throwing him out of my office, I don't know how to stop him."

"Who is he?"

"Antiques dealer. Has a shop just out of town. With the broken wagon wheel sign."

"Oh, him. So what does he claim was stolen?"

"His chairs."

"What chairs?"

"He bought some chairs at auction. Had 'em delivered to his shop."

"And?"

"Someone stole 'em."

"When?"

"If I knew that, I might be able to solve this crime."

"He doesn't know when the robbery took place?"

"He has a barn out back. He stores stuff not immediately for sale."

"The chairs weren't immediately for sale?"

"Stick with me here. No, they weren't. They were rattan, wicker-back chairs. Needed refinishing. Wilbur intended to get 'em done, never got to it. Next time he looked for 'em, they were gone."

"And that period of time would be?"

"Anybody's guess. The best we can tell, the auction was in April, Wilbur filed his first complaint in May."

"A month later?"

"Thirteen months later."

Cora cocked her head. "I can't see why you haven't solved this case, Chief."

Dan Finley's smile was enormous. "You

giving it to her? He's due to come in any day now. Can I say we gave it to her?"

"You can say we consulted an expert. Not that it will matter." Chief Harper picked up his coffee cup, smiled with satisfaction. "I imagine by then he and Cora will have become good friends."

4

The broken wagon wheel sign was the only thing Cora remembered about Wilbur's Antiques. This was not surprising. The white, two-story frame building looked exactly like ninety percent of the houses on the main street of Bakerhaven, which differed from each other only in their choice of black or green shutters. Wilbur had opted for green, the same color as the paint on his sign, which was short and to the point: **ANTIQUES**, it declared, in upper- and lowercase script. The *A* had a pointed top rather than round. The sign was rectangular, about a third wider than it was high.

The sign perched on the broken wagon wheel, which was missing at least two of its spokes. Any missing from the top half would have been hidden by the sign. The wagon wheel was held up by two-by-fours, which kept it at a slight angle from the perpendicular.

Cora pulled up next to the curb and stopped. Her red Toyota was the only car on the block. Apparently, the sign was not packing them in. Cora walked over and peered at the back of the sign, noted that the top spokes were all there. She continued along the front of the house until she could see the barn behind. It was white with green trim. The scene of the crime.

Cora reined herself in. Mustn't make fun. This was important to the gentleman, needed to be treated seriously.

Cora went up the front steps. The windows on either side were not promising. One held a rather ratty Christmas wreath. The other a green vase. Neither instilled in Cora the desire to buy anything.

The front door was wood, not glass, allowing no view of the treasures within. It was also locked. Cora could understand why a man who'd been robbed might be security conscious; still, the whole setup didn't seem conducive to sales. Cora couldn't help wondering how long it had been since anyone had actually *bought* an antique there.

Cora knocked on the door. There was no answer. She knocked again. It seemed from somewhere deep within a faint voice said, "Coming," but it might have been a TV, a creaking floorboard, or her imagination.

The door was flung open by a man Cora knew. Or at least recognized. She had seen him eating lunch in the Wicker Basket, dinner in the Country Kitchen, a muffin in Cushman's Bake Shop. In fact, Cora couldn't recall a time she *hadn't* seen him eating. In light of which, he was most unfairly thin. His face was also most unfairly unwrinkled, considering his age, which had to be close to ninety. He had suspicious eyes, and a narrow line of a mouth that turned down at the corners. It was hard to imagine anyone buying anything from him.

His manner was not welcoming. "What do you want?" he croaked. It was the vocal equivalent of Dorian Gray — only his voice had aged.

"I want to help you," Cora said.

That took him aback. Whatever he'd expected, that wasn't it. He made no move to invite her in. Instead he seemed even more suspicious. "Help me what?"

"I understand you had a theft. Several chairs were taken. So far the police have no leads."

"You want me to hire you to find my chairs?"

"No."

"Then what's it to you?"

"It's a puzzle. I like puzzles."

"Right. You're the crossword puzzle person."

"Yes."

"I don't see the connection."

"There's no connection."

"Then why are you here?"

"I asked Chief Harper if he had any cases he needed help with. He told me about your robbery."

"Oh, so he's given up, has he? Palmed me off on you?"

It was all Cora could do to keep her frozen smile in place. "I prefer to think he called in an expert."

"If he had, he'd be paying you. He paying you?"

"No, he isn't."

"There you are."

"Yes, I am." Cora smiled. "I'm sorry, Mr. Wilbur, but your case isn't interesting enough for me to put up with abuse."

Cora turned, went down the front steps.

Wilbur was caught off-guard. "Hey! Hey!" He stumbled out on the stoop after her.

The door slammed.

Wilbur stopped dead, let out a string of invectives that would have befitted a drill sergeant welcoming the raw recruits.

Cora smiled up at him from the foot of the steps. "I take it you don't have your keys?"

Wilbur compared her to creatures of limited intelligence but impressive sexual prowess.

Cora waited for him to sputter to a halt, then suggested, "How about a back window? You got a ladder?"

Wilbur seemed on the verge of suggesting unorthodox uses for the ladder. Instead he muttered, "In the barn." He clomped down the steps and trudged in that direction.

Cora tagged along behind.

Wilbur reached the barn door, picked up a rock. He turned back to Cora. "You planning on robbing me?"

"It wasn't on my agenda."

Wilbur smashed a pane of glass with the rock, reached in, and unlocked the door.

"Is that how they stole your chairs?"

"Didn't you read the report?"

Wilbur disappeared inside the barn, was back a moment later with a metal extension ladder.

"I read the report," Cora said.

"Then you know."

Wilbur dragged the ladder over to the house. It was built on a slope, so the back windows were higher than the front. Unopened, the ladder barely reached. He leaned it against the side of the house, climbed up, took a crescent wrench out of his pocket, and smashed one of the window-panes. He reached in, unlatched the window, pushed it up, and clambered over the sill.

Cora went around to the front door. She wasn't sure if Wilbur would let her in, but figured he had to move the ladder.

After a few minutes he came out.

"Got your keys?" Cora needled him.

He gave her a look, trudged to the back of the house, took down the ladder, and stowed it noisily in the barn. He emerged with a hammer, nails, and some plywood. He tacked one sheet over the broken window, and locked the barn door.

"You're gonna patch the other window from inside," Cora said. "I know that because I'm a trained investigator. And I saw you put away the ladder."

"You ever *solve* a case?" Wilbur asked her.

"How long have you lived here?"

"Too damn long."

He went up the front steps into the store. Cora followed, found herself in a room full of junk. Granted, what Cora knew of antiques couldn't have furnished your average breakfast nook; still, the stuff in Wilbur's shop looked more likely to be piled up on curbside next to the recyclables than adorning anyone's home or office. The demand, for instance, for a two-wheeled tricycle with no seat couldn't be high.

As for the furniture, while it was certainly old, it was also cracked and covered with dust. Tables, dressers, desks, sideboards, etc., in various periods, styles, and materials were thrown haphazardly together. The desk with the missing drawer was grouped with the director's chair with no back. Cora managed to restrain herself from buying them. She wasn't sure how long she could hold out against the allure of the ripped vinyl settee.

Wilbur shuffled behind what turned out to pass for a desk, though Cora wouldn't have known it. He flipped open an appointment book, took out a pen, and wrote laboriously, moving his lips.

"Police . . . send . . . inspector. Refuses . . . to . . . inspect."

"That's hardly fair," Cora protested. "I'm here. What do you want inspected?"

"You read the file?"

Cora took a breath. "Of course I read the file. You bought some chairs. You reported them stolen. From the barn out back. Under interrogation, you admitted you might have left the door open."

Wilbur dismissed that with a brief, exceptionally pungent comment.

"You didn't admit you might have left the door open?"

"If you knew that, when I broke the window, why'd you ask me if that was how the robber got in?"

So. The guy was sharper than she'd thought. "Why are the chairs important?" Cora asked.

"What?"

"Are these valuable chairs? How much did you pay for them?"

"Isn't it in the file?"

"Is the file accurate?"

"You first."

Cora flipped open the file. "It says you bought the chairs for fifty bucks apiece, but you claim they're worth closer to a hundred."

"They are."

"Is that why you bought them? Because they were cheap?"

"Sure."

"You were looking to make a profit on the chairs?"

Wilbur said nothing.

"That's a hundred percent profit. If you sell 'em at a hundred bucks apiece. You report the loss to your insurance company?"

"What's that got to do with it?"

"I assume you want to get your money back. Of course, you couldn't get a hundred bucks a chair."

"What the hell are you talking about? I don't want the damn money. I want my chairs."

"I understand. How's that working out for you so far?"

Wilbur opened his mouth to retort, closed it again. Tugged at the sleeves of his sweater. Peered at her with crafty eyes. "Okay, lady. You wanna help, I'm glad to have you. Not that I'm letting Harper off the hook. It's a police matter, and you ain't police. If Harper thinks sending you out here takes care of it, he's dead wrong. Now, do I gotta tell him that in person, or will you communicate it to him?"

"I can promise you it will come up in conversation."

Cora had the impression she might have detected a smile at the corner of Wilbur's mouth.

"All right, lady. Find my chairs."

"How?"

"You're the detective. You tell me."

"Let's look at the scene of the crime."

"Why?"

"That's how crimes are solved."

"Not this time. I had chairs. They're gone."

"Can I see where they were?"

"Not gonna help you much."

"So whaddya expect me to do?"

"Find them."

"With nothing to go on?"

"There's a picture in the file."

"You took a picture of the chairs?"

"No. It was in the auction catalogue."

Cora pulled out the photo of a chair. It was a wooden straight-back chair, with curved arms and a woven seat. It looked decidedly uncomfortable. Cora wouldn't have given ten bucks for it, let alone fifty. "They all look like this?"

"More or less. Some needed repair."

"But they all went for fifty bucks?"

"It was a single lot. They all went together."

"All right. You bought 'em at auction. You brought 'em home, you locked 'em in the barn."

"That's right."

"When was the next time you looked for 'em?"

"It was a while."

"Why?"

"I was busy. I bought 'em to sell."

"Did you put 'em on the market?"

"No."

"Why not?"

"They needed work. I didn't get around to it."

"And then you did. The chairs were gone.

There was no sign of a break-in. You reported this to the police."

"That's right."

"Who would have wanted to steal your chairs?"

He shrugged. "I dunno. Antiques dealer."

"Why would an antiques dealer take those chairs and leave everything else?"

"I have no idea."

"You have any enemies? Anyone out to get you? Any rival like to see you fail?"

"Don't be silly."

"Why is that silly?"

"I fail because of a few chairs?"

"That was a generalization. How about it? Anyone you got a blood feud with looking to give you trouble?"

"No."

"The chairs were stolen when?"

"It's in the file."

"Yes, it is." Cora consulted the file. "About a year ago." She snapped the file shut. "Okay. Thanks for your time."

"You giving up?"

Cora smiled her trademark Puzzle Lady smile, though she doubted if Wilbur would recognize it. "Not at all," she told him.

5

Harvey Beerbaum couldn't believe his good fortune. Cora Felton hadn't been at his house in months, and never alone. The last time was when he threw a garden party for the selectmen. Cora wasn't a selectman, but Iris Cooper had suggested she come. Cora had been suspicious that Harvey had pressured the First Selectman to ask her. He had, but Iris didn't let on. At least, not officially. Not in front of him. Now that he recalled, the two ladies had spent a good deal of the party giggling in the azaleas.

Harvey's house befitted the portly cruciverbalist. The walls were hung with crossword puzzle momentos. A framed copy of the first puzzle he'd ever had published in the *New York Times*. A third-place trophy he'd taken in the nationals — he'd have won it, too, if he hadn't written an *E* for an *A,* a simple-enough mistake when one is solving a difficult Saturday puzzle in front of three hundred people with the knowledge that at any moment one of the other two finalists may shout, "Done!" and all will be lost.

Hanging from the ceiling was a huge crossword puzzle grid. Not the one he'd missed, but the one created by ace constructor Merl Reagle for a charity event, and then auctioned off to the highest bidder. Merl had signed it, too, in magic marker, making it well worth the two hundred dollars he had spent for it.

Harvey, thrilled by the company, fluttered about like a mother hen.

"It will only be a minute. The tea, I mean. I love the gas stove. So much faster than electric. Then we'll have our tea. I wish I had some scones. If I'd known you were coming, I'd have picked some up at Cushman's. So nice of you to drop in, of course."

"It's all right, Harvey. You didn't even need to make tea."

"Oh, but I did. I'd be a poor host not to offer refreshment of some kind. Now that you've stopped drinking —" Harvey broke off, flushed. "Do forgive me. I'm somewhat flustered. I don't know what came over me. I would never make any assumptions of the kind. And I wouldn't want you to think people were talking about you. Of course they haven't been talking about you. Well, they

53

have, but only in terms of your notoriety. I don't mean notoriety, I mean fame."

Cora, watching the little man prance back and forth from the couch where she sat to the stove where the watched pot never boiled, was rapidly losing patience. "Harvey, sit down. You're driving me nuts. When the teapot whistles, you can get it."

"It's not the whistling kind."

"I am. I'll see it boiling, and I'll whistle. Now sit."

No golden retriever ever obeyed a command so quickly. Harvey perched on the edge of a chair, a bundle of nervous energy. "It's not a teapot, of course. It's a kettle. Not that I should be telling you words. Still —"

Even the hint of a discussion of syntax was more than Cora could bear. "Harvey, let me get right to the point. I happen to need your help."

Harvey's jaw descended to the vicinity of his navel. "*You* need *my* help? That'll be the day. You do five puzzles a week, fifty-two weeks a year. You construct in your sleep. How could you possibly need my help?"

"Your water's boiling," Cora told him. "Would you like me to whistle?"

Harvey hopped to the stove, filled two teacups with hot water, brought the tray to the coffee table. On the tray was a wooden box with Heinz 57 varieties of tea.

"Which kind would you like? I've got Lemon Zinger, Earl Grey, camomile, Sleepytime —"

"Tea's tea," Cora told him. "You could give me ground oak leaves, I wouldn't know the difference. Harvey, I need a favor."

"Of course, of course. What do you need?"

"I want you to sell something for me."

Harvey stopped dipping his tea bag in his cup. "I beg your pardon?"

Cora wondered vaguely what kind of tea it was. "On eBay, Harvey. I'd like you to sell something on eBay."

"For you?"

"Yes, for me."

"I don't understand."

Cora rolled her eyes. Of course he didn't. It was too easy. There was nothing to wrap his torturous mind around.

"It's perfectly simple, Harvey. You're a registered seller on eBay. You have an account."

"How do you know that?"

"It's not a secret, Harvey. When you put something up for bids on eBay, it's rather public."

"You shop on eBay?"

"Ah. A meeting of the minds. Yes, Harvey. I buy things on eBay."

"You've never bought anything of mine."

"No, I haven't," Cora admitted. "But I've seen your offerings." She repressed a shudder at the thought of the crossword puzzle cuckoo clock Harvey once had up for bids.

"And you have something you want to sell?"

"In a manner of speaking."

Harvey frowned. "What do you mean, in a manner of speaking?"

"Well, I don't want to sell it. I want someone to sell it for me. I've never sold anything on eBay. I don't have an account. But you do. So, if you could sell the item for me, I'd really appreciate it."

"What is the item?"

"A chair."

"What kind of chair?"

"A rattan wicker-back chair. With wooden arms."

"Oh. Like mine?"

Cora followed his gaze to the corner of the room where a square wooden table sat framed by four meticulously placed rattan chairs. It would have been a perfect bridge table, if Harvey only played.

"Mine's a different style. Not that it matters."

"Do you have it in the car?"

"No, but I have a picture of it."

Cora dug into her drawstring purse,

handed over the picture of the chair.

"I see," Harvey said. "So, you'd like me to advertise this: 'Rattan chair, owned by the Puzzle Lady — ' "

Cora put up her hand. "No, no. Don't mention me. I have nothing to do with it. It's just a chair. You're selling a chair. Four chairs, actually."

"Four chairs?"

"Yes."

"How much do you expect to get for them?"

"I have no idea. It will be interesting to see how they go."

"How much would you want for an opening bid?"

"I don't know. Twenty bucks apiece."

"That's all?"

"Well, I wouldn't want to scare anyone off."

"I understand. But that's an inconveniently sized item to sell so cheap."

"What's inconvenient about it? You just scan the picture."

"I mean in terms of shipping. It's hard to move an item when the shipping cost exceeds the purchase price. It makes people reluctant to bid."

"Well, we don't want to do that. How about shipping cost included?"

Harvey's eyes widened. "Are you crazy? If they go for the floor bid, you'll wind up losing money."

Cora sipped her tea. She'd chosen her tea bag at random, was surprised to find it had an orange flavor and wasn't all that bad. "So what? It's not your money."

"No, but I'd hate to see you get taken."

Cora smiled, patted his face. "You worry too much, Harvey."

Harvey looked at her searchingly. "You've got something up your sleeve, haven't you? Come on, Cora. It's me. Harvey. Level with me. What's this all about?"

6

Sherry looked up from the computer. "Cora, have you lost your mind?"

Cora shrugged. "Well, no more than usual."

"You have Harvey Beerbaum selling phony chairs for you?"

"They're not phony. They don't exist."

"Exactly."

"No, not exactly. Doesn't something have to exist to be phony? I mean, you're the wordsmith here. How can you have a phony nothing at all?"

"Cora, I'm not in the mood."

"Marital troubles again? Amazing how you can have them when you're not even married. Of course, I always did. But Aaron's not married either."

"The fact is, you've got Harvey involved in something you shouldn't have. I'm surprised he was willing to do it."

"He likes me."

"That makes it ten times worse. You *seduced* him into doing something he shouldn't."

"I didn't seduce him."

"Oh, no?"

"Oh, yes. Trust me, I know when I've seduced someone." Cora shrugged. "At least, since I quit drinking."

"Was Harvey happy to do it?"

"He got a little snarky when he found out there weren't any chairs."

"Yeah, I would imagine he did. You could ruin his rating."

"What rating?"

"Come on, Cora. You buy on eBay. You check the seller's performance rating. The evaluation he got from his customers. What do you suppose it will be when he gets a reputation for fraud?"

"Reputation, schmeputation," Cora said. "He was actually kind of amused when I told him my plan."

"What's your plan?"

"Well, it all goes back to the Kleinsmidt inheritance."

"The what?"

"The eight Kleinsmidt heirs. They inherited a ten-million-dollar estate, share and share alike. Each heir got a million bucks. Two million was never found. It was rumored to be in diamonds. The famous Kleinsmidt diamonds."

"Cora!"

"The will was read in the Kleinsmidt dining room. At a table with eight rattan chairs. Each heir was entitled to one, but they didn't take them, and the chairs were sold with the estate. It was twenty years later before anyone suspected the diamonds were hidden in the chairs."

"You told Harvey *that?*"

"Well, I had to tell him something."

"Is there such a person as Kleinsmidt?"

"I'm sure there's one somewhere."

"I mean a Kleinsmidt heir."

Cora spread her arms. "I have no idea what any Kleinsmidt, living or dead, may have inherited."

"So, you not only got Harvey to hold a fraudulent auction on eBay, you did it by telling him an outrageous lie."

"Well, I couldn't tell him the truth. I don't *know* the truth. All I know is some guy wants his chairs back. The Kleinsmidt diamonds are as good a reason as any."

"The Kleinsmidt diamonds don't exist."

"Neither do the chairs."

Sherry took a breath. "Cora, I'm not going to argue with you. You know why? Because this has absolutely nothing to do with me.

You and Harvey worked this out on your own. All the e-mail is going to go to Harvey. Harvey is the one who is going to go to jail. You're the one who is going to be accountable."

Cora patted her niece on the cheek. "You worry too much, Sherry. If I went to jail every time I told an outrageous lie I'd have never had time to get married."

"Most lies aren't illegal."

"Well, they should be. When I think of the whoppers Henry told me —" Cora broke off, looked at Sherry searchingly. "Is that your problem with Aaron? Has he been telling lies?"

"Of course not."

"Then what's the problem?"

"There's no problem."

"Right, right. You're just enjoying a young lady's prerogative of behaving like a peevish nitwit. Well, I'm certainly glad there's no problem, because I need a favor."

"Oh?"

"If you wouldn't mind."

"Does this have anything to do with chairs and eBay?"

"It's legal, it's simple, it's right up your alley."

"Why do I want to say no?"

"Your contrary nature?"

"No, your devious one. Whenever you get so conciliatory, Cora, I smell a rat."

"Bite me. All I want is a crossword puzzle."

"What?"

Cora explained about the young mother bashing in her husband's car.

"You want me to write a crossword puzzle to soften up her husband?"

"Well, *I* can't do it."

"That's not the point. The woman's been deceiving her husband and you want to help her out?"

"I want to help her confess."

"You want to make it all better? Why does this woman deserve your help? Why does she *need* your help? She's afraid to tell her husband she smacked up the car?"

"I don't think he'd beat her."

"That's not what I meant."

"Me either. It's just a young airhead mother, trying to make everything hunky-dory."

"I understand. What I don't understand is why you ever agreed to such a thing."

"She came off like she was having an affair. Naturally, I wanted to help. The car bash was a kick in the teeth."

"You were going to help this woman have an affair?"

"Of course not. But I wanted to hear about

it. My own sex life is virtually nonexistent."

"Is that why you're flirting with Harvey Beerbaum?"

"Will you knock it off about Harvey Beerbaum! I'm trying to solve a robbery. I also got finessed into writing a crossword puzzle. Which I'm not capable of doing. You wanna help me out? Or you want me to just fess up I'm not really the Puzzle Lady?"

"Not with the rent coming due."

"Okay, so whip me up a puzzle. It doesn't have to be great, it just has to get me off the hook with Reckless Stroller Mom."

"Have you learned your lesson? About promising things you can't deliver?"

"There's a straight line I'm not gonna touch. So, you'll do it. Great. If you can get it done before I go for coffee tomorrow, I won't have to start making up excuses."

The phone rang.

Sherry scooped it up. Her face hardened. "I told you not to call me." She hung up.

Cora raised her eyebrows. "Dennis?"

"Yeah."

"I see why you and Aaron are having troubles."

7

"It's not my fault he calls me," Sherry protested.

Aaron Grant sipped his wine. "I'm not saying it's your fault. I'm just wondering what can be done."

"It's the same thing, Aaron," Sherry said irritably. "Wondering what can be done implies there's something I'm not doing."

"That's not what I mean."

"That's what the words mean. If you use the words, you're stuck with 'em."

"Words have different meanings."

"No kidding."

"I'm sorry I brought it up."

"You didn't bring it up."

"Yeah, I did. I asked you how you were."

"And I told you I'm cranky, and you wanted to know why. Fine. You brought it up, and now you're sorry. That makes both of us. Can we just have dinner?"

Sherry and Aaron were dining at the

Country Kitchen. From the outside, Baker-haven's homey, colonial restaurant looked like a large log cabin. The inside featured wood. It also featured a salad bar, which Sherry and Aaron had availed themselves of while they waited for their orders.

"Absolutely," Aaron said. "As long as we're both agreed that it's my fault."

"What's your fault?"

"Whatever we're talking about."

Sherry couldn't help smiling. "You're lucky you're cute. Otherwise, I wouldn't put up with you."

"I know. So, we're both agreed it's neither one of our faults if your ex-husband keeps calling you?"

"We're agreed it's your fault if you keep bringing it up."

"Fair enough."

Aaron took a bite of salad.

"That's a lot of blue cheese," Sherry said.

"I like blue cheese."

"You like high cholesterol?"

"Can't get enough."

"It'll kill you."

"No it won't. I really can't get enough. My cholesterol is so low, it doesn't register."

"That's impossible."

"No, hyperbole. Is it hyperbole, or just exaggeration?"

"That would depend on whether cholesterol too low to register is a possibility."

"Well, is it?"

"I have no idea."

"Anyway, it's low. Blue cheese can't hurt me."

"Did you make that up? Do you even *know* your cholesterol level?"

"Do you?"

"Know your cholesterol level?"

"No, yours."

"Yes, I do. And it's fine, because I don't eat that."

"Aren't you supposed to wait until we're married before you start to reform me?"

"What makes you think we're getting married?"

"Haven't I proposed yet?"

"Only half a dozen times. Have I ever said yes?"

"I don't remember."

"What a romantic. No, it's not the type of thing you'd be apt to remember, is it? Here's a hint. If I'd ever said yes, Aaron, maybe you'd have stopped asking."

"Cora thinks we're getting married."

"Oh?"

"Treats it like a done deal."

"I'm not bound by anything my aunt says."

"And Dennis clearly thinks we are."

"I thought you weren't going to bring up Dennis."

"Only in a good context."

"A *good* context?"

"As proof of our intentions."

"You expect to wear me down with this type of banter?"

"No. It's obviously not working." Aaron held up his hands. "Look, it occurs to me the reason you haven't accepted is I've asked you to marry me so many times it's old hat. It isn't special. You don't even have to think about it. You say no as a matter of course."

"I'm glad you see my point of view."

"So, I think some sort of dramatic gesture is needed."

Aaron reached in his pocket, pulled out a plush jeweler's case. To Sherry's amazement, he got up from his chair, sank to one knee, opened the case. Inside was a diamond ring.

"Sherry. Will you marry me?"

Sherry Carter's mouth fell open. Her face turned blazing red.

Heads turned at the sight of the young man obviously proposing marriage. Every eye in the restaurant was on them.

A waitress with a huge tray of food found her way blocked. Her load was clearly heavy, but she wasn't about to interrupt. She shuffled to a stop, shifted the weight of the tray.

Aaron saw her out of the corner of his eye. He smiled up at Sherry.

"You wanna accept me already? We're holding up people's dinner."

8

Sherry Carter couldn't believe it. She'd actually said yes. Was it the ring? Was it the romantic gesture? Was it Aaron making a spectacle of himself? Was it him kneeling in the path of an encumbered waitress, so that unless she accepted four patrons would go without dinner?

Whatever the reason, Sherry had gone against her better judgment, agreed to do the thing that she had sworn she would never do again.

If only her first marriage hadn't been such a disaster. If Dennis had merely been a bum, a philanderer, a drunk, a drug addict, a freeloader. But, no, he'd had to be a wife beater. A violent, dangerous, manipulative —

Manipulative. That was the worst. That handsome, suave s.o.b. could charm the birds out of the trees, could make a credulous girl believe he could change. If she'd stayed with him a bit less. If she'd left a bit sooner. She wouldn't have blamed herself then.

She wouldn't still blame herself now.

Part of the battered-wife syndrome.

The last time he hit her she was pregnant. She lost the baby.

She left the hospital, never went back to him.

Too late.

It was her fault. She didn't deserve a second chance.

She'd said yes.

My God, she'd actually said yes.

She'd said yes to Aaron Grant.

Sherry wished he'd come home with her. But he was beeped by the managing editor, sent back to the paper to cover some late-breaking news. As if it mattered. TV would get there first. No way the paper got a scoop.

Sherry scowled at herself.

That's right. Belittle the man you just accepted. Deprecate yourself by deprecating him.

Make it easier to call the whole thing off.

My God!

She'd really said yes.

A silly grin spread over Sherry's face.

She'd really said yes.

Sherry took a breath. *Hey, snap out of it.*

Back to reality. So she said yes. It wasn't irrevocable. Women say a lot of things in the heat of passion. Not that a salad at the Country Kitchen could be considered passionate. Even so, the guy proposed. So she said yes. She might have meant it. She might not. She might go through with it. She might not. She had all the time in the world to change her mind if that's what she wanted to do. Right now she needed to calm down, get control, take care of business.

Easier said than done. Sherry's powers of concentration were minimal at best. Thank goodness she'd finished the Puzzle Lady column, didn't have that hanging over her head. If she had to construct a crossword puzzle now —

Sherry's eyes widened.

Oh, hell! Cora. The puzzle for Cora. She'd promised to help. Could she put it off? No, there was some stupid deadline. The young mother had to fess up before the young father realized she wrecked the car.

That sounded stupid. How could it be?

Oh, right. Inspection. The damage would be discovered during inspection.

Which was tomorrow, so Cora had to have it in the morning.

Ah, hell.

Sherry clicked on the icon, called up Crossword Compiler. Was offered the standard fifteen-by-fifteen grid. Let's see. Could she get away with anything smaller? Perhaps, but it would be more trouble than it was worth. She was used to 15×15. Anything less and she'd have trouble placing the theme entry.

Which should probably be in rhyme. *Let's see, what was it? Ah, yes, a dented fender.* If that wasn't inspiration. Talk about a muse.

Sorry, dear
I wrecked the car
Had too many
At the bar.

No. Wrong tone. Too many letters. Sounded more like a man than a woman. Aside from that, it was great.

The problem was, there wasn't much precedent on car-wreck rhymes.

All right, how about a general apology.

Don't get mad
Punch my eye
I'm so sorry
I could die.

Sherry giggled.

Uh-oh. Not good. She was losing it. *Come on. Get serious. What's wrong with that?* Aside from the fact the last line had nine letters.

Get serious. Get this done. If it were a Puzzle Lady puzzle, you'd knock it off in half an hour.

If it were a Puzzle Lady puzzle, it wouldn't be that stupid.

Oh, yeah? You just can't think straight because you're getting married.

Oh, my God!

Sherry spiraled around a few more times in her head, drove away the demons.

Okay, what's needed here? A little car-crash poem.

I was out
On a bender
There's a dent
In the fender.

Come on, you're getting giddy.

Getting?

Oh, Cora, Cora. If you knew what you've done to me.

The phone rang.

Good. If it was Cora, she'd beg off.

If it was Aaron . . .

Well, she wouldn't beg off. But she'd express her doubts. Not that he wasn't fully aware of her doubts. But still.

She hoped it was Aaron.

"Hello?"

"Sherry?"

Dennis's voice went through her like a knife.

Not now!

"You have to stop calling."

"I can't."

"Yes you can. If you call again, I'm telling Brenda."

"Yeah. Like she doesn't know."

"Are you drunk?"

"No. Just determined."

"Really? When did you leave Brenda?"

There was a silence on the line.

"When did you leave Brenda?" Sherry repeated.

"What's the difference?"

"You haven't left Brenda, have you? You're still living with her. Still working for her father. You're lucky she hasn't thrown you out."

"Get serious."

"I know. It's not her nature. Even if I told her about this phone call. Even if she believed me. She'd still find a way to forgive."

"I didn't call to talk about Brenda."

"What a surprise."

"I heard a rumor."

"You heard a rumor? What rumor?"

"You're getting married."

Sherry's heart stopped. "Who told you that?"

"Is it true?"

"It's none of your business."

"My wife getting married? It certainly is my business. I at least have a right to know."

"Ex-wife. And if I get married, I'll tell you."

"I'd like to know before you do it."

"Your wishes don't control me anymore."

Sherry bit her lip as she said that. It implied that once they did.

"Damn it, did you accept a marriage proposal tonight? Yes or no?"

"Where'd you hear that?"

"Yes or no?"

Sherry hung up the phone.

That was freaky. Aaron proposes over dinner. Two hours later Dennis knows.

Was he spying on them? Peeking through the window? Was he there at the Country Kitchen?

How the hell did he know?

Sherry had the creepy feeling she was being watched. Which was ridiculous. No one was watching her now. She was in her office, at the computer. There was no one at the window. The blind was open, but there was a full moon lighting up the empty lawn. Nonetheless, Sherry got up and closed the blind. Felt like a fool.

Sherry needed to call Aaron, ask him to come over, even though he had to work. That would be a fine start to the relationship, all clingy the moment he proposed. There was no need. She'd be fine. Put Dennis out of her head. Go on with her life.

Now, what was she doing?

Her eyes lit on the computer screen.

Oh, hell. Cora's puzzle. There was no way she could deal with it now.

On the bottom shelf of the bookcase was a stack of oversized books too tall to stand. Sherry bent down, pawed through. Sure enough, in a cardboard cover and spiral binding was the collection *100 CROSS-WORD PUZZLES FOR ALL OCCASIONS.* Sherry remembered it, particularly since the book offered *one* crossword puzzle for each occasion, as opposed to the hundred the title implied. Sherry dug it out, leafed through.

"My Bad," by Benny Southstreet, sounded promising.

So, *20 Across: Start of message; 31 Across: Part 2 of message,* etc.

Excellent. And that message was . . . ?

Well, *1 Across: "Huh?"* would be *WHAT;* *5 Across: Faultfinder's find;* she'd need to get one of the down clues first. But *10 Across: Hay place* would be *LOFT.*

Sherry shuddered. Bad clue. Obvious and boring. She made a pencil note: *Room at the top?*

And, good lord, *7 Down: Annina in* "Der Rosenkavalier" as a clue for *ALTO?* Talk about obscure! Specialized knowledge required! Sherry scribbled: *Tone of voice?*

There. Much better. And —

What the hell was she doing? The answers were on page 118.

Sherry flipped to the back of the book, checked out the solution grid.

So. The theme entry was:

My apology I'll
Not prolong
I am so sorry
You were wrong

Sherry groaned. A wisecrack, not an apology. Just her luck.

On the other hand . . .

Perhaps, with a few minor changes . . .

Sherry's fingers flew over the keyboard, typing the puzzle into Crossword Compiler.

My Bad
by Benny Southstreet

ACROSS

1 "Huh?"
5 Faultfinder's find
10 Hay place
14 Hopscotch space
15 Loosen up
16 About, in lawyerspeak
17 88 days on Mercury
18 Consume with gusto
19 Bond in court
20 Start of message
23 Chinese shell food
26 Ahead of time
27 Chilean-born pianist, Claudio ___
28 Wander about
31 Part 2 of message
34 Z, as in Zákinthos
38 Falco of "The Sopranos"
39 Unhappy fan, maybe
40 Rock group?

41 Wanton look
42 Part 3 of message
44 Just say no
45 Take the honey and run
46 "Be prepared," for one
50 "Even if it fails . . ."
52 Part 4 of message
56 Had on
57 Oohed and ___
58 Persia today
62 Et ___ (and others)
63 Bump and ___
64 Only
65 Jerk
66 Roll-on alternative
67 Had a big mouth

DOWN

1 A question of motive
2 Break ground?
3 Docs' bloc
4 Long essay
5 Baguette or challah
6 Lutzes and Salchows
7 Annina in "Der Rosenkavalier"
8 Manhandle
9 Industrial show
10 Tripoli's locale
11 Broadcast booth sign
12 Something extra
13 Set for the BBC
21 "What's ___ problem?"
22 Ring stone
23 "Doonesbury" square
24 Eat away
25 Bandleader Shaw
28 Spacious
29 Small bills
30 Farming prefix
32 Off-Broadway award
33 Baguette or challah
34 Animal behavior expert
35 Mistake
36 U. of Maryland athletes
37 Thus far
43 In stitches
44 Unknown John or Jane
46 How "I did it"
47 Mrs. Oop
48 City on the Po
49 Fine-tune
50 Battleground
51 Hot alcoholic drink
53 Poverty metaphor
54 Lawman Wyatt
55 Sound from a fan
59 "Winnie-the-Pooh" baby
60 Part of "snafu"
61 End-of-proof letters

W	H	A	T		B	L	A	M	E		L	O	F	T
H	O	M	E		R	E	L	A	X		I	N	R	E
Y	E	A	R		E	A	T	U	P		B	A	I	L
			M	Y	A	P	O	L	O	G	Y	I	L	L
P	E	A	P	O	D	S				E	A	R	L	Y
A	R	R	A	U			R	O	A	M				
N	O	T	P	R	O	L	O	N	G		Z	E	T	A
E	D	I	E		B	O	O	E	R		O	R	E	S
L	E	E	R		I	A	M	S	O	S	O	R	R	Y
				D	E	F	Y			E	L	O	P	E
M	O	T	T	O				A	T	W	O	R	S	T
Y	O	U	W	E	R	E	W	R	O	N	G			
W	O	R	E		A	A	H	E	D		I	R	A	Q
A	L	I	A		G	R	I	N	D		S	O	L	E
Y	A	N	K		S	P	R	A	Y		T	O	L	D

9

Harvey Beerbaum was so excited he nearly spilled his double skim mocha latte. "We have a bid! Can you believe it! You already have a bid!"

Though pleased, Cora was somewhat less astounded. After all, that's why they'd auctioned the damn thing. "Who is it?"

Harvey's eyes widened. "Why, I have no idea. But he's bid a hundred dollars."

"He?"

"Or she. Whoever it is has bid twenty-five dollars a chair."

"You don't know who it is?"

"Not yet. When he or she gets the final bid, I'll find out his or her name."

"If you say *he or she* every time, I'll strangle you."

"What do you want me to do?"

"I want you to wait out here while I get my coffee. Then I'll be in a much better mood."

"You don't want me to go in with you?"

"No."

"Why not?"

"Because you can't stop talking, and I don't want you spreading this around."

"I can talk about something else."

"I can't. Sit down. Relax. It's a nice morning."

Harvey reluctantly sat on the bench in front of the window.

Cora sighed. That was the problem with letting people like Harvey do you a favor. You had to talk to them. At least she didn't have to marry him.

Cora went into the bakeshop and ordered a cappuccino and an apricot scone. Life immediately looked better. She found Harvey sitting on the bench outside.

"That looks good," Harvey said. "What is it?"

"An apricot scone."

"Oh. I'm having a chocolate croissant. But that scone looks awfully good."

"Oh. Did you want a bite?"

"No. I'm just showing you I can talk about something else."

"You don't have to now," Cora said.

"I know. I was just showing you I could."

"I'm impressed. What about the chairs?"

"You have a bid of a hundred dollars."

"That's the only bid?"

"Yes, of course."

"Why *of course?*"

"That was the asking bid."

"I thought you were going to start at twenty bucks apiece."

"I looked at some other chairs. Twenty-five seemed more in line."

Cora kept the smile plastered on her face, but inwardly she groaned. Harvey was such a fussy little noodge. Why'd she ever get involved with him? "You have no idea who this is?"

"No." Harvey reached in his vest pocket, took out a small, fastidiously folded piece of paper. "I have the e-mail address. If you want to write to him. Or her."

"I swear to God, Harvey, one more *him or her* and you'll bleed from the nose."

"It's sbk@aol.com. That's not much help. It could be anyone. If you want to write this person, you can. Otherwise, I won't know their name until the bidding closes."

"When is that?"

"Next Tuesday night."

"Oh, hell," Cora said. "So, for all we know, this could be someone who just wants cheap chairs."

"Right. There's no way to tell unless someone else bids."

"What are the odds of that?"

"Well, if no one bids in the next twenty-four hours, I'd say they were poor. On some items, of course, people wait, try to put in a bid at the last minute. That's on more expensive items, which generate more interest. On something like this, who could really care?"

"Who, indeed?" Cora said.

The young mom with the stroller came down the block. At the sight of Cora, her face lit up hopefully.

"Oh, how cute," Mimi said. "You puzzle people talking together. Oh, you darling!" she added, as Cora handed her the paper. "Just in the nick of time. I hope this helps."

Mimi flashed them a dazzling smile, and wheeled her stroller into the bakeshop.

"What's that all about?" Harvey asked.

"Oh. She's having trouble with her husband."

"What did you give her?"

"A prescription for Cialis."

Harvey looked astounded.

"Oh, for goodness' sakes," Cora said. "Get a sense of humor. She wanted a crossword puzzle for her husband. To smooth over a spat."

"And you did that for her? You've got a heart of gold, Cora. A heart of gold."

"Yeah, I'm the cat's meow. About this bid . . ."

"Like I say, that's all we can tell for the moment. Unless someone else bids on the item."

"You know anyone would like some nice chairs?"

"Oh, I couldn't have a friend bid," Harvey said. "That would be dishonest."

"Heaven forbid."

"Was that intentional?"

"Was what intentional?"

"The play on the word *bid*."

Cora wondered which answer would get her in more trouble. "Frankly, I didn't notice."

"It's probably automatic," Harvey said. "I bet you could do it in your sleep."

Cora smiled. "That's a hell of a straight line, Harvey, but I'm not gonna bite."

Cora went home, logged on to the Internet, and checked out eBay. Harvey had done a nice job scanning in the picture of the chair. And he had one bid, for one hundred dollars.

It occurred to Cora it would be a shame if that was the only bid. After all, a hundred dollars was pretty damn cheap for four rattan chairs.

Cora bid $120.

10

Chuck Dillinger scowled. "What's this?"

"For you, sweetheart." Mimi had placed Cora's crossword puzzle inside a Hallmark greeting card. On the envelope she'd written *For my sweetheart.*

He looked at her. "This is from you?"

"In a way."

"In what way?" Chuck said.

Mimi could sense the irritation in his voice. He'd had a long day at work, he wanted a drink, and she'd hit him with a puzzle the minute he walked in the door. "Sorry, honey. It's from me, but I didn't do it. I mean, I didn't make it. You'll see when you open it."

That explanation neither enlightened nor appeased Chuck. He appeared not sure what to say next.

The baby's bawling saved him.

"Oh, dear," Mimi said, and rushed for the crib.

Chuck flipped the envelope on the coffee table, went to the mini-bar, and poured himself a scotch. He took off his shoes, loosened his tie, unbuttoned his shirt collar. He sat in an easy chair, put his feet up on the coffee table. Took a huge sip of scotch, exhaled.

Mimi sat on the couch, patted the baby on her shoulder. "Hard day at the office?"

"Well, I didn't make partner, and I didn't get fired."

Mimi was glad to hear it. That was Chuck's whimsical response for an average day. He wouldn't have said it if anything was really wrong.

"Did you open your card?"

"No, I made my drink. What's the card all about?"

"Open it. I'll tell you."

The envelope wasn't sealed, just had the flap stuck in. Chuck pulled out the card. " 'To a wonderful father.' Honey, it's not Father's Day."

"I know."

Inside read: *With love,* signed, *Mimi.*

"What's this?" Chuck unfolded the paper. He stared at the puzzle. "What the hell is this all about?"

"It's a present. I had the Puzzle Lady make it special. Just for you."

"You what?"

"Come on, dear, solve it. See what it says."

"You've got to be kidding."

"No. Go on."

"Mimi. I've had a long day. I'm in no mood to solve a crossword puzzle."

"I'll help you. In fact, you don't have to do anything. Just sit there and have your drink, and I'll fill it in."

"You've got the baby."

"Yes, and what a little angel. See, she's gone to sleep on my shoulder. Come on, here we go."

With her husband's grudging help, Mimi filled in the puzzle. She'd practiced with a xerox copy, to make sure she could. Her husband was not a patient man. It would spoil everything if she had trouble solving it.

When she was finished, Chuck said, "So?"

Mimi pointed.

"See the poem? That's for you.

"My apology I'll
Not prolong
I am so sorry
If I went wrong."

Chuck stared at her. "*Went wrong?* What do you mean, *went wrong?*" He cocked his head. "You went through my things?"

"No, I —"

"What have I told you about going through my things?"

"I didn't go through your things. Let me show you. I'm so ashamed."

"You're so *ashamed!*"

"Don't wake the baby."

"You're so ashamed you come at me with crossword puzzles and you're just afraid I'll wake the baby?"

"Come outside."

"What?"

"I have to show you something."

"And you'd like all the neighbors to see?"

"No one's gonna look at us. If we don't shout," Mimi added. With the baby sleeping on her shoulder, she jerked open the front door.

Chuck followed her out into the yard. "Mimi, what's going on?"

"You notice how I parked the car? Angling away?"

"So you're terrible at parking. I kid you about it. What's the big deal?"

Mimi led him around to the far side of the car. Pointed to the freshly repaired fender. "I backed into a light pole. I'm really sorry. I know how much you love the car."

Chuck looked astounded. "You dented the car?"

"Yes. I'm really sorry."

ACROSS

1 "Huh?"
5 Faultfinder's find
10 Room at the top?
14 Hopscotch space
15 Loosen up
16 About, in lawyerspeak
17 88 days on Mercury
18 Consume with gusto
19 Bond in court
20 Start of message
23 Chinese shell food
26 Ahead of time
27 Chilean-born pianist, Claudio ___
28 Wander about
31 Part 2 of message
34 Z, as in Zákinthos
38 Falco of "The Sopranos"
39 Unhappy fan, maybe
40 Rock group?
41 Wanton look
42 Part 3 of message
44 Just say no
45 Take the honey and run

46 "Be prepared," for one
50 "Even if it fails . . ."
52 Part 4 of message
56 July 4 or 5, e.g.
57 Oohed and ___
58 Invasion site of 2003
62 Turkish military title
63 Bump and ___
64 Only
65 Look for
66 Roll-on alternative
67 Had a big mouth

DOWN
1 A question of motive
2 Break ground?
3 Docs' bloc
4 Long essay
5 Baguette or challah
6 Lutzes and Salchows
7 Tone of voice?
8 Manhandle
9 Industrial show
10 Tripoli's locale
11 Broadcast booth sign
12 Something extra
13 Set for the BBC
21 "What's ___ problem?"

22 Ring stone
23 "Doonesbury" square
24 Eat away
25 Bandleader Shaw
28 Spacious
29 Small bills
30 Farming prefix
32 Off-Broadway award
33 Baguette or challah
34 Animal behavior expert
35 Mistake
36 U. of Maryland athletes
37 Thus far
43 In stitches
44 Unknown John or Jane
46 King with a golden
   touch
47 Old enough
48 Tax of a tenth
49 Fine-tune
50 Battleground
51 Hot alcoholic drink
53 Acts like a shrew
54 Ballpark cover
55 Sound from a fan
59 "Winnie-the-Pooh" baby
60 Part of "snafu"
61 End-of-proof letters

93

W	H	A	T		B	L	A	M	E		L	O	F	T
H	O	M	E		R	E	L	A	X		I	N	R	E
Y	E	A	R		E	A	T	U	P		B	A	I	L
		M	Y	A	P	O	L	O	G	Y	I	L	L	
P	E	A	P	O	D	S			E	A	R	L	Y	
A	R	R	A	U			R	O	A	M				
N	O	T	P	R	O	L	O	N	G		Z	E	T	A
E	D	I	E		B	O	O	E	R		O	R	E	S
L	E	E	R		I	A	M	S	O	S	O	R	R	Y
		D	E	F	Y			E	L	O	P	E		
M	O	T	T	O			A	T	W	O	R	S	T	
I	F	I	W	E	N	T	W	R	O	N	G			
D	A	T	E		A	A	H	E	D		I	R	A	Q
A	G	H	A		G	R	I	N	D		S	O	L	E
S	E	E	K		S	P	R	A	Y		T	O	L	D

ACROSS

1 "Huh?"
5 Faultfinder's find
10 Room at the top?
14 Hopscotch space
15 Loosen up
16 About, in lawyerspeak
17 88 days on Mercury
18 Consume with gusto
19 Bond in court
20 Start of message
23 Chinese shell food
26 Ahead of time
27 Chilean-born pianist, Claudio ___
28 Wander about
31 Part 2 of message
34 Z, as in Zákinthos
38 Falco of "The Sopranos"
39 Unhappy fan, maybe
40 Rock group?
41 Wanton look
42 Part 3 of message
44 Just say no
45 Take the honey and run

46 "Be prepared," for one
50 "Even if it fails . . ."
52 Part 4 of message
56 July 4 or 5, e.g.
57 Oohed and ___
58 Invasion site of 2003
62 Turkish military title
63 Bump and ___
64 Only
65 Look for
66 Roll-on alternative
67 Had a big mouth

DOWN

1 A question of motive
2 Break ground?
3 Docs' bloc
4 Long essay
5 Baguette or challah
6 Lutzes and Salchows
7 Tone of voice?
8 Manhandle
9 Industrial show
10 Tripoli's locale
11 Broadcast booth sign
12 Something extra
13 Set for the BBC
21 "What's ___ problem?"

22 Ring stone
23 "Doonesbury" square
24 Eat away
25 Bandleader Shaw
28 Spacious
29 Small bills
30 Farming prefix
32 Off-Broadway award
33 Baguette or challah
34 Animal behavior expert
35 Mistake
36 U. of Maryland athletes
37 Thus far
43 In stitches
44 Unknown John or Jane
46 King with a golden
   touch
47 Old enough
48 Tax of a tenth
49 Fine-tune
50 Battleground
51 Hot alcoholic drink
53 Acts like a shrew
54 Ballpark cover
55 Sound from a fan
59 "Winnie-the-Pooh" baby
60 Part of "snafu"
61 End-of-proof letters

Mimi waited for the explosion.

Instead, Chuck started to giggle. "That's what this is all about? The car? You thought I'd be upset about the car?"

"You're not upset?"

Chuck took her by the shoulders, kissed her on the forehead. "You're very sweet, you know. You think you're the first housewife ever dented the family car?"

"I was so worried about it."

"And getting that woman to make up a crossword puzzle. If that don't beat all. Come on, sweetie, let's go in."

Chuck put his arm around Mimi and his daughter, and led them into the house.

He glanced over his shoulder as they went in the door. But there was no one there.

11

Mimi couldn't believe her good fortune. Her husband was taking it like a prince. An absolute prince. Chuck had seemed in a cranky mood when he got home. But when he saw the dent in the car, he couldn't have been nicer. Mimi knew why. The puzzle softened him up. But not the puzzle itself. The fact that she'd gone to the trouble to get it for him. Gone so far as to ask the Puzzle Lady. A famous person. A professional. It was like asking a doctor for a diagnosis at a party. It simply wasn't done. But she'd done it. And how it had paid off! Chuck had gone from testy and irritable to virtually calm. He'd read the poem, seen the damage, and that was that. Mimi shuddered to think what his reaction might have been if he hadn't read the poem.

It was a shame nobody knew. It occurred to Mimi that, like most selfless gifts, it would go unnoticed. She wished she could do something about that. Let people know what a savior Cora had been. Cora was famous, yes, but not noted for her good deeds. And stars got such bad press. The tabloids Mimi read on line in the supermarket each week — but of course never deigned to buy — owed their existence to the public's opinion of the foibles of the rich and famous. Celebrities were notorious, always censured, never praised. Any act of generosity went unappreciated. Which was so unfair. If a star visited a children's hospital, either no one knew, or it was regarded cynically as a photo op.

Mimi picked up the crossword puzzle from the desk. It occurred to her she could take it to the paper, give them a human interest story. They'd surely run it, what with it being about Bakerhaven's most famous citizen.

Except Chuck had taken the car. He'd been in such a good mood, he'd kissed her and gone out. That didn't sound right. But he deserved a night out with the boys after her wrecking the car and all that. So she was stuck at home. And Darlene was asleep. Mimi couldn't go anywhere until the baby woke up. Even if she called a cab.

Wait a minute. Chuck had a fax machine. She never used it, and he hardly ever did, but there was one in his study. She wondered if she could figure out how it worked. Chided herself for the thought. In this day and age, not to know how to send a fax!

Mimi grabbed the puzzle off the coffee table, went into the study. The fax machine was on a stand next to the desk. It had a telephone receiver, and way too many buttons. Well, some of them were the same as on a telephone. Others said **COPY**, **START**, and **STOP**. One button said **HELP**. Mimi wondered if she should press it.

She sat down at the desk. Chuck's computer was on. Mimi had used it before, to type lists and letters. She called up WordPerfect, clicked on **FILE**. Clicked on **NEW DOCUMENT**, as she always did to select the custom letterhead Chuck had designed for her. Instead, she scrolled through a series of choices on a series of screens until she found what she wanted. She clicked on it, and a document appeared with the heading:

FAX:

Mimi filled it in, stopping only to look up the number of the paper.

TO: Bakerhaven Gazette
FAX: 203-555-1415
FROM: Mimi Dillinger

DATE: 5/16
SUBJECT: Human interest story
PAGES: (including header) 2
COMMENTS: I banged the fender of
my husband's car. Cora Felton, the Puz-
zle Lady, created a special puzzle, just
for him, to help me break the news.
Chuck loved it. I can't thank her enough.

Mimi printed the document, stuck it in the fax machine. She smoothed out the puzzle, stuck it in behind. Using the keypad, she punched in the number of the *Gazette*. As she did, it appeared in a little window on the machine. But nothing else happened. Mimi frowned. She pushed the button marked **START**, was rewarded by a dial tone, followed by a ring. After two rings there was a scratchy tone, a loud hum, and the two pages were sucked into the machine.

When it was finished, the machine shut off. Mimi was pleased. She'd done it. Except the two papers wound up on the floor. Mimi wondered if there was any way to avoid that, if it was a sign of her inexperience.

Mimi stooped down, picked up the papers, set them on the desk.

There was the corner of a paper poking out from beneath the blotter. She must have moved it using the keypad or the mouse.

Mimi lifted the blotter, pulled out the paper.

It was a hundred-dollar bill. Bright, crisp, new. Not a crease in it.

Well, that was lucky. A quick hundred bucks Chuck must have lost. If she hadn't moved the blotter, she'd never have found it.

Mimi stopped.

There was the corner of something else poking out. Moving the bill must have dislodged it. Could it be another hundred-dollar bill? That certainly seemed unlikely. Even so.

Mimi moved the keypad aside, lifted the edge.

Gasped.

The top of the desk was covered with hundred-dollar bills. New, crisp, clean hundreds. They were not stacked, but spread out thin so as not to make a bulge. It was hard to tell at a glance, but there must have been fifty.

Five thousand dollars?

The phone rang.

That startled her. It was the fax line. Was she getting a fax? If so, how did she do it?

Mimi snatched up the phone, expecting to hear some terrible tone telling her she'd done something wrong.

"Hello? Did you just send me a fax?"

"What?"

"This is Ned Browning, at the *Bakerhaven Gazette*. Did you just fax us something?"

"Oh, it went through? I wasn't sure I'd done it right."

"Good guess." Ned sounded hearty, amused. "You just sent us two blank pages. I assume that wasn't what you wanted."

"Two blank pages?"

"Yes. We're pleased to get faxes, but this one was less than helpful. Can I assume you were trying to send us something else?"

"I sent you two pages."

"I'm sure you did. Tell me, did you read them when you sent them?"

"Of course I did."

"I mean when you put them in the machine."

"I beg your pardon?"

"When you put them in the machine. Could you read what you were sending?"

"Of course."

"Well, that's the problem. You put 'em in backwards, and faxed me the blank side."

"I put 'em in frontwards."

"Yes, you did. With the writing toward you. Put 'em in with the writing away from you, and we'll be in business. What's this about, by the way?"

"Oh, it was nothing."

"You got that right. Fax it to me again. If

it's not self-explanatory, I'll give you a call."

"But —"

The click of the editor hanging up the phone cut her off.

Mimi slammed down the phone in exasperation. Now she didn't want to send the fax. In fact, thinking it over, it probably had been a bad idea. She had more important things to think about. Five thousand of them, to be exact. But the guy had her number — must have caller ID or star 69, or something — and if the fax didn't come through he'd call to ask why. It was going to be more trouble to explain why she wasn't faxing the pages than to just send them.

Mimi put the pages in the right way this time, punched in the number, pressed **START**. She barely paid attention while the pages went through.

What was five thousand dollars doing under the blotter of her husband's desk?

12

Cora Felton opened a bleary eye, gazed up to find her niece glaring down at her.

Sherry was in bathrobe and slippers. She hadn't combed her hair, put on makeup, or even splashed water on her face. She looked like a poster girl for the new horror film, *Zombie Niece from Hell.*

"God, I hope I'm dreaming," Cora muttered.

Sherry shook Cora's arm again. At least Cora deduced it was again, and that an earlier impression of a great white shark eating her arm was just a nightmare.

"Damn it!" Sherry said.

"Well, when you put it that way." Cora pushed back the covers, raised her head. "Sherry, what did I do now? I've been asleep. All I did last night was play bridge. At a tenth of a cent a point. The worst I'm guilty of is gambling. I didn't get busted, and I won twenty bucks."

Sherry flung the *Bakerhaven Gazette* down on Cora's chest. "Page six," Sherry said, and stalked out the door.

Cora grabbed the paper. What now? Had she blurted out that Sherry was getting married? No, she hadn't. Even when the girls hinted at it during the game. With rumors of a proposal right there in the Country Kitchen. Cora had neither confirmed nor denied. She had pled ignorance. A reasonable plea. She was ignorant then, just as she was ignorant now.

Cora folded the paper open to page six.

And there it was.

PUZZLE LADY SAVES THE DAY.

There was her picture. And there was the puzzle she gave Mimi. According to the article, it had won Mimi's husband's heart.

Cora flung the paper down, stumbled into the bathroom, groped around for her toothbrush.

Minutes later, more or less awake, she found Sherry in the kitchen making coffee. Sherry was slamming the dishware around with more than her usual vehemence.

"I don't see what's so bad," Cora said.

"It was a private puzzle for a particular

purpose. It wasn't for general consumption."

"You realize how stupid you sound?"

"Damn it, Cora, this is serious."

"Why? I have puzzles in the paper every day."

"Yes. Written and paid for."

"Is that the problem? That you didn't get paid?"

"Indirectly."

"I'm going to strangle you."

"The feeling is mutual."

"What's the problem?"

"It's not your puzzle."

"No kidding."

"It's not my puzzle either."

"What?"

Sherry told Cora about adapting the puzzle from the one in the book.

"Well, that was pretty stupid," Cora said.

Sherry glared at her.

Cora put up her hand. "Not that I blame you. After all, you have a lot on your mind."

Sherry donated part of what was on her mind to her aunt.

"My, my, such language," Cora said. "I'd be willing to bet some of those words aren't in Webster's."

"You make a ridiculous promise. Then you let that woman put the puzzle in the paper."

"I had no idea she was going to put it in the paper." Cora smiled at her niece. "Come on, Sherry. What's the harm? It's just a dumb old puzzle. Who could possibly care?"

13

Benny Southstreet owed his bookie forty bucks. Which wouldn't have been a problem. Benny *had* forty bucks. Only he'd wagered it with another bookie on Citrus Cloud in the fourth race at Aqueduct. Citrus Cloud had done pretty well. Out of a field of six, the horse had finished third. Unfortunately, Benny had bet him to win. The resultant hole in Benny's bank account had not been conducive to the gentleman's health, as Frankie "the Shirt" (as in "you bet your shirt") Finklestein tended to frown on those who did not cover their marker within a reasonable period of time, reasonable being determined as whatever Frankie decided it was.

Benny needed a hundred bucks, and fast.

Failing that, he'd be happy to take fifty.

Luckily, Benny had a sideline. The same mental agility that allowed him to handicap horses, and might have stood him in good stead had it not been accompanied by the general good luck of your average fruit fly, allowed him to construct crossword puzzles, a skill both scorned and envied by his peers, who didn't understand, but were nonetheless happy to be paid off by the fruits of his labors.

Benny had one such fruit waiting in the computer right now. He printed it out, wondering wistfully as he always did on such occasions just how much he might get for hocking his computer instead of using it to print crosswords. As usual, he stifled the notion, printed the puzzle like a good boy. He crept out the door of his rented room in Hoboken, tiptoed past the door of the landlady he hadn't paid in two months, went outside, and caught the PATH train to New York.

Wally Embers, of Astroturf Publishing, was glad to see him, largely because Benny didn't owe Wally any money. Benny sold Wally crossword puzzles that the editor bought outright, cash on the spot, no royalties, no advance. Neither man ever owed the other a cent. In Benny's case, that made Wally unique.

Wally was working on a layout when Benny hunted him up in the hole-in-the-wall office that served as his publishing house.

"Look what the cat dragged in. You got a puzzle for me?"

"You bet."

"Eleven by eleven?"

"Fifteen by fifteen."

"I don't need a whole page."

"But I bet it would fit."

"That's not the question. The question is, why would I pay fifty bucks for a fifteen by fifteen, when I can pay twenty bucks for an eleven by eleven?"

"I take it the answer isn't 'because you're a nice guy.' How about because it's less work."

"How is that less work?"

"Because you don't *have* an eleven-by-eleven puzzle. It's easier for you to cut half a page out of the story that's leaving you this eleven-by-eleven space. Plus you save the two cents a word you're paying the writer."

"Three cents."

"Oh, big spender. Okay, so you do the math. See how much buying my puzzle — which is right here, in hand, ready to go — is gonna actually cost you, when you factor in half a page saved at three cents a word."

"You know, if you put as much effort into legitimate business, you'd be rich."

"So they tell me."

Wally looked the puzzle over, cut a check.

"You can't pay cash?"

"You can't go to the bank?"

"My creditors are always waiting at the bank."

Wally chuckled dutifully. That was one of those jokes that was probably true.

Benny took the check, said, "Hey! *Forty* bucks? What the hell is that?"

Wally shrugged. "It's a compromise. I want a twenty-dollar puzzle. You want to sell me a fifty-dollar puzzle. That's more work for me, plus I won't save thirty bucks at three cents a word. I'm more than splitting the difference. I would say it's damn decent."

"It's still a fifteen-by-fifteen puzzle."

"Which I don't need."

"I could always sell it to somebody else."

"Who?"

"I don't know."

"Exactly."

Benny folded the check, stuck it in his pocket. "You're robbing me blind, Wally." A newspaper on the editor's desk caught his eye. "What's that?"

Wally looked. "Oh. You know the Puzzle Lady, does the daily column? She's got two today."

"So?"

"So, how the hell'd she do that? I'm always interested in how people get publicity. And it's always the same thing. Human interest

111

angle. Gets 'em every time. You might want to give it some thought."

Benny wasn't listening. He was staring at the puzzle in the paper. "That's funny."

"What's funny?"

"Son of a bitch!"

14

The man looked like a crook. There was no other way to say it. He had a high forehead, a thinning hairline, a narrow face, a trim mustache, and shifty eyes. The type of guy you'd pick out of a police lineup. Even if you didn't recognize him. Figuring he must be guilty of something.

Buddy seemed to think so. The toy poodle squirmed in Cora's arms as if eager to get at the intruder.

Cora made no move to let the man in. For once she wished Buddy were a Rottweiler, snarling on his iron leash. "Yes?" she demanded, in as discouraging a tone as she could muster.

He looked up at her from the stoop. It occurred to Cora he'd have been looking up at her even had they been on the same level. A short man, his head permanently cocked to one side, as if from a lifetime of looking up at people.

"Miss Felton? Miss Cora Felton?"

It was a question Cora didn't want to answer. The type of question you said yes to and the next thing you knew you were named corespondent in a divorce complaint.

"What do you want?"

"I want to see Cora Felton. That would be you. It would be rather silly to pretend not to be, with your picture in the national news."

"You're not answering my question."

"What do I want with you? My name is Benny Southstreet. I'm a crossword puzzle constructor. Perhaps you're familiar with my work."

"I can assure you I'm not."

"That's weird."

"Not really. I know a lot less puzzles than you think."

"Fewer."

"Huh?"

"Fewer puzzles. As I'm sure you know."

Buddy, offended on his owner's behalf, contributed a warning growl.

Cora soothed the tiny poodle, and favored Benny Southstreet with an evil eye usually reserved for wayward husbands. "I'm terribly sorry. I don't review people's puzzles. I don't introduce people to Will Shortz."

"I know Will."

"Oh?"

"At least, I've met him. At the tournament. I'm not sure he'd remember me."

That was good. Cora's own conversations with Will Shortz had consisted largely of trying to avoid talking shop.

"At the risk of seeming redundant, what do you want?"

"Repetitive."

"Huh?"

"Not redundant. Repetitive." Benny Southstreet frowned. "Are you *sure* you're Cora Felton?"

"Not at all. In fact, now that you mention it, I'm pretty sure I'm not. Why don't you try the house down the road."

"I was told you have a sense of humor."

"By who?"

"By whom. I see. You're doing it deliberately, to throw me off the scent. Well, it's not going to work. You're the Puzzle Lady, all right. No matter what verbal misconstructions you concoct."

Cora concocted a verbal misconstruction usually not heard outside of a penitentiary shower room.

Benny took a step back. "I beg your pardon?"

"You have it. Now, unless you'd care to attempt the contortion I suggested, perhaps you'd prefer to take a hike."

Benny smiled. "Nice try. But you know perfectly well who I am, and perfectly well why I'm here."

"Of course. Because I'm psychic." Cora put her hand to her head. "Wait, wait. It's coming to me. You're the serial rapist we were warned about."

"Very funny."

"You're not? Damn. That's disappointing. Well, do you *know* a serial rapist? I've been rather lonely lately."

"Any time you get good and ready, you wanna tell me why you stole my puzzle?"

"What, are you nuts? I never stole any puzzle."

" 'My Bad.' "

"Damn right, you're bad. You're also demented."

"Ha-ha. You know what I'm talking about. You changed a couple of the first clues, and a few at the end. Like *Invasion site of 2003* for *IRAQ* instead of *Persia today.* As if that would disguise the fact that you ripped me off. It just shows you knew what you were doing."

"I don't even know what I'm *hearing.* What the hell are you talking about?"

"And then you change the theme entry from a clever little rhyme with a humorous twist to a boring, pathetic apology. It's embarrassing to claim I wrote the damn thing. I have to keep explaining it's not my fault."

"Maybe you can write a little puzzle that does that."

Benny stared at her. "Talk about divas! I've met rude celebrities before, but you take the cake! Christ, lady, didn't you hear what I just said?"

"I heard you. I've seen you. And I'm done with you." Cora chucked the little poodle under the chin. "Now get lost before I sic Cujo here on you."

15

Mimi made up her mind. She'd been stewing about it all day, ever since she dropped Chuck off at the train. Somehow, she'd managed to hold off during breakfast. And then during the ride in the car. Of course, she didn't want to talk in front of the child. Not that the child could understand, but still. That had been sufficient excuse to put off the decision.

The night before, he'd come home drunk — well, not *drunk* drunk, but certainly tipsy — after his evening out. She couldn't say anything then. Break in on his mood. When he'd tumbled into bed and gone right to sleep, she'd been almost grateful.

What a day. What an awful day. This morning she'd peeked under the blotter, to see if it was still there. And it was. She'd barely heard anything the other women said in the bakery. All she could think about was the money. She'd have to ask him about it. There was no way out. She had to ask him. And no matter what he said, it would be bad. Because she'd have to explain how she found it. It was too much on top of the dented fender incident. He'd been so good about that. To try his patience with something else. He'd be angry. Very angry.

Still, he had the money. He was the one in the wrong. How could he justify that? Was it her fault for pointing out his transgression? Could he really hold that against her?

Of course he could. He could hold anything against her if he wanted to. That was the way men were. Or at least the way Chuck was. If he had a bad day, it was her fault.

No, that wasn't fair. Chuck was a good guy. But there was no reason to deliberately rile him.

Like today. Making a doctor's appointment for four forty-five. Yes, it was the only one she could get. And, yes, Darlene was running a fever. And Chuck had been nice about taking a cab home. Even so, she wished she'd been able to pick him up. Though she'd dreaded picking him up at the station, because she wouldn't want to bring up the money until they got home, and she'd feel awkward not talking about it. Just as she felt awkward about the cable TV guy flirting with her, if that's really what he was doing, at any rate getting a little too familiar. She felt awkward not mentioning that, though not nearly as awkward as she would have felt mentioning it. So she hadn't looked forward to the ride home in the car.

Of course, she hadn't *deliberately* scheduled the four forty-five appointment. That was the one she was offered. Surely they wouldn't have been able to give her an earlier one just because she had to pick up her husband. Of course, she hadn't asked. She would have felt funny asking. Everyone had problems. They couldn't rearrange the office schedule just to accommodate her.

Darlene had strep. Thank God. If it had been nothing, she'd have felt terrible about the appointment. Instead, she felt terrible about being glad Darlene had strep throat. Still, she felt vindicated as she stopped off at the pharmacy to pick up the antibiotic.

Now Mimi parked the car in the garage, took Darlene out of the car seat, and went in the house to tell her husband his child was sick and ask him what five thousand dollars in cash was doing hidden under the blotter of his desk.

Chuck was indeed already home. His jacket was over the back of a chair, his briefcase on the floor by the portable bar.

Mimi took a breath, braced for the occasion. With a child in one arm, and a bottle of medicine in the other, she stalked into the office.

Chuck was on the phone when she came in. He had a glass of scotch in one hand. He saluted her with it, said, "Just a second, Dave. Hi, honey, be right with you. Look, Dave, my wife is home. I gotta get off the phone. Anyway, I checked out the movie money and you're in the clear. It's not counterfeiting if the bills can be distinguished from the real thing by reasonable effort. You just have to make a few changes. For starters, the serial number. I talked to the producer myself. The stuff is gonna be bundled, there is absolutely no reason for a different number. It's not gonna play on camera. If it did, they could always use a real bill on the outside of the pack. The guy doesn't much care. He says it's like how all movie telephone numbers are 555. Anyway, if you're doing ten million in hundreds, just run the same bill with the same number. Your problem is, you're doing too good work. Cut a few corners for a change."

Chuck put down the phone, smiled at his wife. "So, how are you?"

Mimi was totally at sea. How could she bring up the money now? Chuck had just accounted for it. If it really was the money under the blotter he was talking about. Was that money fake? It must be. But how could she tell? She couldn't ask. She'd have to admit she'd been snooping. Which she could get away with if he was in the wrong. But to admit to going through his things and finding *play* money . . .

Chuck frowned. "Honey? What's the matter? You look upset."

Mimi was having a panic attack. What could she tell him? What could she say?

Then she remembered.

Mimi slapped on a concerned face, and tried not to sound relieved.

"Darlene has strep throat," she told her husband.

16

Benny Southstreet couldn't believe it. The woman lied to his face. First she rips him off, then she lies to his face. The great pooh-bah of puzzles and cereal. A liar and petty thief. Here he was, a decent, honest, hard-working puzzle constructor, getting ripped off by the queen of words herself. She probably figured she was so high-and-mighty no one would take his word against hers.

Even though he had the documentation. Even though he could prove his case. Who would listen? The grid was the same, and most of the entries. And most of the clues. The theme was different, but not that different. There was no way it was a coincidence. No way. It was a ripoff, plain and simple, and she would not, no, she would *not* get away with it.

Scrunched down in the front seat of his rental car, Benny Southstreet watched Cora Felton's Toyota pull out of her driveway and

123

head for town. The yappy little dog's nose was out the back window. That was a break. Benny had puppy biscuits in his pocket just in case, but he was happy not to have to use them.

The minute Cora's car was out of sight, Benny slipped out of his car and crept up the drive. It was early evening, not yet dark. Anyone in the house could have seen him coming. But Benny was sure it was empty. Cora's niece had gone out about an hour earlier with a young gentleman, and from what Benny had been able to pick up nosing around town, they were the only ones who lived in the house. Even so, Benny knocked on the front door. He wasn't sure what he was going to say if anyone answered it. Luckily, no one did.

Benny tried the knob. The door was unlocked. He figured it might be. People in the country so seldom locked their doors. Benny slipped inside, began his search. In a modest ranch house, it wasn't difficult. The office was the first door down the hall.

There was a pile of papers on the desk. Benny pawed through them. Many were crossword puzzles, none of them his. Benny frowned, glanced around the office. The bottom shelf of the bookcase caught his eye. The oversized paperbacks looked suspiciously like crossword puzzle collections.

They were.

One of them looked damn familiar. Benny had sold so many puzzles to so many magazines it was hard to keep track. But he could have sworn he had one in that collection. He pulled it out, leafed through.

There it was! "My Bad," by Benny Southstreet.

There! That proved it! All he had to do was call the police and —

Get caught for breaking and entering.

Not only that, he'd be accused of planting the puzzle book. Even if he wasn't, the fact that she had it wouldn't prove that she used it. It would certainly raise the inference. But he wanted proof.

All right. When she changed his puzzle into hers, most likely she did it on the computer.

Benny checked out the icons on the screen. Sure enough, the Puzzle Lady had Crossword Compiler. Benny called it up, clicked on **OPEN** to see a directory of the puzzles. The title "My Bad" seemed almost too much to hope for.

It was. The puzzles didn't have titles, merely numbers and dates. Benny clicked on "#5134, 5/06." The puzzle that appeared was one he had seen in the paper. Benny couldn't care less about solving puzzles. If he was going to, it wouldn't be some ditzy old lady's. But he'd been checking out her column since she stole his puzzle. And this was one of the ones he'd seen.

So, where was his puzzle? Had she deleted it?

She must have. Which made sense. She wouldn't want to keep the evidence around.

Unless . . .

Benny clicked on an icon, opened Cora's mailbox. Half a dozen e-mails came in, mostly spam. Benny didn't want **RE-CEIVED MAIL**. He moved the mouse, clicked on **SENT MAIL**.

The woman who had given the puzzle to her husband was named Mimi Dillinger. There was no such person listed. But Benny knew e-mail addresses didn't always reflect people's names. He called up all the letters that had been sent in the last week, looking for one with an attachment. There was none. Well, another idea down the drain.

Benny guessed that was all he could do. Except he knew a bit about computers. With a little effort, he could figure out where Cora had been. Of course, that had nothing to do with the crossword puzzle. It would be a wholly unjustifiable intrusion into Cora's personal space. There was no reason whatsoever for him to do so. Except in the hope of finding something scandalous and embarrassing about her. Like a penchant for S&M porn sites, for instance. Stuff he had no right or reason to know.

Benny opened Netscape Navigator, checked for recent use. Discovered Cora had just been on eBay. Well, that was certainly none of his business. He wondered what she had been trying to buy. It was easy enough to find out. He scrolled through the list of recently opened eBay screens, clicked on one.

Huh. Chairs. Cora was bidding on chairs. And who was she bidding against?

Benny glanced out the window just to make sure no car was coming up the drive, then busied himself at the keyboard.

17

Chief Harper frowned at his coffee. It was late morning, the goodies from Cushman's Bake Shop were long gone, and the chief was making do with a cup of sludge from the station pot. "Solve the case yet?" he inquired.

Cora Felton graced him with a look usually reserved for Amway salesmen. "No, I have not solved the case. Though I must say I probably put in as much work in three days as you did in a year."

"That's because I have other cases. I can't concentrate on just one."

"Yeah. Look, I got my dog in the car. What do you want?"

"You left your dog in the car?"

"I'm taking him for a haircut. Yesterday I took him for a shot. I swear, I should get a chauffeur's license."

"A shot?"

"Rabies. Distemper. I don't know. Some yearly vaccine the vet thought up to make money. Now he needs a trim because poodles don't shed, and there goes another sixty bucks."

"I think there might be a local ordinance about leaving an animal unattended in a motor vehicle."

"So bust me. Come on, Chief. You called me in here. If you just want a progress report, I haven't got time."

"I see you have time to get your name in the paper." Harper pointed to the *Gazette,* open to the puzzle page. "Awfully nice of you, helping out the young woman."

"There's nothing nice about it. She tricked me into it."

"Still, to go to all the trouble of making a puzzle."

"You don't make a puzzle, you construct it. Don't you know anything?"

"When it comes to crossword puzzles, not much. Anyway, whatever you want to call it, you did it. And you did it all by yourself."

A chill ran down Cora's spine. "What do you mean by that?"

"Exactly what I said. The puzzle you gave to the woman. It's just like the ones in your column. You didn't get paid for it, but, aside from that, it's just like all the rest."

"Why wouldn't it be?"

"I have no idea. But it's not copyright, or

whatever it is, when you put a puzzle in the paper. Not that this puzzle's not in the paper, but you know what I mean."

"I don't know what you mean. And I really don't care."

"Maybe not. But while we're on the subject, can you assure me you had no outside help in coming up with it?"

"I'm not going to dignify that with an answer."

"So, if someone said you ripped off his puzzle, that person would be lying?"

"Would he ever. I've never ripped off anyone's puzzle in my life."

"I'm glad to hear it."

"Why, Chief? What's this all about?"

"After the puzzle appeared in the paper I had a phone call. Some guy askin' if you'd ever been charged with literary theft."

"You mean plagiarism? What did you tell him?"

"I told him no, of course not. He asked me to make sure you wrote the puzzle in the paper."

"So, what did you do?"

"Nothing. I'm not going to put any faith in an anonymous voice."

"The guy didn't give a name?"

"If he had, he wouldn't be so anonymous."

"But you asked me about it anyway."

"Give me a break. I didn't ask you to *ask* you. I asked you to *tell* you."

"You called me in here," Cora reminded him.

"Not for that. I got another case for you."

Cora brightened immediately. "Really?"

"Yes, and it's right up your alley. Chuck Dillinger, the husband of the woman you helped, lodged a complaint this morning that his office was broken into."

"His office? In the city?"

"No, in his house."

"He has an office in his house?"

"Not his office. His study."

"His *study* was broken into?"

"You find that strange?"

"He locks his study?"

"What's wrong with that?"

"Do *you* lock *your* study? I bet your study doesn't even have a lock."

"My study doesn't even have a door."

"There you are. The guy locks his study. Did you ask him why?"

"No."

"What kind of a lock does he have on it?"

"I don't know. I haven't seen it."

"Of course not. You just spoke to him on the phone. Tell me, Chief, do you do *all* your work over the phone? Do you ever leave your office?"

"Why should I? I'm the chief. I've got people to handle things for me."

"Like who?"

"Like you. Wanna go see the wife? You got a relationship with her already. Why don't you run out there, ask her what's what."

Cora looked pained. "Oh, come on. I'm trying to get away from the woman."

"You're looking for a crime. What's wrong with breaking and entering?"

"Breaking what? The study door you're not even sure the guy has?"

"There you are. That's something you could find out for me."

"Yeah, great. Tell me, Chief, what were you going to do about this if I hadn't come in?"

"Probably wait to see if the guy called again. Then I'd know if he was serious."

"I don't know when *you're* serious, Chief. Are you as lazy as you sound, or are you just pulling my leg?"

"A little of both. Actually, I sent Sam Brogan out there. He hasn't reported in yet. That's why I'm sure it's nothing."

"Sam probably scared her to death," Cora observed dryly. Bakerhaven's crankiest officer had reduced interrogations to a Zen art that often reduced witnesses to tears.

"Sam's a good boy. If he found anything, he'd have reported in."

"He didn't," Cora said. "So, why do you want me to go out there and do it?"

"Because you're just that much better than Sam."

Cora scowled suspiciously. But Chief Harper kept a straight face.

18

Mimi Dillinger seemed hassled. "What do you want?" she said, stopping Cora at the door.

Cora frowned. Mimi had the baby on one hip and a diaper over her shoulder; still, one would have expected a slightly warmer greeting for the savior who bailed her out with hubby. "I hear you had a break-in."

"Who told you that?"

"Chief Harper."

Mimi frowned. "Why is he telling everyone our business?"

"It's not like he made a public announcement. I stopped by the station and he asked me to help him out." Cora took a breath, said, "I sometimes help people out."

Mimi, prompted, chimed in with belated thanks. "Well, you certainly helped me," she gushed. "Chuck took it so well. I can't thank you enough."

"You didn't have to put it in the paper."

"I suppose that was a bit impulsive. But once I sent the fax I didn't know how to get it back. Is it a problem?"

Cora waved it away. "What's done is done. But about this break-in . . ."

"Oh, it was nothing. The police were here."

"Sam Brogan?"

"Yes." Mimi frowned. "Is he always like that?"

"Yeah," Cora said. "Anyway, Chief Harper would like to get the facts without the attitude."

"Oh. Well, then, come in."

It was, to Cora's thinking, a rather grudging invitation. She followed Mimi into the living room of a modest two-story colonial. The decor was what Cora referred to as functional-modern. As opposed to what Cora referred to as ultramodern. Or silly.

Cora gazed wistfully at the portable bar. It was not that long since she'd given up drinking.

Mimi put the baby in a playpen in the corner. Darlene immediately began bawling.

"Was your husband here when Sam Brogan came?"

"No, he was at work."

"So you had to deal with him?"

"Yes. And you'd think the man never saw a baby before. 'Madam, could you keep that

135

kid quiet!' Can you believe it? He actually said that."

Cora, who shared Sam's sentiment, merely nodded. "So, when did this break-in occur?"

"Sometime last night."

"Can you pin it down any?"

"Not really. We didn't discover it until this morning."

"Was anything taken?"

"No. But it's the principle of the thing."

"You mention that to Sam Brogan?"

"Yes. He wasn't happy."

"No, I don't imagine he was. How did the thief get in?"

"The policeman said since nothing was taken, he's technically not a thief."

Cora snorted in disgust. "Yeah, I know. But *person-who-broke-in* is such a cumbersome phrase. How about *prowler*? How did the prowler break in?"

"Through the kitchen window."

"Oh?"

"He smashed a pane of glass in the back door of the kitchen, reached in, and unlocked it."

Cora frowned. "Hmm."

"What's wrong with that?"

"Chief Harper said the study was broken into. According to you, the kitchen was broken into."

136

"It was. You can see for yourself."

"Then why did your husband say it was the study?"

"Obviously the prowler broke in through the kitchen to get to the study."

"Yeah, but nothing was taken. If nothing was taken, how do you know the prowler was even *in* the study?"

"I don't know. Maybe things were messed up."

"Is that what your husband said?"

"He called the police from work. I wasn't there."

"Well, what did he tell you?"

"Someone broke in."

"You knew that from the glass on the floor. Did he tell *you* it was the study?"

"I don't remember."

"Hmm."

"What's the matter?"

"Can I look at the study?"

"Why?"

"To see if anything's missing."

"But you don't know what was there."

"What's your point?"

Mimi looked at Cora in exasperation. She clearly didn't want to show Cora the study, but it was hard to refuse someone who had done her such a big favor. "You can look, but don't mess up Chuck's things. He doesn't like people messing with his things."

"Did the prowler mess with his things?"

"I don't know. I think it's the fact that he might have."

"Uh-huh. So where's the study?"

Mimi led Cora to a room down the hall. The door was open. There was a keyhole in it.

"Chuck keep this locked?" Cora asked.

"No."

The study was a small room dominated by a wooden desk and an office chair on wheels. It was an armed chair of the type you could tip back to put your feet up on the desk. Cora hated them. She seldom put her feet up on the desk, and the chair was wobbly.

There came a loud wail. It was either the baby objecting to the playpen, or someone strangling a cat. At any rate, the sound sent Mimi charging out of the room. Cora was glad. The woman had no useful information, and it was easier to toss the place without her.

Not that Cora knew where to look. Or what to look for. There'd been a break-in. Nothing had been taken. But the husband had specifically named the study. He was either omniscient, a moron, or lying. If the latter — no, the last, sequence of three — oh, hell, she was starting to think like Sherry, what a depressing prospect. If Mimi's husband was lying, if something was stolen, it was something he didn't want to report. Now, what could that be?

Drugs immediately came to mind. The guy was a dope dealer, someone ripped off his stash, naturally he couldn't tell the police. But he could report a break-in. Which might result in the police getting a line on his nemesis. Which would serve as a hell of a warning not to do anything of the kind again.

Okay, so where did the guy hide his drugs?

The bookcases seemed too easy, but Cora checked them anyway. There was nothing behind the books. Nothing in the file cabinets, unless pressed thin as wafers and slipped in the file folders. Nothing in the desk drawers. Nothing behind the desk drawers.

The kid was still howling, and Cora loved her now. She was a perfect distraction.

Okay, suppose nothing was stolen. Suppose something was just looked at.

The computer was on. And Cora had recently learned a little about computers.

Cora sat in the tippy armchair, wheeled it up to the desk. The keyboard was on the desktop, a little high for her liking. There was no mouse pad, the mouse sat on the ink blotter.

The blotter was slightly askew. The left front corner had been moved about a half inch to the right, creating a diagonal line in the dust on the desk.

Someone had moved the blotter. Why? Was there something under it?

Cora pushed the keyboard aside, raised the edge of the blotter. Saw nothing. Of course, the monitor was holding most of the blotter down. Should she move it?

In the living room, Mimi was reasoning with her child, with little success. From what Cora could tell, they had a lot more to discuss.

Cora pushed the monitor back, raised the blotter.

There was nothing there.

Except . . .

Was that something in the upper right-hand corner? Where the edge of the monitor still held the blotter down?

She hadn't moved the monitor far enough. She had to move it again.

Uh-oh!

Darlene was quiet. The child from hell screams for fifteen minutes, and now she's quiet?

Damn!

Cora's left hand snaked out from under the blotter, grabbed the top of the monitor, tipped it up. Beneath the blotter her left hand was no longer holding up, her right hand fumbled forward, touched something, gripped it between her fingers.

The monitor began to fall.

Cora leaped to her feet. The desk chair shot across the room, banged into a small bookcase.

Cora lunged across the desk. Her right hand flew from beneath the blotter, grabbing the monitor as it went over. She wrestled it back onto the desk with her right hand, knocking the keyboard and mouse to the floor with her flailing left.

The ensuing racket was slightly louder than a busboy dropping a tray of dishes, slightly less than an atomic blast.

The baby wailed again. Its surprised tremolo could only mean Mimi had snatched it from the playpen.

Cora only had a second to straighten up the den.

Fat chance.

The monitor was sideways. The keyboard and mouse were on the floor. The desk chair had knocked a glass, a vase, and a framed photograph off the bookcase. Miraculously, none of them were broken, merely strewn across the floor.

Footsteps hurried in the direction of the study. Cora had approximately half a second to make things right.

She flung herself to the floor. She did it so convincingly she banged her head on the leg of the desk.

Mimi burst into the room. "My God! What happened?"

Cora looked up ruefully, rubbed her aching head. "I fell. I went to sit on the chair, completely lost my balance. I'm afraid I messed up the desk. Oh, dear! And the bookcase! Did anything break?"

Mimi glanced around the room, then looked back at the prone woman on the floor with the impatient feigned tolerance the young reserved for annoying infirmities of the elderly, and Cora knew she was home free.

19

Cora slammed the red Toyota to a stop, dragged her drawstring purse off the passenger seat, and practically flew up the path. She was eager to see what she'd found under the blotter of Mimi's husband's desk, if she had indeed found anything. It felt like the tiniest scrap of paper. Or cardboard. Or plastic. Or light metal, such as aluminum foil. Or cloth. It could have been a piece of a letter, a playing card, or a paper napkin without surprising her in the least.

If it was something so innocuous, Cora might have trouble figuring out what it was. She had plunged it deep within the recesses of her drawstring purse, where several similar objects presumably lay.

Cora burst in the door, bellowed, "Sherry!" There was no answer. She must be out with Aaron. Otherwise, she'd be home, since Cora had the car.

Cora went into the kitchen, lit up a cigarette. She took a saucer down to use as an ashtray. Sherry was always hiding the ashtrays to discourage her from smoking.

Cora sat down at the table, regarded her purse.

Should she dump it, or take out the items one by one? Dumping seemed good. Were there any items that shouldn't be dumped? Ah, yes. She removed her gun, set it aside. Then, taking hold of the bottom corners of the drawstring purse, she turned it upside down and slid the contents out on the table.

It was a fairly imposing pile of junk.

Cora quickly removed the objects she knew to be hers, which included a makeup mirror, a knitting needle, and several ornate cigarette lighters, none of which worked, but all of which had sentimental if not intrinsic value.

An autograph book from her more lighthearted days, if such a thing was possible, boasted, among others, inscriptions from James Taylor, Reggie Jackson, and Paul Newman.

There was also a hairbrush. Cora couldn't remember the last time she'd used it. Maybe it wasn't hers. Even so, it wasn't what she found under the blotter.

Cora pawed through the remaining articles, found birth control pills, a diaphragm, three condoms, and spermicidal jelly. Maybe it was just as well she hadn't unpacked in front of Chief Harper.

A coin purse. A wallet, with ID cards and money. A number of pencils with broken points. A number of pens, none of which worked. A church key, left over from her drinking days. Damn. Cora could remember turning the house upside down to open a beer bottle, and she had a church key all the time.

Never mind. What did she find under the blotter?

There were a number of small pieces of paper in her purse, mostly receipts.

Whoa! What was this? A small green and white paper. What the hell was that?

Cora held it up, squinted at it.

It had a right angle, and a jagged, torn edge.

She could make out the upper half of what appeared to be numbers.

One, zero, zero.

Cora whistled.

It was unmistakably the corner of a hundred-dollar bill.

Cora couldn't recall the last time she'd had a hundred-dollar bill loose in her purse. Granted, there were huge stretches of her life she couldn't recall all that clearly; still, the presence of large sums of money would have been apt to make some impression.

Hot damn!

Wait till Chief Harper saw this!

Cora snatched the phone from the wall, punched in the number. "Chief? Cora. I'll be right over. I found something in the Dillinger house," she said, and slammed down the phone before he could argue.

Cora's moment of elation was dampened by the pile of junk on the kitchen table. She couldn't leave it there. She had to sort through it, throw stuff out.

Like hell.

Cora held her purse up to the edge of the table, pushed her precious belongings back into it. She snatched up her gun and her car keys and tore out the door.

As Cora's Toyota sped down the driveway, Dennis Pride stepped out from his hiding place in the hall closet.

Well, that was interesting as all hell.

What had Cora found in the Dillinger house?

20

Chief Harper squinted up from the bill. "So?"

Cora pointed. "That's a piece of a hundred-dollar bill."

"I can see that. So what?"

"It may have come from under the blotter on Mimi's husband's desk."

"May have?"

"There's a very good chance. You could almost assume it did."

"Why would I have any doubt?"

"It could also have come from my purse."

"Aha. And when's the last time you cleaned your purse?"

"I believe Nixon was in the White House."

"That's not encouraging."

"It should be. A bad witness swears up and down they're right no matter what. A fair witness, who acknowledges the fact they might be wrong, has an opinion I can take to the bank."

"That's well argued. It does not cheer me." Harper sighed. "All right. I guess I gotta ask the husband about this."

"No, you can't do that."

Harper looked at Cora in surprise. "Excuse me?"

"If you ask her husband, Mimi will know I was snooping."

"So?"

"I'm not going to be invited into many people's homes if they know I snoop."

"You're investigating a break-in. You're not supposed to look around?"

"Not under the blotter."

"Oh, for pity's sake." Chief Harper raised his head, bellowed, "Sam!"

After a pause of several seconds, from the deep recesses of the police station came a rather exasperated, "Yeah?"

"Come in here a minute?"

Sam didn't answer, but after a while there came the sound of police boots stomping down the hall, and Bakerhaven's crankiest police officer trudged in. He saw Cora, scowled, stroked his mustache. "What do *you* want?" he demanded.

"You ever have to sneak up on a suspect, Sam?"

"No, but I got one ready for booking. If I can get the paperwork done. Which I can't really do in here. What's she got you involved in now, Chief?"

"That break-in you covered."

"Nothing to it. Nothing taken, nothing damaged, except one small pane of glass. Case closed."

"Not quite."

"Why not?"

"You found something in the study."

"No I didn't."

"Yes, you did." Chief Harper held out the plastic evidence bag with the corner of the bill. "You found this under the blotter in the study."

"You planting evidence now, Chief?"

"No, just accounting for it."

"I see." Sam gave Cora his most withering look. "He means you found it."

"Don't worry, Sam," Cora said sweetly. "I won't tell anyone you overlooked it."

Sam nearly choked on his mustache.

21

Becky Baldwin's law office was over the pizza shop. Today's special was sausage and peppers. Becky, with a fashion model figure to maintain, had grown immune to the aromas. Her clients were not so lucky.

"Damn, I missed lunch," Benny Southstreet complained, sniffing the air.

Becky ignored the digression. She had few enough clients, she didn't intend to lose one to a pizza. "But you have a problem?"

"Yes, I do. And you seem to be the only lawyer in town." He put up his hand. "No offense, of course. I'm not saying you're not good. You're pretty young for a lawyer."

Becky smiled. "How old do you think a lawyer should be?"

"I know that's stupid. But you're a girl. Not that there's anything wrong with a girl being a lawyer. I seen some pretty tough woman lawyers. The one who handled my divorce was built like a tank." Benny shuddered at the thought. "Damn, that pizza's driving me nuts."

Becky wanted to tell him to get some lunch and come back, but she was afraid he wouldn't. She smiled, said, "You must be in a lot of trouble to pass a pizza place to get to my office."

"I'm not in trouble."

"I'm glad to hear it."

"No you're not. If I were in trouble, you could make a buck. That's how you lawyers think."

Becky was pretty sure that was how Benny Southstreet thought. "What can I do for you?"

"You know any law?"

"One or two."

"Is that a joke? I'm sitting here starving, and you're making jokes?"

Becky'd had enough. "You ask me if I know any law. That's either a joke or an insult. You think you just rent an office and hang up a sign? I'd like to see you pass the bar, mister."

Benny nodded approvingly. "Spitfire. I like that. Not much muscle, but a lot of moxie. Think I should trust you?"

"I know what I think. I have no idea what you think. Or who you are. Can you afford a cash retainer?"

Benny put up his hands. "Hey. Just a minute. Who said anything about cash? We're talking lawsuit, here. It's not cash. It's contingency."

"Just my luck," Becky said dryly. "Guy knows two legal terms and one of them's *contingency.*"

"Yeah, well, that's right, isn't it?"

"In a negligence suit, maybe. Is this a negligence suit? A personal injury?"

"Sure. I'm the injured party."

"And how were you injured?"

"Not physically. I was stolen from."

Becky shook her head. "That's a matter for the police."

"No it's not. They'd just laugh at me."

Becky was sure they would. An incoherent, two-bit gambler who looked like he'd stepped out of a production of *Guys and Dolls*. "What was stolen, Mr. Southstreet?"

"My crossword puzzle."

Becky blinked. "I beg your pardon?"

"See? See? You're laughing at me too. It's not funny. The damn bitch stole my puzzle!"

Dennis Pride barged in. That was the biggest problem with Becky's office, aside from garlic and onions. No waiting room. No privacy. Anyone entering from the street interrupted any client conference. Dennis did so now, just in time to hear Benny's complaint.

Dennis grinned. "So, some bitch stole your puzzle. Who might that be?"

"Dennis, could you wait outside?" Becky said.

"I could, but I'm not gonna. I'm supposed to check in with my lawyer. I'm doing it. Unless you got something else, I'm outta here."

"I'd like to talk to you."

"I'd like to talk to you too. But someone stole this guy's puzzle. Some bitch, I believe he said."

"You see?" Benny Southstreet said. "You see? This is the reaction I can expect. No one cares."

"I think it's an outrage, but you got no case. Unless the person who stole it was someone famous."

"Oh, yeah? It's the Puzzle Lady, for Christ's sake. You think I got a case now?"

"The Puzzle Lady stole your puzzle? I like it. This is really good."

"Dennis."

"I'm going, I'm going. I would not want to interfere with this. You got a live one here. This could be worth some money."

Dennis grinned at Becky, and ducked out the door.

Becky watched him go, then turned back

to her prospective client.

Benny's arms were folded. His head was cocked in an I-told-you-so pose. "Well," he demanded, "what do you think now?"

22

Dennis ambushed Benny Southstreet outside the pizza parlor. He'd meant to ambush
him outside Becky Baldwin's, but Benny
foxed him, ducking in for a quick sausage
and peppers. Benny was holding it over a
greasy paper plate and feeding one end of
the folded slice into his mouth when Dennis
came walking up. "Get any satisfaction?"

Benny chewed the pizza, swallowed. "God,
that's good! Yeah, she's taking the case."

"You mind walking away from here so she
doesn't come out and see me?"

"What's the problem?"

"I'm supposed to check in with her. I
checked in with her. I don't need a lecture."

"How come you gotta check in?"

"I'm on probation."

"For what?"

"Possession of drugs. And it wasn't even
my drugs."

"Yeah, sure."

"The court agreed it wasn't my drugs. Not that they cared. Never mind. Tell me about your case."

"I'm not supposed to talk about it." Having made that virtuous pronouncement, Benny couldn't *stop* talking about it. He filled in Dennis in between bites of pizza.

Dennis frowned. "So, the Puzzle Lady ripped you off?"

"You find that hard to believe?"

"I find it very interesting. That a woman with so much to lose would take such a chance."

"Well, she didn't know it was going to be in the paper."

Dennis put up one finger. "I wouldn't be so quick to concede that. Not with a lawsuit pending. How do you *know* she didn't expect it to be in the paper? Maybe she knew the type of woman this Mimi What's-her-name was and *expected* it to be in the paper."

"Are you saying she did?"

"Not at all. I'm exploring possibilities. Which is what you should be doing. This woman she wrote the puzzle for — what do you know about her?"

"Housewife and mother. Husband works for some law firm in New York."

"They got money?"

"Why?"

"You're suing them. It would help if they had money."

"They have some."

"What kind of house they got?"

Benny shrugged. "Small two-story colonial. No great shakes."

"You seen it?"

"Why do you ask?"

"I hear they had a break-in."

"Are you accusing me?"

"Should I be?"

"Not unless you want a fat lip."

"So what did you find?"

"Where?"

"At their house."

"I'm warning you."

"Yeah, yeah. Sure."

"Why are you so interested?"

"The Puzzle Lady's niece."

"What about her?"

"I used to be married to her."

"You still got feelings for her?"

"None of your damn business."

"Any chance of a reconciliation?"

"Not much."

"How come?"

"I remarried."

Benny raised his eyebrows.

"I don't want to talk about it."

Benny grinned. "Ah! Struck a nerve."

"We're not talking about me. We're talking about you. If Cora Felton searched their house, what might she have found? That was important enough to turn over to the cops. We're talking something small enough for her to stick in her purse. That she'd have to sort out from her other junk."

"I have no idea."

"Neither do I." Dennis cocked his head at Benny. "Luckily, whatever it is can't send *me* to jail."

23

Chuck Dillinger's office was small. It also faced the interior court instead of the street. What good was an office on Madison Avenue if your office wasn't *on* Madison Avenue? True, it was a Madison Avenue address, but it wasn't *his* address, it was the partnership of Hendricks and Sloane, and he wasn't Hendricks or Sloane, so he had a small office on the interior court.

Chuck Dillinger was a young associate, hoping to make partner. It wasn't cheap raising a family, especially in Connecticut. Not in a house as nice as his, on the good side of town. Without help, he couldn't make it. He'd have to move to upstate New York, or even New Jersey. Not the direction his life should be heading. Not the direction at all.

Chuck checked his appointment book. He had no client meetings today. Which left him with paperwork. He hated paperwork. That was what his paralegal should be doing. Only

Chuck didn't have a paralegal. He relied on the switchboard girl, who didn't type and didn't file. Which left him typing and filing.

The phone rang. It was, of course, the switchboard. Either that or his wife. Only she had his direct line. Chuck was surprised to hear a man's voice.

"Mr. Dillinger?"

"Yes."

"This is Officer Brogan, Bakerhaven PD."

"Oh?"

"I'm working on the break-in at your house."

"Oh." Chuck's pulse raced. "Caught the guy?" he asked casually.

" 'Fraid not. So little to go on. Just wanted to follow up. You said your study was broken into, is that correct?"

"I'm not sure it was broken into, since nothing was taken."

"No, but you said so. Isn't that right? Not that it was broken into, but the fact you reported it was?"

"I may have said something like that."

"Why would you have thought such a thing?"

Chuck's head was coming off. What the hell was this all about? "Officer, I don't even remember saying such a thing, but if I did, uh, there's nothing in the house worth stealing, so I would naturally think the study."

"There's things worth stealing in the study?"

"Well, my computer's there. And some expensive cigars."

"You thought someone broke in to steal your cigars?"

"No. Of course not. I have no idea why anyone might break in. I have nothing worth taking. Nothing *was* taken. I assume the thief broke in, looked around, was disappointed, and left."

"That sounds quite reasonable."

"Good. I hope that clears things up, Officer."

"Yeah, but that's not why I called."

"Oh?"

"There was something under the blotter of your desk. Which probably wouldn't mean anything. Except with your claim someone broke into the study . . ."

"You found something under the blotter of my desk? You didn't mention anything about that."

"Neither did you."

"What?"

"You didn't mention keeping anything under the blotter of your desk."

"I don't know what you're talking about. What did you find?"

"The torn corner of a hundred-dollar bill."

There was a silence on the phone. Sam Brogan continued, "Do you have any idea what that was doing there?"

After another brief silence, Chuck said, "Oh, is that all. You had me worried."

"You know what the bill was doing there?"

"Yes, of course."

"You wanna share that information?" Sam said dryly.

"I often keep a couple of hundreds under my blotter for emergencies. The corner must have torn off one of them."

"So these were your hundred-dollar bills?"

"That's right."

"And you think the burglar took them?"

"No, I don't."

"Why not?"

"Because I spent them."

"Oh?"

"I ran out of cash and spent the bills. The corner must have torn off when I pulled them out."

"Okay. So you're saying what we're dealing with is the corner of a genuine hundred-dollar bill, it's your hundred-dollar bill, and it wasn't stolen?"

"No. I'm sorry, Officer. If you're looking for leads, I'm afraid it's another dead end. But I certainly appreciate your taking the time and effort. Was there anything else?"

"No, that'll do."

Chuck hung up the phone. Son of a bitch! The cop would have to find a piece of a bill. He wondered if it was foolish to have claimed it was his, but what else could he do? His wife had bought the stage money explanation, but the cop was another story. Mimi would never check, but the cop might. When there wasn't any movie money, there'd be hell to pay. No way to lie his way out of that.

Of course, there'd be hell to pay if the cop checked with his wife. But that would be easier to explain. The bills were his personal secret stash. His wife didn't know about it. He couldn't admit it to her. No way.

Wait a minute! Mimi hadn't seen the corner of a hundred-dollar bill. She'd seen a whole stack of 'em. Five thousand dollars' worth. How could he reconcile that?

Chuck was sweating profusely, and his office had air-conditioning, one of the few perks of the job. Good lord, how would he handle that?

Chuck hyperventilated, trying to calm himself. It wasn't so bad. Why would the cop bother to check with his wife? There was no reason to, and —

Icy terror gripped him.

What if he already had?

What if the cop knew Mimi's story, and was just baiting him? What if the cop was merely waiting to spring the trap?

The phone rang.

Chuck stared at it in horror. Oh, my God! That was the cop calling back. "I checked with your wife. Would you like to reconsider the story about the hundred-dollar bill?"

Good God! Maybe he should duck into the men's room, pretend he was out of his office. No, that would never do.

Chuck scooped up the phone. "Hello?"

"Mr. Dillinger?"

Chuck had never been so relieved to hear the receptionist's voice. "Yes?"

"Someone to see you. A Mr. Dennis Pride."

24

Dennis Pride was grinning like he'd just won the lottery. A cocky, insolent grin. He glanced around the office as if making an unflattering value judgment.

Chuck wanted to wipe the smug smile off his face. But what if he was a new junior partner? Younger morons were being wooed away from more and more firms these days. There was no way to know them all. He didn't dare be overtly hostile.

The young man was wearing a suit and tie — granted, not the quality one would expect from a hotshot attorney; still, he could be someone's eccentric nephew. There was no reason not to tread cautiously.

Chuck extended his hand. "Mr. Pride, I'm Chuck Dillinger. Come in, sit down. What can I do for you?"

"I was hoping we could help each other out." Dennis shrugged. "Actually, I was hoping you could help *me* out. Anything that helps *you* would be entirely incidental."

"What are you talking about?"

"Benny Southstreet."

Chuck frowned. "Who?"

Dennis nodded approvingly. "That's good. Very good. You're either a terrific poker player or you've never heard of him."

"I've never heard of him. Who's Benny Southstreet?"

There was one comfortable client chair in the office. Dennis lolled back in it, crossed his legs. "I understand you had a break-in at your house."

"Are you a cop?"

"Good lord, what an idea. Wait'll the boys in the band hear that. I mean *band* as in rock group. This is my day job. I actually sing."

Chuck just gawked.

Dennis chuckled. "That's your cue to say, 'You sing a funny tune,' or something equally square and cliché."

"Damn it, what about the break-in?"

"Ah, the man lives. I understand you were pretty upset, considering nothing was taken."

"Well, nothing was."

"Then why were you so upset?"

"How'd you like someone to break into your house?"

"I haven't got a house. But I concede the

166

point. Let's talk about something else."

"What?"

"Cora Felton."

Chuck's mouth fell open.

Dennis grinned. "That's a pretty good barometer. I think we could safely say you've heard of Cora Felton and you haven't heard of Benny Southstreet."

"Of course I've heard of Cora Felton. She's the Puzzle Lady."

Dennis laughed out loud.

"What's so funny?"

"Nothing. It's just that's the only thing you've told me so far. That Cora Felton is the Puzzle Lady."

"Well, everyone knows that."

"Yes, they do. That's why I find the information less than useful. I understand you've had particular reason to know about the Puzzle Lady."

"I don't know how that puzzle got in the paper."

"Didn't your wife put it there?"

"I suppose she did."

"And you knew that, didn't you? But you automatically lied. It's like a reflex action with you. Is it because you're a lawyer? Is that why you do it?"

"I've had enough of your insolence. What do you want?"

"Do you know Cora Felton searched your house?"

"What?"

"Your wife didn't tell you that. I wonder what other things she hasn't told you."

"What are you implying?"

"Nothing at all. That was just for fun. Cora Felton found something, stuck it in her purse. I don't know what it was, but she told the cops about it." Dennis was watching Chuck's face. "Ah, I see that means something to you. You know what she found. What was it?"

"I have no idea."

Dennis shook his head. "There you go again. The automatic lie. Just when we were having fun. This Benny Southstreet that you never heard of — you know who he is? He claims he wrote the puzzle Cora Felton gave your wife that got printed in the paper."

"What?"

"That's what he claims. Personally, I think he's the guy who broke into your house. He knows where it is, he knows what it looks like. And he needs to find evidence to back his lawsuit."

"Who is this guy?"

"Ah, now you're interested. Can I assume something valuable was taken?"

Chuck clamped his lips in a tight line.

"I'll take that as a yes. And Cora Felton found evidence of the theft. Did Benny drop something, I wonder, something that might have his fingerprints on it, something that would implicate him?" Dennis studied Chuck's face. "No, that's not it. And you *know* that's not it. Now, how do you know that's not it? Did the cops ask you about it? Aha! The cops *told* you about it. Asked you if you know what it is. Did you lie to them? I'll bet you did. That would be your immediate reaction. Even if you didn't have to. I wonder if you had to. Now, why would that be? Let's see. Suppose it was drugs. That's a biggie. Did Benny rip off your drugs? No, that doesn't work. If the cops found evidence of drugs, you wouldn't be here. No, it's gotta be something embarrassing but not illegal. You have a porn site, by any chance? That Benny Southstreet found on your computer? Did Cora discover it and write down the URL?"

"Now you're just wasting my time. Who the hell are you? What has any of this got to do with you?"

"Ah, the crux of the matter. I'm an interested party, and I'm not the police. If you lost something valuable, perhaps I can get it back. For a percentage, of course. Should we say half?"

"Are you a private eye?"

"Oh, my God. This gets better and better. First a cop, now a private eye. You're missing the point. I'm the guy who can help you out. I'm the guy who can get back what was stolen."

"What makes you think you can do that?"

"I'm in a wonderful bargaining position. I have nothing to hide. I haven't done anything illegal. I can act on your behalf, and I can act on Mr. Southstreet's behalf, and I can effect a reconciliation. And neither one of you will complain, because you don't want to involve the police.

"Now then, let's start again. What did Benny Southstreet take from your study that you would like to have back?"

25

Mr. Wilbur rubbed a hole in the sludge on his dirty windowpane, and peered out to see who was knocking on his door. The man on the doorstep didn't look like an antiques dealer. There was something way too cagy about him. Not that antiques dealers weren't cagy. The most knowledgeable people in the world were antiques dealers. But this guy was different. This guy looked like he knew nothing about antiques, and couldn't care less. There were a fair share of them in the business too. They had the look. Wilbur knew it well. The look of someone hoping to screw you out of one particular item.

Wilbur opened the door on a safety chain. "Yes?" he demanded.

Benny Southstreet put on his most ingratiating smile, which didn't fool Wilbur for a moment. "Are you open?"

"Depends what you want."

"I want to see some antiques."

"Name one."

"Excuse me?"

"What antique do you want to see?"

"Just browsing."

"I'm not open for browsing. You think what you want, come back."

Wilbur slammed the door in his face.

Benny Southstreet stood on the front steps and assessed the situation. It was not the first time he had had a door slammed in his face, so he was not astounded by the occurrence. He mused for a moment how a man with so few people skills managed to stay in business. He assumed the guy owned the house and had next to no overhead.

Benny knocked on the door again. When it opened a crack, he said, "Rattan chairs."

The door slammed shut.

Not the right magic words.

There came the sound of the chain being removed.

Ah. Open sesame, after all.

Wilbur opened the door, but still stood blocking the doorway. "What about the chairs?" he demanded.

"I'm interested in them. I'm wondering who else is."

"You wanna buy some chairs?"

"I'm interested."

"Would your interest be reflected in cash?"

"Are you asking if I want to pay for the information?"

"I'm asking if you want to pay for the chairs."

"You got chairs for sale?"

"I might."

"But you don't right now?"

"Not at the moment."

"That doesn't sound promising. Maybe I should buy 'em on eBay."

"You'll get taken."

"Oh?"

"You'll pay too much for bad quality. Your furniture will fall apart."

"You wouldn't advise buying on eBay?"

"Only if you want to throw away your money."

"Then why are you doing it?"

"Huh?"

"You're bidding on chairs on eBay. I don't know why you're doing it, but you are."

"How do you know that?"

"Don't worry, I won't blow your cover. I just find it interesting that you're bidding. And who you're bidding against."

"What do you mean?"

"You're bidding against Cora Felton. Did you know that?"

"What!?"

"Yeah. That's gotta be a kick in the crotch.

The famous Puzzle Lady muscling in on your business."

"How do you know that?"

"It's my job to know. What I don't know is what's so all-fired important about these damn chairs. If I were you, I'd let her buy 'em. When a woman gets her mind set on something, it's hard to stop her."

Wilbur squinted at Benny suspiciously. "What's this got to do with you?"

"The woman ripped me off. I'm wondering if she's ripping anybody else off. If she is, I'd like to know it."

"You say she's the one bidding against me?"

"That's right."

"How do you know that?"

"I'm staying in a motel outside of town. The Four Seasons. Unit 12. You find out why the Puzzle Lady's bidding against you, you let me know." Benny rubbed his chin. "Unless you know now. You know now, you can save yourself the trip. No reason we shouldn't work together."

"No reason we should," Mr. Wilbur said, and slammed the door.

26

Cora ran into Mimi Dillinger outside of **CANINE CUTS,** the dog groomer in the mall. Mimi had Darlene in the stroller. A bag of freshly purchased Pampers hung from the handlebars.

"Oh, what a pretty dog!" Mimi exclaimed. "Darlene, look at the pretty dog!"

"Thank you," Cora said without enthusiasm. For her money, Buddy looked thoroughly humiliated, all poofy and blow-dried with a blue bandana around his neck, and she was sure the little poodle couldn't wait to get home and roll in the mud.

Darlene paid no attention to the dog, probably just to spite Mommie.

Cora sized Mimi up, ventured, "So, about the break-in . . ."

"The police don't seem to be making any progress."

"Oh, they have something now. Something interesting."

"What's that?"

"The corner of a hundred-dollar bill. It was discovered under the blotter of your husband's desk."

Mimi's eyes twitched. "Oh?" she said cautiously.

Cora caught it. She wondered what the woman was trying to hide. "So, the police figured if there was money there, that was something might be stolen."

"I see."

"Yeah. Unfortunately, it was a dead end. Turns out your husband liked to keep a couple of bills under the blotter for emergencies."

"A couple of bills?"

"Yes."

"Any chance it was more?"

"Why do you say that?"

"I don't know. It's just, if it was a lot of money, there might be a reason to break in."

Cora nodded. "That's a good point."

"And you think the prowler stole the money?"

"No. Apparently your husband spent the bills and never bothered to replace them."

Darlene chose that time to cry.

Mimi stooped, said, "There, there," and

stuck a pacifier in her mouth, a little more abruptly than a candidate for Mom of the Year. "So, this bill you found. You had no reason to test it?"

"Test it?"

"To see if it was real."

"Why wouldn't it be?"

"I don't know. I just mean if it really was a clue. Wouldn't you want to test it?"

Cora shrugged. "Not my department. You'd have to ask the police."

"And the police told my husband about finding the bill?"

"Sure. That's how they know where it came from."

The baby squealed again.

"Oh, it's time for her nap," Mimi exclaimed. "I have to get her home."

Cora watched Mimi load Darlene into the car seat of her Chevy. She wondered which fender Mimi had damaged.

She also wondered about the baby. It had been crying almost every time Cora had seen it. She wondered why this time it meant the baby needed a nap.

Could it be that Mimi had gotten uncomfortable with the conversation? Had suddenly realized she was asking too many questions? Or saying too much?

It was hard to say.

But it was certainly interesting that Mimi wanted to know if the police had tested the money.

And thought there might be more bills.

27

Harvey Beerbaum woke up to the sound of breaking glass. The little cruciverbalist was dreaming. In his dream he had just won the American Crossword Puzzle Tournament, and Will Shortz was handing him the trophy. But he couldn't quite reach it. It was slipping from his fingers. The prize slipping away. Victory so near and yet so far. The glass trophy shattering on the marble floor. Dashing his elusive dreams.

Wait a minute. The trophy wasn't glass. And the floor of the Stamford Marriott wasn't marble. And yet the sound . . .

Harvey sat up in bed. It *was* glass. He was sure of it.

Harvey slung his legs over the side of the bed, pulled on his slippers, which were right where he'd left them, at the edge of the shag rug. He slipped on his dressing gown, the extra-large, let out a bit in the middle to accommodate his portly frame. He carefully tied the sash around his waist in a bow, and padded to the top of the stairs.

A flashlight beam played around the living room.

A chill ran down Harvey's spine. He should call the police. But the phone was in the kitchen. He'd meant to put an extension in the upstairs bedroom, but it seemed an unnecessary expense, particularly when he had a cell phone. Only his cell phone was in his briefcase. And his briefcase was in his study.

Downstairs.

Harvey took a deep breath. What could he do? He didn't have a gun. No weapon of any kind.

His first thought was he could hide. But what if the prowler came upstairs? There was no lock on his bedroom door. Could he hide under the bed? Could he *fit* under the bed? Could he climb out the window? Could he yell for help? The neighbors were close enough to hear. But they'd be asleep. What was the chance they would wake up and get to him before a prowler could?

It came to him. The pool cue. He'd won

it in a local tournament. A nontraditional prize, donated in someone's memory, given in lieu of cash. Harvey didn't play pool, knew no one who did. It made a strange trophy, a two-piece cue in a little case, not the type of thing one could hang on the wall. It was in the bedroom closet. On the high shelf. Under a pile of sweaters and vests, put up until cooler weather.

There was a straight chair next to the door, where Harvey sat to tie his shoes. He fumbled for it in the dark, found it, picked it up, carried it quietly to the closet, set it down. As he stepped up he wondered, would it hold his weight? It always had sitting down, but that was different somehow. Harvey hadn't majored in physics, nor done well in math. Linguistics was his stock-in-trade. He knew all the synonyms for *weight-bearing,* just not the formulas.

Not to fear. The chair was sturdy. It didn't even creak. Standing on it, Harvey reached for the top shelf. His hand groped under the sweaters, and moments later he was climbing down with the case. Hard leather with two push-button snaps, the kind that locked, unlocked, thank God. He popped them open, careful not to make a sound, lifted the lid.

Inside lay the two halves of the pool cue. Harvey took them out of the velvet pockets, screwed them together, Fast Eddie about to take on Minnesota Fats. He gripped the cue in the middle, the handle up like a club, and tiptoed out the bedroom door.

The flashlight beam no longer showed. Maybe the prowler was gone. Harvey prayed it was so. He hesitated a moment, then started down the stairs.

They creaked.

Harvey automatically stepped back off the tread. It was so loud anyone would hear. He was like a freight train, coming down the stairs.

Harvey cocked his head, listened. There was no sound. Either the prowler had heard and was laying low, or there was no one there.

Harvey waited in the dark for what seemed like forever, but was probably less than a minute.

A car door slammed.

An engine roared.

It faded in the distance.

Harvey let out a sigh of relief. Even so, he held the pool cue at the ready as he crept down the stairs.

He reached the bottom, switched on the lights.

Harvey blinked in amazement.

His dining room chairs were gone.

28

Harvey Beerbaum wasn't happy. "We have to go to the police."

"And tell 'em what?" Cora said.

"What do you mean, tell 'em what? My chairs were stolen."

"Why do you suppose that is?"

"I know why that is. Because of the stupid eBay auction."

"Are you prepared to tell Chief Harper that?"

"Why shouldn't I be?"

"It's probably a violation of sorts. Advertising things you don't own."

"You're the one who told me to do it."

"You're absolutely right. I'm undoubtedly as guilty as you. I'm sure that will be some consolation when we're both in the pen."

"Damn it, Cora!"

"Such language."

"I'm sorry."

"I'm kidding. Nice to know you've got a

pulse. Harvey, we know who took your chairs. This s.o.b. at aol.com."

"Sbk," Harvey corrected. "That's right. So the police will know who to arrest."

"Yeah. You and me. Which, I think you'll agree, we don't want. We also don't want the police to arrest the guy who stole your chairs."

"Yes we do."

"No, we don't. You just want your chairs back. If we get them, what's the big deal?"

"My house was broken into."

"Which wasn't any fun. We should probably get a promise it won't happen again."

Harvey stared at Cora, then shook his head. "I can't even tell when you're serious."

"Does it matter? The point is, we don't want the police to arrest Mr. Aol.com."

"It could be the other guy," Harvey pointed out.

"What other guy?"

"The other guy who's bidding."

"Oh. Yeah."

Harvey's eyes widened in comprehension. "Cora!"

"Harvey, let's not get sidetracked."

"Sidetracked! You let me tell you about the other bid. Though totally unnecessary, I take it."

"Not at all. It was necessary for you to tell

me so that I would know that you knew."

Harvey's blank stare could have meant anything from a total lack of comprehension to the contemplation of homicide. "So, if you were the other bidder . . ."

"We have only one to worry about. Because I didn't take your chairs."

Harvey looked sideways at Cora.

"No, I *really* didn't," Cora protested.

"How can I trust you?"

"Come on, Harvey. You may be upset, but don't abandon simple logic. *Why* would I take your chairs?"

"I have no idea why you do what you do."

"Harvey, don't be cranky. *I* know I didn't take your chairs, which helps me a great deal. The other guy did. I can concentrate on him."

"And who's the other guy?"

"Well, that's the thing. Ordinarily, I'd have Sherry trace You're El."

"Your what?"

"You're El. You're El. You Are El. Like Toys R Us. It's where the guy lives."

"Oh. His URL?"

"Isn't that what I said?"

"I have no idea what you're saying. Or whether it might be the truth."

"Harvey, that's unkind."

"Unkind? Did I steal your chairs?"

"Did I steal yours? Granted, I may have *caused* them to be stolen."

"Cora."

"The point is, Sherry's not too keen on helping me right now."

"How come?"

"Oh." The answer was because the crossword puzzle wound up in the paper. Cora couldn't tell Harvey that. "Prewedding jitters. Perfectly understandable, but a pain in the fanny."

"So there's no way to find the bidder?"

Cora smiled. "Oh, I got a pretty good idea who he is."

29

Cora Felton finished the last sip of the coffee just as crotchety old Mr. Wilbur shuffled into Cushman's Bake Shop. The timing was no coincidence. Cora had been nursing her coffee a good half hour. The sight of the cranky antiques dealer was a blessed relief. Cora's skim latte was like cold mud.

Cora flicked the Styrofoam cup in the garbage can, muttered a few parting words to the gaggle of women with whom she'd been conversing, yawned, stretched (wondering if that was overdoing it), and went out the door.

Cora's red Toyota was parked across the street. Cora walked unhurriedly to it, opened the door, slipped into the driver's seat, started the engine. She backed up slowly, and drove leisurely out of town.

The moment she was out of sight, Cora executed a maneuver that would have done a NASCAR driver proud, going from zero to sixty in a heartbeat and not stopping there. Cora whizzed by two Subarus, one coming, one going, both drivers terrified, and covered the mile and a half out of town in what had to be the modern-day record.

Cora whizzed by Wilbur's Antiques as if it were the finish line, slammed on the brakes, and skidded a U-turn into the Sunoco station.

"Fill her up," Cora said, brandishing a hammer at the startled attendant, and set off down the road as if the devil were at her heels.

Wilbur's Antiques was locked up tighter than a drum. A drum that had recently been broken into. With surprising strength, dexterity, and speed for a woman of her years, Cora pried the plywood off the barn-door window, reached in, and unlocked the barn door. She hauled out the extension ladder, propped it against the house, climbed up, and pried the plywood off the window. Cora reached through the broken pane, unlocked the window, pushed it up, and climbed in.

There was no time for a search. Cora barely noted the contents of the shop as she hurried to the front door. She unlocked it and stepped out. Learning from Wilbur's example, Cora propped it open with a pottery gargoyle lawn ornament, an objet d'art too hideous for purchase.

Brandishing the hammer like a crazed serial killer, Cora flew around the house and vaulted up the ladder. The piece of plywood was hanging by a nail. Cora spun it over the window, pounded it back on. She practically slid down the ladder, grabbed it, wrestled it into the barn. She paused a moment to make sure no rattan chairs were present, then locked the door and pounded the sheet of plywood home.

Cora was panting as she ran around to the front of the house. She'd been a fool to trust the gargoyle. Surely it had cracked under the weight of the door just to spite her. Or slipped out. One way or another the damn thing would be gone and the door would be shut.

It wasn't. The gargoyle had held. It was a beautiful piece of pottery. She might even buy it.

Cora slipped in, moved the gargoyle, closed the door.

Okay, where to start?

It would have been nice if the chairs were in the middle of the room, but then she would have fallen over them. And it made no sense Wilbur would leave stolen property out where anyone could see. Even so, Cora gave the shop a once-over. The merchandise was as ugly as ever, and there was no sign of the chairs.

There was a door on the side wall. Cora tried it, found a small staircase. Was there more shop upstairs?

No, it was the living quarters. But it was a close call. The layout suggested Wilbur's domicile. But it had clearly been furnished from his wares. The writing desk, for instance, might have been worth more on *Antiques Roadshow* had it had all four legs, but the stack of cinderblocks seemed to be propping it up perfectly well. As for the bed, the brass headboard looked formidable enough to lash unsuspecting virgins to, though Cora found it hard to imagine even the dimmest of naive young lasses having anything to do with the old reprobate. Cora realized she was projecting — she had nothing to reprove him for.

Except his taste in furniture. Good lord. It was doubtless pulled out of his shop, but even so. How many men had an ottoman in this day and age? And that lamp shade. Was the design an attempt to illustrate *Moby Dick,* or just a really ugly fish?

There were no chairs in sight. Which, Cora had to admit, ended whatever tenuous right she might possibly have to be there.

Cora glanced at her watch. She had made

191

amazing time, fantastic time. It was a mere eighteen minutes since Wilbur had arrived at the bakery. Hell, the contrary old son of a bitch sometimes took that long just choosing a scone. And after all her work, it would be a crime not to look around.

Cora frowned. The poorest of rationalizations, but one's own.

Certainly sufficient to rifle his desk.

The three-legged desk boasted a telephone and answering machine, surely the most modern pieces in the room. Except for the small box next to it, the function of which Cora could only guess at. A fax line? No, then it would need a printer.

Oh, well.

The pencil drawer had pencils, a small disappointment. It also had an assortment of standard pencil-drawer junk, from paper clips to pennies, to a plastic pencil sharpener, to a roll of 35-millimeter film, which appeared to be exposed, since it wasn't in a can. Cora wondered briefly if she should take it in and develop it.

Very briefly.

The three drawers on the right side of the desk looked much more promising. At least they were deeper than the pencil drawer, could hold something more substantial.

The top drawer did. A laptop computer.

Folded up, but open a crack. Cora fished it out, set it on the desk, pushed up the top.

It was on.

That was weird. The computer in the drawer left on. Why would that be?

The answer immediately presented itself in the form of a small AOL mailbox icon at the bottom of the screen.

Of course. The machine near the phone was a modem, of the dial-up variety. Wilbur would plug it into the back of his laptop, and go on the Internet.

Should she connect the laptop? Why not? How hard could it be? She could go on-line and check his mail.

Wait a minute! She didn't need to be on-line. She wasn't going to pick up the guy's mail, just check it.

Cora moved the mouse, clicked on the AOL icon.

The mailbox opened.

There on the screen was a list of the headings of the last e-mails Wilbur had received. All she wanted was his You're El. Now, why wasn't it there?

His last e-mail was open. It seemed to be a mailing from some sort of antiques society, where a lot of members wrote in. Now, didn't Sherry call that something? Something to do with tennis. Now, what the hell was that? A McEnroe journal? Not likely. Ah, right. A list-serve.

Which didn't really help her. Where was the damn heading? Not heading. Header. That was it. **VIEW FULL HEADER IN PREVIEW**. Cora moved the cursor, clicked on it.

And there it was. Proof positive.

Wilbur was *sbk@aol.com.*

Now, was there anything else?

Cora skimmed through the e-mail, didn't find anything interesting, aside from the fact that Wilbur had neglected to delete an offer of **HOT ASIAN NYMPHOS**, clearly an oversight.

Cora shrank the mailbox icon, closed the laptop, put it back in the drawer. After a moment she took it out of the drawer, opened it, clicked on the AOL icon, then clicked on **VIEW SHORT HEADER IN PREVIEW**. Wilbur wouldn't necessarily remember whether he'd left the full header on or off, but there was no reason to take a chance on arousing his suspicions.

Cora put the laptop back in the top drawer, then searched the bottom two. She found nothing of interest. On inspiration she slid the drawers out, held them up, looked underneath. She found the bottoms of the drawers.

Cora returned the last drawer to the desk, stood up, and looked around.

Under the mattress, perhaps?

It occurred to Cora it might have been useful if she'd known what she was looking for.

The phone rang, snapped Cora back to reality. She glanced at her watch. Twenty-two minutes.

The phone rang again.

Should she pick it up, rasp hello, see what the person said?

Probably not wise.

The answering machine rendered the decision moot. Wilbur's voice croaked, *"I'm not in. Whaddya want?"*

A voice said, "Geez, you sell a lot of merchandise with that line?"

That had been Cora's exact thought. She grinned, until she heard, "This is Benny Southstreet, if you can't tell. So, that info help, about who was bidding against you? There's more where that came from. I'm a wealth of information. You won't believe what else that woman's been up to. You interested, call the motel. Four Seasons. Unit 12. I'm going out, be back after two. Give me a call, you'll be glad you did."

Cora was furious. That son of a bitch! Something else she'd been up to? Evidence of her plagiarism, no doubt. Of all the dirty tricks. And she couldn't even defend the charge, since it was true. He'd probably planted something in her office.

Cora was roused from her musing by the sound of the front door.

Oh, my God!

Wilbur had been quicker than usual with his coffee. Of all the days. How was she going to explain her presence in his bedroom? She might have to seduce him. Cora shuddered at the thought.

Was there a window?

It didn't matter if there was. It would be too high.

Says who? She could climb down.

Climb down what?

Who cares *what? Just open it!*

It wouldn't open. It was nailed shut. Or stuck. Or never meant to open in the first place. It was too high anyway.

So where to hide?

The closet?

No, no closet. Metal standing closets. The kind that made a lot of noise and didn't hold a lot of clothes. She'd climb in and the damn thing would tip over. Or he'd hear her and stick a broomstick through the metal handles and she'd be locked in there like Alec Guinness in the oven in *Bridge on the River Kwai.* Granted, he got an Oscar; still, she'd never last like he did. Besides, he probably got to get out between takes.

Oh, my God, here he comes, what the hell to do?

Cora dived headlong under the bed.

It was dusty, dirty, and littered with knick-knacks that probably dated back to 1962. Maybe she'd find Hank Aaron's rookie card. No, that was the '50s, not the '60s. Like the Guinness movie. Was she really that old?

Shhh! Here he comes! Quiet! Head down!

Her head *was* brushing the box spring. Cora prayed Wilbur hadn't brought home one of the hot Asian nymphos.

He hadn't. He headed straight for the bathroom.

Why hadn't *she* thought of the bathroom? If she had, he'd have found her, but she'd be more comfortable.

Go to the bathroom! Go, go, go, you old geezer! Close the door and stay in there forever!

He didn't close the door. Instead, he turned on the water in the sink and began brushing his teeth.

His teeth? After a cup of coffee he brushes his teeth? He shouldn't even have *teeth. He's gotta brush 'em at the sink, right by the open door, where he can see someone crawling out from under the bed.*

Like a commando, Cora slithered across the bedroom floor, avoiding antiques and antiques dealers alike, until she reached the stairs.

Stand up or slide down?

Compromise. Cora slid until her feet cleared the top step, then squirmed into a crouch, and scurried the rest of the way. She hit the ground running, zigged and zagged her way through the shop. A flowered vase paid the price, toppling from a pedestal and shattering on the floor. Cora gritted her teeth, plunged on.

It was not until she was out the front door and hurrying down the street that Cora's heart stopped pounding too hard for her brain to catch up and process what she'd just heard.

Oh, was Benny Southstreet going to get it!

30

The Four Seasons Motel was just the kind Benny Southstreet would choose. The sign read, **CABLE TV: $29.99**. That, Cora figured, was either an expensive TV or inexpensive room. Cora drove right in as if she owned the place, pulled up in front of Unit 7.

The service cart with linens and toiletries was outside the open door to Unit 8. The chambermaid was inside. Cora realized *chambermaid* was a rather sexist concept. Surely a man could hold the position.

He didn't. The chamberperson was a woman, not much more than a girl, from Cora's perspective, though perhaps in her early twenties. She had freckles, red hair, and green eyes. She was chewing gum, which, in Cora's humble opinion, made women seem unattractive. Not this one. She seemed bright and perky.

Cora put on her friendliest smile. "Hi there."

"Oh, hello."

"Cleaning the rooms?"

The girl popped her gum. "You must be psychic."

"I'm Cora Felton."

"Yes, I know. I'm Marge O'Connell."

"Hi. So what's it like?"

Marge frowned. "What's what like?"

"Cleaning the rooms."

"Why?"

"I have a . . ." Cora hesitated over the bogus relationship. She'd been about to say "niece," but Sherry was her niece. Cora couldn't bear to claim a granddaughter, even an imaginary one. "I have a friend whose daughter's looking for a job. She's right out of high school. Nice girl. Bright. Wants to put some money away before college."

Marge looked amused. "Does she, now?"

"Yes. So I was wondering if you could give me a few tips on the trade."

"You'd like some pointers on the fine art of being a chambermaid?"

"What are the hours? What's the pay? Do they try to take advantage of you?"

"You mean sexual harassment?"

"Yes." Cora noticed the girl's eyes were twinkling. "You're putting me on?"

"Well, Mr. Haney's close to ninety. His wife's close to a hundred, wears the pants in the family. I'm not sure he remembers what sex is. Anyway, I bet your friend's daughter could outrun him."

"Sounds good. Well, don't let me keep you."

Marge took a set of towels off the linen cart. She turned around to find Cora standing there. "You're still here."

"I was wondering if I could watch you work. Get an idea what the job is like."

Marge put her hands on her hips in a saucy manner, and popped her gum. "Yeah, sure. Which unit you interested in?"

"I beg your pardon?"

"Give me a break. You're an amateur detective. Always snooping around. What is it this time? A murder?"

"I really can't say. You know how it is."

"You mean you have a client."

"I didn't say that."

"Is that what you can't say?"

"I can't say."

"Then I'm afraid I can't help you."

"Could you answer a question?"

"Depends what it is."

"This is Unit 8."

"That's your question?"

"No, that's an observation."

"What's your question?"

"You working your way up or down?"

Marge was working her way up. Cora sat in her car and smoked while Marge cleaned Units 9 and 10, and was there to intercept her when she finished 11.

"Pretty impressive," Cora said. "You did those rooms in fifteen minutes each."

"That's with an audience," Marge said. "Ordinarily, I'd take my time."

"You didn't seem hurried to me. How about I put a stopwatch on you?"

The girl's mouth fell open. "Is that it? Old man Haney sent you to check up on me?"

"I wouldn't do that. Scout's honor."

"Then what's with the watch?"

"Nothing. I'd take it off and put it in my purse, except I'd never find it. Go ahead. Do the room. I won't make a peep."

Marge walked up to the motel door, put the key in the lock. Cora was right behind her.

"So, you're interested in this room?"

"Did I say that?"

"No, you didn't. You expect to watch me clean it?"

"Would that be a problem?"

"Not unless you get me fired."

"I'm not here to get you fired."

"You could do it anyway."

"Yeah, but I'd really have to try."

The girl smiled. "Okay, you can look. But

you're not touching anything."

Cora knew that before Marge said it. Cora had no intention of touching anything. Except the motel room door lock, which she hoped to fiddle with surreptitiously, twisting the little gizmo to unlocked, so that when Marge went in to clean 13 Cora could slip in and ransack 12. It occurred to Cora she had a perfidious nature, if that was what the word meant.

Marge clicked the door open, entered the unit. Cora went in right behind her, took a look, and stopped dead.

In the middle of the room were four rattan chairs.

31

"I'm sorry, but this changes things," Cora said.

The chambermaid frowned. "I beg your pardon?"

"Did those four chairs come with this room?"

"Of course not."

"Do you know what they're doing here?"

"I have no idea."

"Well, I have. They were stolen from a friend of mine."

"Uh-oh."

"So I'm going to take them back."

"Wait a minute. Wait a minute. You can't do that. You'll get me fired."

"For recovering stolen property?"

"I let you look around. Which was fine, as long as you didn't touch anything. You take those chairs, I'm in trouble big-time."

"I told you I wouldn't get you into trouble. So let's go find Mr. What's-his-name, the manager, and I'll explain the situation."

"It's Mr. Haney. And what are you going to explain?"

"I came here to see Benny Southstreet. You were cleaning his room. I looked in the door and there they were."

"You know whose room it is?"

"Of course I do. Come on, give me a break. You knew I was snooping around. You really surprised I had something in mind?"

"You were looking for these chairs?"

In point of fact, Cora was looking for Chuck's hundred-dollar bills. The idea Benny might have taken the chairs never occurred to her. "Absolutely. I came here to ask Benny about the chairs. He wasn't here, but the chairs were. You think Mr. Haney will buy that?"

"It isn't the truth?"

"It's close enough."

"Well, Mr. Haney isn't here. He went shopping at the mall."

"How about his wife?"

"She went with him."

"Who *is* here?"

"Ralph."

"I take it Ralph doesn't have the authority to handle this?"

"Ralph barely has the authority to tie his shoes."

"Okay," Cora said. "We could call the police, but that would be messy, and we don't want things to be messy."

Marge shook her head. "Uh-uh."

"Or I could wait until Benny Southstreet comes back and talk to him about it."

"Perfect," Marge said.

"Only he won't be back till after two, and I'm not waiting around till then."

"So come back."

"Fine. In the meantime, we have these chairs."

"What about them?"

"I don't want to leave them here."

"Well, you can't take them."

"In that case, you're a witness. You'd better look them over carefully, because you're the only one besides me who knows they're here."

"Oh, come on."

"Hey, if these things disappear it'll be my word against his. I'll need you to back me up. You better be ready to identify the chairs."

"Hey, listen, you tell your friend's daughter this is one hell of a tough job."

Cora grinned. "Kid, I like your style. Let me see if I can let you off the hook."

"What do you mean?"

Cora fumbled in her purse, held up a disposable camera, and smiled her trademark Puzzle Lady smile, just as if she were doing a commercial for Kodak. "Let's document the evidence."

32

Cora had purchased a disposable camera, not because she gave a damn about photography, but because the dreamy new guy at the mall Photomat had looked promising, until the clueless son of a bitch had the gaucheness to inquire if her niece was married. Cora hadn't taken a picture since.

The Photomat booth attendant seemed totally unaware of his previous faux pas. He shook his curly dark hair out of his eyes, favored Cora with a goofy, endearing grin. "Miss Felton, good to see you."

"Yeah, yeah." Cora plunked the disposable camera on the counter. "How soon can I get prints of these?"

"One hour."

"I'll try to be back."

Cora drove out to Harvey Beerbaum's. The little man was in the process of constructing some god-awful crossword puzzle when she came in.

"It's a cryptic," Harvey said. "Care to solve it?"

The phrase *when pigs fly* occurred to Cora. "I got more important things, Harvey. I found your chairs."

"Really. Where are they?"

"I can't tell you that."

"What!?"

"I promised."

"Cora, please tell me you're kidding."

"Sort of. I know who took your chairs. I'm going to get 'em back. What more do you need to know?"

"You're sure they're mine."

"Absolutely. If you don't believe me, I'll show you a picture."

"You have a picture?"

"Not yet, but I will."

"Cora —"

"The main thing is, I've seen your chairs and I'm going to get 'em back. Now then, did you make a report to the police?"

"Of course I did."

"Too bad. When I produce the chairs they'll wanna know why. If I don't tell 'em they'll accuse me of compounding a felony and conspiring to conceal a crime."

"Are you doing that?"

"Of course I am. But it's for your own good. You don't want to advertise that your house is so easy to break into. You'll have a gaggle of robbers outside waiting their turn."

"A gaggle of robbers?"

"I know it's geese, but I don't think they steal things. Is there a term for robbers? What would it be, a theft of robbers?"

"So what can I tell the police?"

"Tell 'em you got new chairs."

"That would be a lie."

"So don't tell 'em anything. It's not like they're gonna come running to ask if you got your chairs back. It's an unsolved crime. If you don't mention it, they won't mention it."

"And you won't tell me who took them?"

"I can't."

"Was the person who took my chairs the guy who was bidding on them?"

"No."

"What? Then how did you ever find them?"

"That's a long story."

"I've got time."

"I can't tell you, Harvey. When I can, I will."

"Does the person who took my chairs know that you've discovered that he took my chairs?"

"You're assuming it's a man?"

"Is it a woman?"

"I can't tell you, Harvey."

"Then why'd you bring it up?"

"To avoid the question."

"What question?"

"Good. It's working."

Cora beamed at Harvey, and ducked out the door.

33

Benny Southstreet wasn't back by two o'clock. Cora knew because she was there at one forty-five, hoping to beat Mr. Wilbur to the punch. But Benny wasn't back.

Either that or he'd come and gone. What a revolting development that would be. Particularly if he had taken the chairs. No, they were there. Cora could see them through the gap in the curtain.

There was no sign of the chambermaid. She must have finished her rounds. Evidently it wasn't a full-time job. That was something her feigned friend's daughter ought to know.

Cora got in her car, drove across the street to the Ace Hardware parking lot, and settled down to wait.

Benny never showed. Neither did Mr. Wilbur. Two o'clock came and went without so much as a single car. By two-fifteen, Cora was fed up.

Okay, what now?

Well, for one thing, the photos would be ready.

Cora pulled out of the hardware store parking lot, headed for the mall.

She never got there.

A car going the other direction looked suspiciously familiar. Cora pulled into the next driveway, turned around, and gave chase.

Sure enough, the car was being piloted by a feisty redhead with a chip on her shoulder and fire in her eyes.

Brenda Wallenstein drove straight into town, pulled up, and parked. She got out of the car and walked down the side street to the pizza parlor.

And Becky Baldwin's office.

Cora parked in front of the library, crossed the street, and peered down the alley. Sure enough, Brenda Wallenstein had not driven all the way from New York City just for a Coke and a slice. Instead, she went in the door with the modest sign **REBECCA BALDWIN, ATTORNEY-AT-LAW**.

Cora wished she could follow. Brenda was Sherry's best friend. And her ex-husband's wife. If this had anything to do with Sherry's impending marriage, Cora had to know.

Could she follow her upstairs and listen

213

through the door? Not a good idea. Becky's one-room office shared the landing with a pediatrician. Cora would stand out like a sore thumb. On the other hand, it was a nice day. Becky would be likely to have her window open.

Cora knew right where the window was. Becky always made her sit on the sill to smoke. Cora hurried past the pizza parlor, and ducked around the corner. Sure enough, the window was open. Cora wondered if she'd be able to hear.

She needn't have worried. In college Brenda'd been a cheerleader who always projected to the back of the bleachers.

Becky Baldwin, on the other hand, was an attorney. She only raised her voice when necessary. Cora never heard her greeting, but it wasn't hard to figure out.

"What the hell do you think I'm doing here?" Brenda stormed. "I don't like being played for a fool. Do I look like a fool?"

Becky evidently refrained from comment.

"It's a yes or no question, Becky. Does he have to check in with you or not?"

Apparently Becky sidestepped the issue.

"I'm not asking you to violate a confidential communication. I'm asking for a rule of law. Does a client on probation have to check in with his lawyer?"

Brenda must not have liked Becky's answer because she had a few particularly choice comments regarding Becky's chosen profession. Cora considered taking notes.

When Brenda slammed out the door unenlightened five minutes later, Cora was right on her heels. Keeping in the shadows, Cora followed Brenda back to her car.

Ordinarily, Cora would have confronted Brenda, demanded to know what the hell she thought she was doing. But it was a ticklish situation. Sherry's impending marriage was fragile enough. The least little thing might shatter it. And Brenda was not a little thing. Brenda was a force of nature, an insanely jealous woman with the predatory instincts of a tigress. If she made a move on Sherry, Cora would reluctantly hurl herself in Brenda's path, sacrificing herself for her niece. But if the woman had no such intention, there was no reason to rile her. Let her leave town.

Brenda did head out of town. Unfortunately, it was also in the direction of Sherry and Cora's house. Cora followed along reluctantly, plotting when to make her move. She had to cut Brenda off before the driveway, or there'd be hell to pay.

Why couldn't Sherry be more like her? Cora wouldn't let a jealous wife keep her from a perfectly good marriage. Even the wife of the groom. Well, that hadn't been one of her finest hours. Had that marriage been annulled? Cora couldn't remember.

They were coming up on the moment of truth, the point of no return, or whatever the hell other cliché Cora couldn't think of at the moment. Basically, the road to Sherry and Cora's house. Once Brenda took that, it would be impossible to cut her off without creating a scene right at the foot of the driveway. On the other hand, if Cora tried to cut her off now, she'd drive straight into the milk truck bearing down on them from the opposite direction. What the hell was a milk truck doing out in the afternoon? Didn't people get milk in the morning? Of course a New York City girl, Cora got milk all day long, from the corner fruit stand. But here in the sticks . . . What, the milkman couldn't make a living working three hours a day?

As luck would have it, the milk truck passed Brenda just at the turnoff.

And Brenda kept on going. Right out of town.

Suddenly Cora loved the milkman. She'd have bought him a beer, if she hadn't stopped drinking. Could she buy him a glass of milk? Or would that be coals to Newcastle, whatever the hell that meant? The type of thing Sherry would say.

Cora slowed the car, pulled into the driveway, turned around. She realized she was free-associating. Her mind was on overload, with chairs and money and weddings and eBay and thefts. Two thefts. One chairs, one money. Assuming any money was stolen. Wait. Three thefts. Two chairs, one money. One set of chairs recovered, one not. Well, not recovered, but found. She could prove it. Cora checked the dashboard clock. The photos were long done.

Cora drove out to the mall.

The Photomat booth was closed.

Closed? True, it was a one-man operation. But it was right in the mall. If the guy got hungry, he could call out for pizza. He didn't have to close. Yet he had. Cora shouldn't have been surprised. It was that type of day. The guy was closed for the same reason Benny Southstreet wasn't at the motel.

It occurred to Cora maybe Benny had gone back to the motel. In fact, he surely should have gone back. He told Wilbur he would be there. He was simply late. If he wasn't back now, he was really late. At any rate, she should check it out.

There was a car in front of Unit 12, which

was a good sign. It would have been a better sign if the lines for the parking spaces had been painted with any degree of intelligence. But the car parked in front of Unit 12 was also parked in front of Unit 13. Cora had a vague recollection of seeing Benny Southstreet's car in her driveway, but whether this nondescript Ford Taurus was it, she had no idea. If this was Benny's parking space, he was in. But if Benny's parking space was the empty one straddling Units 11 and 12, he was out.

Cora stepped up to Unit 12, knocked on the door.

No answer.

Cora tried the knob.

It turned!

Whoa!

The door was unlocked, just as she would have left it had the chambermaid been a little less vigilant. And here it was, an open invitation. Or at least an unlocked invitation. She could go in and search the room.

Except for that car. It would be a little embarrassing if Benny was here. Cora wasn't clear on protocol, but it was probably considered gauche to break in on someone accusing you of plagiarism. She'd have to look it up in *Emily Post's Etiquette*.

Or on Google.

Cora knocked again, louder. She pushed the door open a crack, called, "Benny South-street!"

There was no answer.

Cora looked up and down the row.

A young man in a baseball cap stood watching her for a moment, then disappeared into the motel office. That, Cora figured, would be Ralph, the kid the chambermaid told her about. It would also be the end of her reputation.

If any.

Cora wondered if the young man was watching her through the office window. Just in case, she smiled and said, "Hi, Benny," as she pushed the door open and stepped in.

The room was empty. The light was on. The bed was made; no surprise, she'd watched the chambermaid make it.

The four chairs were still there. Thank God. Cora never would have forgiven herself if they'd been gone. But, no, they were right where she'd left them.

Cora looked around. Was there any evidence of Benny Southstreet having been there?

Yes. The briefcase on the desk. It hadn't been there when the chambermaid had made up the room.

Cora popped the briefcase open. Did she

have any right to search it? Absolutely. The man was a thief. He'd stolen the chairs. What else might he have stolen?

The jackpot would be hundred-dollar bills. That would sure rock 'em in their sockets.

There were none. The briefcase contained letters, computer printouts, and, ugh, crossword puzzles.

Cora closed the briefcase, having found nothing of interest.

Whoa! What was that on the nightstand? Benny Southstreet had a gun. A snub-nosed revolver. Looked like a .38. Cora picked it up and sniffed it. Unlike in mystery books, it had not been recently fired. Benny probably never fired it. He wasn't the type. Though he might have used it to intimidate people. Good thing he hadn't tried to intimidate her. Cora's gun was bigger.

Cora put the gun back on the nightstand, and proceeded to take the motel room apart.

There was nothing in the bathroom. Nothing in the closet. Nothing taped to the bottom of the drawers of the desk or the nightstand. Nothing under the bed.

If Benny Southstreet had stolen the bills from the Dillingers' study, they were on his person.

Cora went to the door and looked out. There was no one in sight. The assistant manager was probably watching TV, or playing Nintendo, or on-line poker, or whatever it was young men did in this day and age. It occurred to Cora that if there had been on-line poker when she was married to Henry, it would have taken a good chunk out of the family fortune.

If there was on-line poker when she was married to Melvin, there would *be* no family fortune.

Okay. Moment of truth. She'd gotten Harvey into this. Maybe she couldn't tell him who'd taken his chairs, but she could damn well get 'em back.

Cora went out to her Toyota, popped the trunk. Frowned. It was going to be tight. She brought a chair out. It just fit, but barely. Another might require some doing. Cora got a second chair, and, amid great sputtering, fuming, and imprecations the likes of which the motel had probably never heard, managed to nestle it next to the first one. She slammed the trunk, delighted to find it closed.

Cora stuck a third chair in the backseat from the driver's side, a fourth from the passenger's side. The chairs fit easier than the ones in the trunk.

Cora left the motel room door unlocked, exactly as she had found it.

As Cora pulled out of the motel parking lot, in the rearview mirror she could see the kid in the baseball cap come out of the office and stand there, watching her go.

34

Harvey Beerbaum was delighted. "You brought my chairs back!"

"Well, I felt responsible."

"Yes, but . . ."

"But what?"

"How did you do it?"

"Trade secret, Harvey."

"Yes, but if you found my chairs, you must know who took them."

Cora put up her hands. "Now, let's be very careful here, Harvey. Technically, *legally,* I don't know who took them. I know who *had* them."

"You're splitting hairs."

"That's what the law does."

"Yes, but just between you and me . . ."

"Just between you and me, we got your chairs back, Harvey. Be glad you got 'em. That's the best advice I can give you. That and lock your door."

Cora drove by the motel, but nothing had

changed. The Ford Taurus was in the spot between 12 and 13, but no car was in the spot between 11 and 12. That was too bad. Cora wasn't sure what she wanted to say to Benny Southstreet, but she couldn't wait to hear what Benny Southstreet had to say to her. Would he accuse her of taking his chairs? That would be interesting as all hell. Then he'd have to admit to having them in the first place. Cora was looking forward to it. Well, maybe later.

Cora got home to find Buddy tied up in the yard. Buddy wasn't happy about it, and told her so in no uncertain terms. Cora unhooked the tiny poodle, and he scampered after her into the house.

Cora dumped some kibble in a bowl, added a spoonful of canned food, and mixed it around. She put the bowl on the floor, gave him fresh water, and went to check the answering machine.

Beep.

"This is Chief Harper. I've had a complaint of a break-in at Wilbur's Antiques. Would you know anything about that?"

Oops.

Beep.

"Cora, it's Harvey. Thank you for getting my chairs back. It's all very well for you to say not to worry, but how can I? I had an intruder in my house. In the middle of the night. It is totally unsatisfactory not to know who that is. Please call and tell me."

Beep.

"Sherry, it's Bren. What's going on? You're not home, and Dennis isn't home. Did you know he's in town? He claims he has to check in with his lawyer, but Becky won't say whether he does or not. And, anyway, what difference does that make if he checks in and doesn't leave. I'm worried, because you've got a wedding coming up, and I think that's making him a little crazy. Has he called you? Have you seen him? Is that where you are now? Please let me know. This is getting serious. I'm afraid someone is going to get hurt."

Oh, hell. Wait till Sherry heard that. Maybe she should delete it. Cora wondered if she knew how. Did this answering machine have a delete button? Or was the only way to erase it to record over it?

Beep.

"Sherry, what's going on? I just heard Brenda's message. Are you out with Dennis? I can't believe you're out with Dennis, I don't care what the circumstances are. The guy is no good, and never has been. He doesn't deserve whatever you're giving him. . . . I don't mean that like it sounded.

225

But he doesn't deserve to be heard. He's had his chances. I don't know where I'll be, but call me on my cell phone. This is ridiculous."

Beep.

"Aaron! What do you mean, picking up my messages? I'm not out with Dennis. I wouldn't be out with Dennis. I can't believe you would think such a thing. But that's not the point. You're picking up my messages and blaming me for them? Ah, hell. I tried your cell phone and it's switched off. Which makes no sense since you asked me to call. So I left a message there, and I'm leaving a message here. If you pick up the message here, I'd like to know why you're picking up my messages. Anyway, call me. You can *leave* a message."

Beep.

"Sherry, how are you going out? I thought Cora had your car. Did someone give you a ride?"

Beep.

"I can't believe you're calling me. Your cell phone's still off, and you're still picking up my messages. Dennis —"

There was a long pause.

"Sorry, Aaron. You had me confused. Damn it, turn your damn phone on, will you?"

There it was. A veritable soap opera on the

226

answering machine. Cora wanted no part of it. As far as she was concerned, if anyone else called, the answering machine could pick up again.

Cora left the young lovers to their own devices, and trudged down the hall to bed.

35

Marge, the chambermaid, looked at the door to Unit 12 and frowned. There was no **DO NOT DISTURB** sign. But a car was parked in front of the unit. Actually, *two* cars were parked in front of the unit. One in the space straddling 12 and 13, and one in the space shared by 11 and 12. Either could be Mr. Southstreet's car. On the other hand, it was equally possible neither car was. Due to the vagaries of the parking lot, the car between 11 and 12 could be for Unit 11, and the car between 12 and 13 could be for Unit 13, leaving no space at all for the car for Unit 12. Which sometimes happened. Usually, the guest in question would simply choose another space, but occasionally one got really ticked. Marge could remember an instance when the police had to be called, another when an irate guest had to be comped a room. Thank goodness she hadn't had to deal with them. Ralph had been driven nuts.

So, what to do about Unit 12? It was after ten o'clock. By rights the guest should be up and out. Of course, she could skip his room and move down the line, but what if the car meant someone was in Unit 13?

Marge frowned. She would have to intrude. The thing she liked least about her job. Waking people up. Disturbing them in the shower. Or at even more embarrassing times. Like when that old couple was having an affair. That old couple were in their early forties, but that seemed ancient to Marge.

Associating, perhaps, Marge glanced down the row to where her genuinely old employers were having an argument in front of the motel office. Marge hated it when they bickered. Moms always won, and Pops always took it out on Marge. Without even realizing.

So, there was no hope for it. Marge fished out her passkey, went to the door, and —

The door was open. Just a crack, but still.

Marge pushed it slightly farther open, called, "Housekeeping."

No answer. No rustle of anyone turning over in bed. No sound of running water.

Marge pushed the door wider. "Housekeeping."

The first thing she saw was the bed. It was just the way she'd left it when she made up the room yesterday.

That was odd. Benny Southstreet hadn't come back. Well, less work for her.

Marge opened the door, stepped inside.

The chairs were gone.

This was not good. This was *really* not good. Not after she'd let Cora Felton see they were there. Photograph them, even. And figure out how to unlock the door. No, that wasn't fair — just surmise on her part. But somehow while they photographed the chairs the button on the door had been disengaged. Marge had made a point of locking it again when Cora was watching.

So the missing chairs could hardly be her fault. Because it would have to be someone with a key who took them. Which explained things. Benny Southstreet came back, took his chairs, and left. Forgetting to pull the door tight behind him. Perhaps because he had an armful of chairs. He had left, and someone had parked in his spot, and none of it was her fault.

Except for the briefcase on the desk. He might have taken his chairs, but he'd certainly left his briefcase. Not a bright move, under the circumstances, with the door left unlocked.

So, the guest might not have slept in the bed, but this was still an occupied room. Which needed to be made up. Let's see . . .

The glasses on the tray next to the ice bucket had the protective paper over the top. The bucket was dry. The wastebaskets were empty. Nothing had been touched.

Did he need any soap and towels?

Marge pushed open the bathroom door, stopped, and gasped.

There was a gun on the tile floor next to the bathtub. It was lying on a piece of paper.

A crossword puzzle.

The shower curtain was half-closed.

Marge grabbed it, yanked it open.

Benny Southstreet lay in the bathtub. He was fully clothed. His tie was even tied. His hair was slightly mussed, but his eyes were wide-open in a look of weary resignation. Aside from his prone position, he could have been waiting in line at OTB.

He was clearly dead.

ACROSS

1 Grounds for a suit
5 "__ Frutti" (Little Richard song)
10 Erie Canal mule
13 African lilies
15 Reaction to, "Pick a cod, any cod"
16 "¿__ pasa?"
17 Start of a message
19 Beehive State athlete
20 Polo or Garr
21 It's under foot
22 Feel poorly
23 Classic Ford model
26 Threatening sentence-ender
28 TV broadcast band
29 Message part 2
32 Synthesizer inventor
34 Gets bored with
35 Bio by Molly Ivins
37 Have a couple of eggs?
38 Xerox competitor
42 "I'm OK with it"
45 Iditarod race place

46 Message part 3
50 Links number
51 All told
52 Falls in New York
54 "___ whillikers!"
55 Till bills
58 Hoofbeat sound
59 Easy mark
60 End of message
64 Cobra kin
65 Bungled play
66 Streamlined
67 Fourth of July?
68 Oceans, in poetry
69 Connecticut campus

DOWN
1 Mai ___
2 Long in the tooth
3 Is a fan
4 Basic belief
5 ___ Friday's (restaurant chain)
6 Big coffee containers
7 Brouhaha
8 Makes fit
9 Lower-ranking
10 Violent gust of wind
11 Pediatric mental disorder
12 Actress Sobieski
14 Lamb, at large
18 North Dakota city
23 ___ the word
24 "Oops!"
25 Jury verdict
27 Small and lively
30 Garbage
31 "Yo, dude!"
33 Enthusiasm
36 Closed, as a sports jacket
39 Confess to less
40 "The Mod Squad" costar Epps
41 Juno, to Greeks
43 Mined over matter?
44 Cager Strickland or Dampier
46 Puzzle cutter-upper
47 On edge
48 Treeless tract
49 Some surrealistic paintings
53 "Holy smokes!"
56 "To be," to Henri
57 "Cut it out!"
61 Surgery sites, briefly
62 Brooks of "Blazing Saddles"
63 Barely manage, with "out"

36

The motel parking lot had never been so full, with the police cars, the medical examiner's car, and the ambulance. Chief Harper wasn't about to park on the road. He pulled into the last available space, blocking the ambulance, and got out.

Officers Sam Brogan and Dan Finley were there to meet him.

"What have we got, boys?"

Sam popped his gum. "Male, Caucasian, thirty-five to forty-five, black hair, blue eyes —"

Harper had no patience for it. "Oh, for Christ's sake, you're not on TV, Sam. What the hell happened?"

Dan Finley chimed in. "Someone popped Benny Southstreet."

Harper sighed. "If we could hit a happy median."

Sam frowned. "Huh?"

"Just tell me what happened."

"The occupant of Unit 12 is dead. The chambermaid went in to make up the room, found him in the bathtub. The doc's in with him now."

"Any sign of a weapon?"

"There was a gun on the floor. I photographed it and bagged it."

"Was he shot?"

Sam shrugged. "Ask the doc. I didn't see a bullet hole. But there's blood under his head."

"If he was shot, any chance it was self-inflicted?"

"I don't know. But if I ever climb into the tub and shoot myself, I promise I'll leave a note."

"And there wasn't?"

"Not as such."

"What the hell does that mean?"

"There was a crossword puzzle." Dan Finley seemed proud of the announcement.

Harper groaned. "Tell me there wasn't."

"Yeah, there was," Sam said. "Right under the gun. I bagged it too."

"In the same bag?"

"No. Separate bags. Was that wasteful? Should I have been more thrifty?"

Harper ignored the sarcasm. "You dust the place for prints?"

"I will when the doc gets done leaving his."

"Now, Sam, Barney Nathan's a pro."

"Yeah, sure. I got his prints on file for elimination, all the same."

"Any witnesses?"

"Chambermaid who found him." Sam jerked his thumb.

Harper looked, saw a young woman in front of the motel office being comforted by an elderly couple.

"That's the owners of the place," Sam said. "They don't know squat and the chambermaid's hysterical. Wanna talk to her?"

"Guess I better." Harper walked over. "Hi there. You the owners?"

The man looked close to ninety, with lonesome wisps of hair, and sagging skin that hung as loose as his flannel shirt and fishing vest. "That's right."

His wife, just as thin but hard as nails, jumped in. "How long you gonna tie up the parking lot? Guests can't get in and out, and no one's gonna rent a room."

"One of your guests is dead, ma'am."

"Well, I didn't do it," the woman groused. "It's not our fault, either, but whaddya wanna bet some damn shyster decides to sue?"

"That's out of my hands, ma'am." Harper turned to the chambermaid. "You're the one who found him?"

236

"Yes, sir."

"Well, that's gotta be a shock. You feel up to talking about it?"

Marge had recovered some of her composure. Still, she had been dreading the questions. "I guess so."

"How'd you come to find him?"

"I was doing my job. Cleaning the rooms. I got to his. I didn't know whether he was there. The car was out front, but there was no **DO NOT DISTURB** sign. So I knocked."

"And?" the Chief prompted.

"And the door was open. Just an inch or two, but definitely unlocked. I pushed it farther open, called, 'Housekeeping.'" She stole a look at the elderly owners, as if not wanting to say the wrong thing in front of them. "Which is what I'm supposed to do. The guests shouldn't be disturbed, but the rooms have to be cleaned."

"I understand. What did you do?"

"No one seemed to be there, so I went in."

"What did you find?"

"The first thing I saw was the bed was made. Hadn't been slept in. Just the way I left it yesterday."

"Could it have been slept in and made?"

"It could, but I don't think so. The bed was made perfectly, the way a chambermaid

237

would make it, with the top sheet folded over and the blankets tucked in. A guest wouldn't bother."

"You thought the guest never came home?"

"At least never slept there. That was my first thought. The bed hadn't been slept in."

"So you didn't have to make up the room."

"Right. I just had to check if he needed new towels. I went in the bathroom and there he was."

"Must have been a shock. Did you have any idea who might have done this?"

"Not at all."

"You work here every day?"

"Five days a week."

"Anyone ever visit him? As far as you know. He ever have company in his room?"

Marge chose her words carefully. "As far as I know, he never let anyone into his room."

Harper wasn't happy with that answer. He was sure the girl wasn't lying, but still. Why had she hesitated?

Before Chief Harper could frame another question the Channel 8 News van came screeching up, and on-camera reporter Rick Reed, young, handsome, and bright as your average fireplug, emerged, followed by a camera crew.

"Chief Harper," he cried. "What have we

got here? Wait. Don't tell me. Hang on a minute." Rick squared his shoulders, faced the camera. "This is Rick Reed, Channel 8 News, live, at the Four Seasons Motel, where a grisly find in one of the units hints of a potential tragedy." Rick paused for a second, to see if that made any sense. Wasn't sure. He plunged ahead. "Chief Harper, what can you tell us? Do we have a homicide here?"

"It's too soon to say."

"Yes, but is it true someone has been killed?"

"We don't want to jump to any conclusions."

"Of course not. You were talking to that young woman. Is she a witness?"

"She's an employee." Eager to deflect the news team from the chambermaid, Chief Harper led Rick Reed in the direction of the unit. "A man was discovered dead in Unit 12. The doctor is examining the body now to see if there is any sign of foul play."

"What is the chance that there was?"

Chief Harper smiled. "Well, there's three police cars here. You do the math."

Rick Reed lowered the microphone impatiently. "I can't use a remark like that on the air."

"I thought you were live."

"We're live on tape."

"What the hell does that mean?"

"I was live when I said it."

Harper smiled. "Were you really?"

The soundman was waving frantically for Rick's attention. "We *are* live," he hissed.

"What?"

"We're *live!*"

"That's right," Rick Reed said, picking up the cue. "We are coming to you, live, from the scene of a tragedy. The discovery of a dead body in Unit 12 of the Four Seasons Motel. Wait! I think I see the medical examiner now."

Barney Nathan came out of Unit 12, as usual in his trademark red bow tie.

Rick Reed stepped forward eagerly. "This is Rick Reed, Channel 8 News, bringing you a live, exclusive interview with Dr. Barney Nathan."

Chief Harper grabbed the doctor by the shoulders and marched him aside.

"Just as soon as he's talked to the chief of police," Rick finished lamely. He brightened immediately as the Emergency Medical Team bumped a gurney out of the motel room door. "Hang on! They're bringing out the body now!"

While the news crew shot the departure of

the corpse, Chief Harper conferred with the doctor.

"Okay, Barney, what have you got?"

"He was killed sometime yesterday."

"Killed?"

"Murder or suicide. But it's a violent death."

"Are you sure?"

"Absolutely. Bullet wound in the head just above the hairline. Whether it's self-inflicted is your call."

"Could it have been?"

"It *could* have."

"Do you think it was?"

Barney tugged at his bow tie. "I couldn't give you a medical opinion on that."

"How about a nonmedical opinion?"

"A guy fully dressed climbs into a bathtub and shoots himself? What's the point?"

"You could say that about any suicide."

"I mean climbing into the bathtub. A man about to shoot himself isn't concerned with getting blood on the carpet."

"Did he?"

"Get blood on the carpet?" Barney shook his head. "Not at all. Not a lot of blood in the bathtub, either."

"What do you make of that?"

"Guy didn't bleed much." At Harper's look, the doctor shrugged. "It happens."

"Could he have been shot through a pillow or a towel that soaked up the blood?"

"Not in this case. You got powder burns around the wound. Of course, if you didn't, it couldn't be suicide, it would have to be murder."

"Anything else? That would indicate it *wasn't* suicide?"

"Wound's in the *back* of the head, not the temple. You could do it, but it would be awkward. And the gun would wind up in the bathtub, not on the floor."

The ambulance doors slammed.

Barney Nathan glanced in that direction, said, "Well, gotta go do my autopsy. I suppose you want the bullet."

"Try not to scratch it any more than you have to."

"You mean I shouldn't dig it out with a butter knife? Thanks for the tip."

"And avoid Rick Reed if you can."

"My pleasure."

When the news crew descended on the doctor, he smiled and kept going. Undaunted, Rick Reed pounced on the chief. "I'm here with Chief Dale Harper, who just finished with the medical examiner. Anything to report, Chief?"

"The doctor is accompanying the body to the morgue to perform an autopsy."

242

"Autopsy? Then it *was* a murder?"

"That's what the autopsy will determine."

"Well, what did the doctor say?"

A blast from the ambulance siren drowned out any possible answer.

Chief Harper looked, said, "Oh, hell, I'm blocking the ambulance," and went to move his car. He took advantage of the camera crew filming the departure of the corpse to sneak back to the crime scene.

Dan Finley popped out of the motel room door. "The place is lousy with prints."

Chief Harper groaned. "You auditioning for a cop show, Dan? Don't tell me about it, just dust 'em and lift 'em."

"There's an awful lot of 'em."

"So I gather. Just get on with it."

"There's prints on the gun."

Harper's eyes widened. "You lifted prints from the gun?"

"Three beauties. We'll be able to get a match."

Harper pulled Dan aside and lowered his voice. "You label the prints from the gun?"

"Of course."

"Well, double-check 'em. Some smart defense attorney's gonna claim they jumped around."

Dan smiled. "Who's doing the tough-guy lingo now, Chief?"

243

"Take the gun and the prints and run them down to the lab. I want a ballistics report, and I mean now."

"I gotta get the bullet from the doc."

"Pick it up on your way."

"What about the crime scene?"

"Sam can finish up. You get on down to the lab."

"Right." Dan Finley gathered up the evidence, hopped in his police car, and took off.

Watching Dan go, Chief Harper felt a tremendous rush of adrenaline. He had to compose himself, put on his best poker face before walking past the TV crews. It wasn't easy.

Finding prints on the murder weapon was an incredible break.

Now if he could just match 'em up.

37

Mr. Wilbur parked out on the road, strode through the parking lot, and glared at the crime-scene ribbon across the door to Unit 12 as if it were an inconvenience placed there primarily to tick him off.

"What the hell's going on here?" he demanded of no one in particular.

Chief Harper tore himself away from the unrewarding task of interrogating the other motel guests to intercept him. Otherwise the cranky antiques dealer might have ducked under the ribbon and gone in.

"What do you want, Wilbur?"

"I want to see Benny Southstreet. What's the matter? He under arrest?"

"He's dead."

Wilbur considered. "In that case, I *don't* want to see him."

"What's your business with Benny Southstreet?"

"That's between me and him."

"Not anymore."

"Good point. Okay, I was hoping he could get my chairs back, seeing as how you weren't doing squat."

"What made you think he could do that?"

"He said so."

"When?"

"Yesterday."

"You saw him yesterday?"

"No, on the phone."

"What did he say?"

"He said he had some chairs I might be interested in."

"Were you?"

"If they were my chairs? What do *you* think?"

"Were they?"

"How the hell should I know? I figured I'd check it out."

"Did you?"

"No."

"Why not?"

"He wasn't there. He said he'd be here at two o'clock. I called the number, he didn't answer. I drove by, knocked on the door. He wasn't there."

"Are you sure?"

"Sure I'm sure. I waited around, in case he was in the can, knocked loud. He wasn't there. You say he's dead?"

"Yes."

"So what about the chairs?"

"What chairs?"

"Have you heard a word I said? The guy had chairs. If he's dead it's a damn shame, but where are they?"

Harper frowned. "Wait a minute. You're saying Benny Southstreet had chairs in his motel room?"

"Or his car. Why am I telling you? Did you find his chairs or not?"

"Not in his motel room."

"How about his car?"

"Which one's his car?"

"You're asking me?" Wilbur shook his head. "Sheesh, you got any plans to solve this thing?"

The zapper on the keys found in Benny Southstreet's pocket flashed the lights and unlocked the doors of the Ford Taurus. The chairs weren't in it.

"There you are," Wilbur declared. "The killer took the chairs."

Rick Reed, close enough to overhear, chimed in, "Chairs? What chairs?"

"Oh, hell." Chief Harper dragged Wilbur away from the reporter. "If you want to spout a lotta nonsense, I suggest you don't do it in front of the TV camera. You don't know this guy ever had any chairs. You don't know chairs have anything to do with it. But we have a violent death, and if it turns out to be a murder, your interest in your damn chairs is going to make you a suspect in the eyes of the public."

"Oh, sure. Like people will really think I did it."

"Someone did. Why not you?" Harper said bluntly. "Now shut up about the chairs until we find out if they ever existed. Will you do that?"

"I don't see how I can refuse, considering how much progress you're making."

Chief Harper walked over to where the chambermaid was hanging out with the rest of the motel help. "Can I talk to you a minute?"

Marge seemed concerned. "I told you all I know."

Harper smiled. "Humor me."

He led her away from the others.

"What do you want now?" Marge asked.

"Tell me about the chairs."

Marge stopped, and her mouth fell open. "What about them?"

"You didn't mention the chairs. I was wondering why not."

"I don't understand. What's important about the chairs?"

"I don't know, but I mean to find out.

What do you know about them?"

"Nothing. The guy had four chairs. I don't know why. I had to clean around them."

"Where are they now?"

"I have no idea."

"You knew they were gone?"

"Well, I didn't see them."

"You didn't think that was worth mentioning?"

"Are you kidding? The man is dead. Who cares about some stupid old chairs?"

"That remains to be seen. The point is, it's not up to you to evaluate the evidence and decide what is important enough to tell us. You think of anything, you let us know."

"Okay."

"Is anything else missing? Anything you noticed before that you don't see now?"

"No, that's it."

"The last time you saw the chairs was when you cleaned yesterday? You have no idea where they went? Or when?"

"No."

"You had no idea they were missing until you went in there just before you called the police?"

"No, I didn't. You mean he was killed for his chairs? But that's ridiculous."

"Why is it ridiculous?"

"It just is. I mean, I can imagine someone

stealing the chairs. I can't imagine someone killing someone over them."

"And you have no idea who might have taken them?"

"I don't know how anyone could. The door was locked."

"I thought you said it was unlocked."

"I mean yesterday. When I made up the room. The door was locked when I left. No one could have gotten in there without a key. Unless Mr. Southstreet let them in."

"You're sure the door was locked when you left?"

"It's one of the rules. You clean the room, you leave it locked."

"Maybe you forgot?"

Marge shook her head. "I tried the knob. Like I always do."

Chief Harper's cell phone rang. He dismissed the chambermaid with a nod, yanked the phone out of his pocket, strolled away.

"Chief, it's Barney. Your boy came by, picked up the bullet."

"Fine."

"No, it's not fine. I have a job to do. I don't need some young whippersnapper hounding me to hurry."

"Dan's got a gun with fingerprints, Barney. He'd love to match it up."

"I'm sure you would too. But I have to follow procedure."

"I understand. Give him the bullet when you can."

"I *gave* him the bullet. He's long gone. I just don't like to be rushed."

"I'll let him know. How's the autopsy coming? You got anything for me yet?"

"I can give you an approximate time of death. Yesterday afternoon, between twelve and four."

"That ironclad?"

"Hell, no. But as a working hypothesis, I'd take it to the bank."

Chief Harper hung up the phone, to find a vaguely familiar young man bearing down on him. He was relatively young, probably on the good side of forty. He wore a black T-shirt and blue jeans.

"Chief Harper."

"Yes?"

"I'm Paul Fishman. I run the Photomat stand at the mall."

"Yes, of course," Chief Harper said. That explained his daughter Clara's sudden interest in photography.

"I saw it on the news. About the murder. Are you calling it that yet?"

"It's too soon to say."

Paul jerked his thumb. "It's not too soon for the TV guys. They said a murder at the

Four Seasons Motel."

Harper's face darkened. "Did they really?"

"They may have said *potential,* or *alleged,* or whatever newsmen say when they're not allowed to tell you something obvious."

Harper nodded. "It's probably a murder, but don't quote me on it."

"Anyway, they showed a shot of the crime-scene ribbon, and it's Unit 12, isn't it?"

Harper's eyes narrowed. "Yeah. Why?"

Paul Fishman put up his hands. "Look, I don't know how these things work. Whether I need a lawyer, or what. Doctors have professional privilege, or client confidentiality, or something like that. I'm just a guy in the Photomat. But I don't want to violate anyone's right to privacy."

Chief Harper glanced around for the TV crew, saw that Rick Reed had moved in on the chambermaid. "I haven't got time for this. You want a lawyer, I'll get you a lawyer. But just between you and me, what the hell are you talking about?"

"I have some pictures that might have something to do with the crime."

"Photographs?"

"Yes."

"You mean a roll of film that you developed?"

"That's right."

"You don't want to violate anyone's privacy by turning them in to the police?"

"You see my problem?"

"I see your problem. And if I don't see your photographs, I'm running you in on obstruction of justice. You're not violating anyone's privacy here. I'm *ordering* you to turn the pictures over. If you'd rather hear it from a judge, you and your photos can wait in jail until I get a court order for you to turn 'em over." Harper looked him right in the eye. "The point is, you're not surrendering them voluntarily, you see what I mean?"

"Yes, I do."

"So let's have 'em."

Paul produced a packet of four-by-six prints. "They're just from a throwaway camera, but they're pretty clear. I do good work. Brightness, definition, color correction. Take a look."

Chief Harper pulled out the prints. The first was a shot of the motel sign.

"They're in reverse order," Paul volunteered. "That's the last shot on the roll."

The next-to-the-last shot was a close-up of the number *12* on the door. Then came shots of the chairs. Long shots. Close-ups. All four together. A single chair. Close-ups of the detail work. In the longer shots, the chairs were clearly in the motel unit.

Chief Harper's pulse quickened. Here it was, a good solid lead. He flipped to the next photo, and stopped dead.

It was a shot of Sherry Carter, young, lithe, and tanned, in a string bikini, a wide-eyed smile, and her hand up in an unmistakable don't-take-my-picture pose, as she lounged in a deck chair on the front lawn of her house. Sherry looked positively gorgeous, but the allure was lost on Chief Harper, so great was his surprise.

He didn't let on, said casually, "Whose pictures are these?"

"Cora Felton's. She dropped them off yesterday, never picked them up."

"What time yesterday?"

"Early afternoon."

Sam Brogan came up, practically dragging a young man wearing a baseball cap. "This kid was on the desk yesterday. Whaddya think he saw?"

"Don't make me guess, Sam," Harper said irritably.

"Tell him," Sam ordered.

"A woman loading chairs into a car."

"You're kidding! When?"

The kid was sulky, probably figured he was in trouble for not reporting this before. "I dunno. Sometime in the afternoon."

"Tell him from where," Sam prompted.

"Unit 12."

"You recognize the woman?"

"Yeah. It was that Puzzle Lady woman."

"Are you sure?"

"Sure I'm sure. It took a while. She had to load 'em one at a time."

"The guest didn't help her?"

The kid crinkled his nose. "Guest?"

"The guy who rented the unit," Harper said impatiently. "Mr. Southstreet. He didn't help her carry the chairs?"

"I didn't see him. Just her."

"Oh. So you don't even know if he was there."

"He was there, all right."

"I thought you didn't see him."

"I didn't. Not then. But when she got there, I saw him let her in."

"You *saw* him?"

"I didn't *see* him. She knocked on the door. It opened. She said, 'Hi,' and went in."

"She said, 'Hi'?"

"Yeah. I think she said his name, but I couldn't tell. Not through the office window."

"You saw this through the office window?"

"When she got there. Not when she took the chairs. I was outside then."

"And you're sure it was Cora Felton?"

"Oh, yeah."

"And Mr. Southstreet let her in?"

"Sure he did. That's how I knew it was okay she took the chairs. He gave 'em to her."

Chief Harper's cell phone rang. He jerked it out, growled, "Yeah?"

"Chief, it's Dan. I'm down at the lab. The bullets match. And that's not all."

"What do you mean?"

"You know the fingerprints we keep on file — you, me, Sam, the doc, all the other likely people who might have touched something at a crime scene — so we can eliminate 'em?"

"What's your point?" Harper said irritably.

"You're not going to believe whose prints are on the gun."

38

Down at the station Chief Harper and Dan Finley took the handcuffs off Cora Felton and offered her her one phone call. Since Becky Baldwin had been present when she was arrested, Cora didn't need it.

Becky looked across the visiting-room table. "I feel funny about this, Cora. Benny was my client."

"He's dead. Doesn't that resolve the conflict of interest?"

"Not if you killed him."

"I didn't kill him."

"That's going to be tough to prove."

"Whoa! Hold on a minute! You're a defense attorney. You don't have to prove I didn't kill him. The prosecution has to prove I did."

"They can. Which throws the ball back in our court. Once they prove you killed him, we have to prove you didn't."

"Maybe I should hire another lawyer."

"Feel free. They're just going to tell you the same thing. Your fingerprints are on the murder weapon. You took pictures of the stolen chairs. As if the pictures aren't damaging enough, the chambermaid's caved in and admitted you were the one who took them."

"The pictures, not the chairs."

"The boy from the front desk saw you take the chairs. Even if I could shake his testimony, they can prove you took them, because you gave them to Harvey Beerbaum yesterday afternoon. Which is double-plus-ungood, since it means you took 'em right around the time the doctor says Benny was killed. According to the chambermaid, you photographed the chairs around eleven-thirty, the guy from the Photomat says you dropped off the film around noon, and Harvey Beerbaum says you called him at three-thirty and came over by four."

"The guy from the Photomat's pretty dreamy, isn't he?"

"I beg your pardon?"

"He ask you out yet?"

Becky blushed. "Cora, you're charged with murder."

"Yeah, but I didn't do it. Just between you

and me, isn't the guy a hunk?"

"How can you even think about such a thing?"

Cora shrugged. "Be a nice break for Sherry. Get you out of Aaron's way. Head off any pass the guy might make at her."

"You think he'd hit on Sherry?"

"You didn't see the shot of her in a bikini."

"Cora, stick with me here. You're in jail."

"Yes. You will get me out, now, won't you?"

"I don't think you understand how serious this is."

"Oh, yes, I do. I'm charged with murder. Unless Benny Southstreet turns out to be a police officer, it's as bad as it gets. Can you arrange bail?"

"It's not easy in a capital case."

"Oh, come on. I'm not a flight risk."

"I'll certainly raise the issue. Right now I'm trying to get the puzzle."

"What puzzle?"

"The puzzle found on the body. The police think it's yours. Please tell me it isn't."

"Hand to God."

"Are you sure? Did you get a good look at it?"

"I haven't seen it."

"Then how do you know it isn't?"

"Becky, trust me on this. I had nothing to do with the puzzle found by the body."

"What if it's the one you gave that house-wife?"

"Becky, honey, in that context, *housewife* could be seen as a pejorative term." Cora hoped it was. It sounded like something a linguist might say.

The phrase rang no alarm bells with Becky. Though other things did. "If it's the same puzzle Benny claimed you stole from him, that would make a pretty tough case."

"I thought it was pretty tough anyway."

"You're not being very helpful."

"I don't know anything that will help. Stop torturing me with what-if-it's-the-same-puzzle, and go find out if it is."

"I can do better than that," Becky said. "I'm gonna get a copy and bring it in here for you to solve."

"Oh, for Christ's sake! You think I wanna sit in jail solving a puzzle?"

"Maybe it will get you *out* of jail."

"Yeah, yeah, right. The guy died with a crossword puzzle by him, and when you solve it it says, 'Cora didn't do it.' Gee, Becky, come back to planet Earth."

"You don't wanna see the puzzle?"

"Give it to Sherry. She's good enough at solving them."

"I thought she was busy with her matrimonial problems."

"What's more important? Her wedding, or my murder?"

"Your loopy logic is hard to follow, at best. Do you have anything practical to add in your defense? Aside from the bald assertion that you didn't do it?"

"I'd take a good hard look at Chuck Dillinger."

"How come?"

"Southstreet may have ripped him off for some money."

"What makes you think so?"

"Evidence would indicate."

"What kind of evidence?"

"Circumstantial."

"How solid is this circumstantial evidence?"

"Actually, it's more of an inference."

"Cora."

"What do you care? You're not presenting this to a jury. I'm just telling you how things are. There is a strong possibility, which I can't begin to prove, that Benny Southstreet may have ripped Chuck Dillinger off. Chuck Dillinger might be a perfectly good suspect."

"That's not very promising."

"Yes it is. We're way ahead of the police on this one. We know the chairs had nothing to do with it. I stole the chairs, and I didn't kill him."

"What if he was killed for *not* having the chairs?"

Cora whistled. "Whoa, Becky, you surprise me! What a great idea!"

"You think it's right?"

"No, I think it's dead wrong. But it's a *great* idea."

"Thanks a heap. What's all this about Chuck Dillinger?"

"He filed a report with the police that his study was broken into. The person who broke in was probably Benny Southstreet."

"You got anything to back that up?"

"Not a thing."

"Well, what do you expect me to do about it?" Becky said irritably.

"Get me out of here."

Becky took a breath. "Cora, you're not making any sense. You're spewing out a lot of unrelated facts that don't add up to anything. This isn't like you. You may be a little nuts, but you're generally smart as a whip. Now, is there anything you want to tell me? You haven't fallen off the wagon, have you?"

Cora's face hardened. "Well, that's a hell of a thing to say. No, I am not drunk, thank you very much. Do I smell like a brewery? Do I look like a lush?" She realized she was wearing her Wicked Witch of the West outfit, complete with cigarette burns and liquor stains. "Okay, scratch that. The point is, Miss Smarty Pants, I've never been arrested for murder before. There's been men I'd like to murder — my fifth husband, for instance — but I've never actually done it. Or been suspected of it. I'm in jail charged with murder, and it isn't very nice. And the facts are so jumbled and sketchy I don't know how to explain it. What the hell am I going to tell Chief Harper?"

"You're not going to tell him anything," Becky said. "You're not talking. You're not talking to the cops, you're not talking to the prosecutor, you're not talking to the media. The only things you're saying are 'No comment' and 'See my attorney.'"

"Then how do I explain to the police —"

"You don't. You don't go near the police. I'm not even sure you should tell Sherry. Because she'll tell Aaron Grant, and he's a reporter."

"Aaron wouldn't do anything to hurt us."

"Probably not a great time to test that theory. What you tell your niece is your business. What you tell the cops is mine. You tell 'em nothing. Not a damn thing. When I get you out of here, you stay away from Chief Harper. He comes near you, you walk away.

He calls you on the phone, you hang up. He asks you a question, you just smile. You don't give him the time of day. Do you understand?"

Cora nodded. "Perfectly."

39

Chief Harper banged his coffee cup down on the counter. "Are you kidding me?"

"Not at all," Cora told him. "That's the facts of the case as I know them."

"But it makes no sense."

"You think it makes more sense I killed the guy to get some chairs?"

"And protect yourself from a plagiarism suit that could cost you your career."

"Then I'm not very bright," Cora said, "trading a plagiarism suit for a murder rap."

"Well, you didn't expect to get caught."

"Of course not. Not when I was clever enough to leave my fingerprints on the murder weapon. It was the perfect crime."

Chief Harper took a sip of his coffee, grimaced, and glanced around the grungy diner. It was your typical greasy spoon, with glare lighting and Formica tabletops. He and Cora were the only customers. They sat opposite each other at a booth in the back. Cora wore a conservative skirt and blouse she'd picked up at the mall. The Wicked Witch of the West getup in which she'd been arrested was in her drawstring purse on the seat next to her. Harper was in uniform. Otherwise, they could have passed for illicit lovers involved in a low-rent affair.

"Why are we having coffee here?" Harper asked irritably.

"We're hiding from the media. So they won't hear me confessing."

"You're not confessing. You're telling me you're innocent."

"I'm glad to hear you take that attitude. Some policemen might quibble about the theft of the chairs. Which isn't really a theft, it's a retheft, stealing stolen property back. Is there a law that covers that?"

"There must be a precedent somewhere. At the moment you're not charged with that crime."

"That's why I was careful to say 'hypothetical' when I told you about it. I did say 'hypothetical,' didn't I?"

"I don't remember."

"Well, this whole conversation is hypothetical. Like, 'Suppose we discuss the crime.'"

"You mean, suppose I listen to your ideas? All right, I've listened. And I'm no wiser than when I started. In fact, I'm even more confused. Tell me again why you went to the motel."

"I hoped to find some evidence of Benny Southstreet breaking into Chuck Dillinger's apartment." Cora had adopted that version of the story, so she wouldn't have to mention breaking into Wilbur's Antiques. There was no reason to bog Chief Harper down with too many details.

"Instead you found the chairs he had stolen from Harvey Beerbaum."

"That's right."

"Which Harvey had advertised for sale on eBay."

"Absolutely not."

"Oh? I thought you said he did."

"No. Benny *thought* they were the chairs on eBay. They weren't. They were simply Harvey's dining room chairs."

"What made him think they were?"

"What made him think I ripped off his puzzle? The man was simply weird."

Harper frowned. "Come on, Cora. You know better than that. You don't dismiss a suspect's actions on the grounds they must be crazy."

"Benny Southstreet's a suspect in his own death? You're telling me it's a suicide?"

Harper ignored that. "So you went out

there while the chambermaid was making up his room and peeked in the door?"

"Well, I didn't have a key."

"You saw the chairs?"

"Yes, I did."

"We don't even need that admission. We have photographic evidence."

"You say that as if it were a strike against me. How many murderers photograph the crime scene beforehand and drop the film off at Photomat?"

"If you want to argue you couldn't be that dumb, it would help if you started showing even the least bit of sense. Selling chairs on eBay, for God's sake."

"Hey, who asked who to investigate Mr. Wilbur's robbery?"

"I said investigate, not set up some crazy Internet sting."

"What do you mean, crazy? It worked, didn't it?"

"Like a charm. You got Benny Southstreet to steal Harvey Beerbaum's dining room chairs. What could be better?"

"I also got Wilbur to bid on them."

"So? The guy's been trying to find his stolen chairs for months. Of course he's looking for someone to put 'em up for bids."

"Yeah, but Benny Southstreet wasn't. What the hell was he doing in the picture?"

"Getting killed, mainly. With your prints on the gun."

"Well, if you're gonna make an issue of that."

"I'm not the one making the issue. It's in Henry's hands now."

"Henry Firth? That twerp?"

Chief Harper choked on his coffee. "Hey! That's the county prosecutor you're talking about."

"He's still a twerp."

"You shouldn't take this personally, Cora."

"It isn't personal. I thought he was a twerp *before* I got arrested. Can you talk him out of prosecuting me? For his own good. He's gonna make a fool of himself."

"Not if you get convicted. It'll be like busting Martha Stewart. He'll be the prosecutor who put away the Puzzle Lady."

"You're not cheering me up, Chief."

"Well, I would strongly suggest you come up with some evidence in your favor. Right now, everything works against you. What time were you at the motel? Hypothetically, of course."

"Right around three o'clock."

"That when you saw the gun?"

"The hypothetical gun? Yeah, it was right there on the nightstand."

"You picked it up?"

"I wanted to see if it had been fired."

"You picked it up and sniffed it?"

"So?"

"Isn't that the sort of thing they do in detective stories?"

"That doesn't make it wrong."

"In the detective stories do they usually leave their fingerprints on it?"

Cora didn't dignify that with an answer.

"Had the gun been fired?"

"No, it had not. The gun hadn't been fired. Benny wasn't in the motel room. I took the chairs and left. Sometime after that Benny Southstreet came back to the motel room, the killer came to the motel room, took the gun, and shot Benny in the head. By which time I was long gone."

"Not very long, according to the medical examiner. There's a rather small window of opportunity for killing this guy. Autopsy report puts the time of death between noon and four. If you left around three, there's only an hour this could have happened. And that's pushing the edge of the time limit."

"I can't help that. The facts are the facts."

Chief Harper eyed Cora as skeptically as he'd regarded the diner's coffee. "Are they really? Why do I get the feeling you're selling me snake oil?"

"You're a cop. You have a suspicious nature. It's too bad. I'm giving you the straight goods."

"Then the straight goods don't help you much. You're in the soup, and everything you say just makes it worse."

"Okay. You got anything that makes it *better?*"

"I beg your pardon?"

"Come on, Chief. I told you what I know. You got anything that helps me?"

"Not really."

"Thanks a heap. Let me put it this way. What do you know that I don't?"

Harper scowled. "I shouldn't be telling you this."

"You're not. We're talking hypothetically."

"There wasn't a lot of blood. Which would indicate the shot was muffled by something that soaked it up."

"Was there a towel or pillow missing from the unit?"

"No. And there were powder burns around the wound which there wouldn't have been in that case."

"What if he was killed somewhere else and the body moved?"

"With the gun you were playing with in his motel room *after* the time the medical examiner says he died? The gun you claim *hadn't been fired?* He was killed somewhere else with *that* gun?"

"Am I correct in assuming you don't think much of that theory?"

"You see the problem? I wish I could tell you something that helps. But nothing does. All the evidence we turn up indicates you killed the guy."

"Great. I'm so glad we had this little talk. So what do you advise me to do?"

"Keep a low profile."

40

There were half a dozen news crews camped out at the foot of the driveway. Cora kept a low profile as she plowed through them, flooring the Toyota and sending camera, light, and sound technicians diving for safety. She zoomed up the drive, screeched to a stop, and was in the front door before anyone recovered in time to get a shot.

Sherry sprang up from the couch to meet her. "Cora, are you all right?"

"Fine. Where's Aaron?"

"On the computer."

"Oh?"

"Filing his story." At her aunt's look, Sherry said, "Well, he has to cover it, Cora. I told him to go, but he won't leave."

"True devotion."

"He's just afraid Dennis is still around."

"Is he?"

"How the hell should I know? He left with

Brenda, so I assume she's got him under control."

"This whole mating ritual used to be easier." Cora flopped down on the couch, took her cigarettes out of her purse.

"You're not going to smoke in here."

Cora shrugged. "I need practice. Cigarettes will be like money in the pen."

Aaron came down the hallway. "So, you're out. Did you make bail, or are you on the lam?"

"That has a nice ring to it. I suppose I could try a combo, and skip bail."

"Pardon me for asking, but what happened?"

"Off the record?"

"Why does it have to be off the record?"

"Well, Aaron, if you want a confession, it's gotta be off the record. Otherwise, you're an accessory, and you can go to jail."

"Confession?"

"She's just kidding you, Aaron."

"The hell I am. I didn't kill Benny Southstreet, but I'm guilty of so many other things, I don't know where to begin."

"Give it a shot."

"Aside from plagiarism, which Sherry did for me, I'm guilty of fraud, false advertising, using the Internet to defraud, conspiracy to commit fraud and false advertising, and all that, in addition to bidding on my own object to drive the price up, which I'm not sure of the name of, but it can't be good. Then there's breaking and entering, two counts, criminal trespass, two counts, burglary, larceny, and/or petty theft, depending on how much Harvey's chairs are worth. When you add in the murder charge, which is the only thing I *didn't* actually do, it hasn't been a really great day." Cora settled back on the couch and sighed. "You know what I'd like right now?"

"A visit from Harvey Beerbaum?" Sherry said from the window.

"Not even close." Cora's eyes widened. "What, you mean he's here?"

"Coming up the walk." Sherry went and opened the door.

"Come in, Harvey, join the defense team," Cora said. "You wanna be a character witness or an alibi witness? To be an alibi witness you have to fib a little. To be a character witness you have to outright lie."

"It's not funny," Harvey said. "You know what the police did?"

"You mean arrested me, Harvey? Yeah, I noticed."

"They took my chairs. My dining room chairs. How do you like that? First Benny takes my chairs. Then you get them back.

Then the police take them."

"Why did they take the chairs?" Aaron asked.

"They said they're going to fingerprint them. It's very unsettling. Suppose they find my fingerprints?"

"So what if they find your fingerprints, Harvey, they're your chairs," Cora told him.

"I know, I know." Harvey slumped down on the end of the sofa. "I'm just upset because I feel bad."

"You feel bad about what?"

"The puzzle they found with the body. The police wanted me to solve it. Ordinarily, they'd ask you. That's what they always do. Not that I mind being second choice. Even so, under the circumstances, knowing they were only coming to me because you were the suspect . . ." Harvey shook his head.

"You're saying you solved the puzzle for them?"

"I felt bad about it, but if I didn't, someone else would."

"So you solved it. Do you remember what it said?"

"I can do better than that. I made a copy."

"The police let you make a copy?"

"No. I reconstructed it from memory."

"You can do that?" Cora said.

Sherry coughed warningly.

"Of course I can. I'm sure you could too. Not that I can remember every puzzle I ever solved, but when I needed to, it wasn't any trouble." Harvey took a folded piece of paper out of his jacket pocket, passed it over. "There you go."

"Let's see the theme entries." It was all Cora could do to keep from side-spying up at Sherry to see if her niece was giving her points for remembering the term *theme entries.*

"It's a ditty," Harvey said.

"A ditty?"

"A rhyme, really. Have a look. See?" Harvey said. He recited:

"I don't mind if
You thrill me
Just try hard
Not to kill me."

Cora offered a comment that could hardly be construed as constructive criticism.

"Miss Felton!" Harvey said, astonished.

"It couldn't just be a simple nursery rhyme. No, there has to be a sinister element."

"Of course. Otherwise, what would be the point?"

"What's the point at all?" Cora demanded.

ACROSS

1 Grounds for a suit
5 "__ Frutti" (Little Richard song)
10 Erie Canal mule
13 African lilies
15 Reaction to, "Pick a cod, any cod"
16 "¿__ pasa?"
17 Start of a message
19 Beehive State athlete
20 Polo or Garr
21 It's under foot
22 Feel poorly
23 Classic Ford model
26 Threatening sentence-ender
28 TV broadcast band
29 Message part 2
32 Synthesizer inventor
34 Gets bored with
35 Bio by Molly Ivins
37 Have a couple of eggs?
38 Xerox competitor
42 "I'm OK with it"
45 Iditarod race place

46 Message part 3
50 Links number
51 All told
52 Falls in New York
54 "___ whillikers!"
55 Till bills
58 Hoofbeat sound
59 Easy mark
60 End of message
64 Cobra kin
65 Bungled play
66 Streamlined
67 Fourth of July?
68 Oceans, in poetry
69 Connecticut campus

DOWN
1 Mai ___
2 Long in the tooth
3 Is a fan
4 Basic belief
5 ___ Friday's (restaurant chain)
6 Big coffee containers
7 Brouhaha
8 Makes fit
9 Lower-ranking
10 Violent gust of wind
11 Pediatric mental disorder
12 Actress Sobieski

14 Lamb, at large
18 North Dakota city
23 ___ the word
24 "Oops!"
25 Jury verdict
27 Small and lively
30 Garbage
31 "Yo, dude!"
33 Enthusiasm
36 Closed, as a sports jacket
39 Confess to less
40 "The Mod Squad" costar Epps
41 Juno, to Greeks
43 Mined over matter?
44 Cager Strickland or Dampier
46 Puzzle cutter-upper
47 On edge
48 Treeless tract
49 Some surrealistic paintings
53 "Holy smokes!"
56 "To be," to Henri
57 "Cut it out!"
61 Surgery sites, briefly
62 Brooks of "Blazing Saddles"
63 Barely manage, with "out"

"I mean, come on. Some moron's littering the crime scene with cryptic crosswords hinting at a homicide? Give me a break!"

"It's not a cryptic," Harvey corrected. "It's a simple fifteen by fifteen."

"I'm going to hurt you, Harvey. You happen to tell the police when I brought you the chairs?"

"Right around four-thirty."

"*Four*-thirty? Harvey, it was *three*-thirty."

"Are you sure?"

"Yes, I'm sure. I've reconstructed my whole day."

"I haven't, of course, but it seemed like four-thirty."

" 'Seemed like' isn't the same as 'is.' "

"Well, I could be mistaken."

"That's the stuff, Harvey. How badly might you be mistaken?"

"I don't know."

"Well, I do. You've got that clock on the wall. You know the one I mean."

"It's a trophy. From a regional tournament."

"Right. The miniature grandfather. With the hands and the pendulum. It works, doesn't it? It tells time?"

"Of course."

"When you thought it was four-thirty, maybe the big hand was on the six. That's where you got that impression. But the little hand, which is pretty little, who's to say whether it was between the three and the four or the four and the five. You see what I mean?"

"You think I made a mistake?"

"That's entirely possible, Harvey." Cora stood up, prompting Harvey to do the same. She put her hand on his shoulder. "Here's what you should do. You should go home, take a look at the clock. Try to imagine where you were when I brought you the chairs. What angle you might have seen the clock from. Remember, you wouldn't be paying much attention to the clock, because, after all, you were excited about getting the chairs back."

"I suppose so."

"Excellent, Harvey. Go home now, think it over. Because the last thing in the world you want to do is tell the police something you're going to be cross-examined on in court. And then some snide defense lawyer's gonna ask you how you know for sure. If that defense attorney's got blond hair, long legs, and a skintight sweater, she may make you jump through hoops."

Harvey's eyes were wide. "But . . . but . . ."

"Go home, take a good look at the clock, and search your memory. Because you don't want to be that type of witness who's so sure of himself he trips over his own feet."

Cora winked, pushed him out the door.

Harvey pointed. "What about them?"

The news vans were still parked at the foot of the drive.

"You didn't talk to them on your way in, did you, Harvey?"

"No."

"And you're not going to talk to 'em now. If they try to stop you, keep on going. It'll be harder, because they'll wanna know what we said. Ignore them. Pay no attention. Just keep on driving. Run over a few of them if you can."

Harvey looked aghast. "But —"

"Attaboy." Cora clapped him on the shoulder, banged the door shut.

Aaron Grant spread his arms. "Well, there's my story."

"You wouldn't write that," Sherry said. "Cora, what do you think you're doing?"

"Harvey's mistaken. I brought him the chairs at three-thirty."

"There's no chance *you're* mistaken?"

"Sure there is. That's not the point. I gotta give myself a little wiggle room. The guy was killed between twelve and four. Even stealing the chairs at three-thirty's cutting it close. Four-thirty fries my fanny."

"Why?" Sherry said. "You didn't have to take 'em straight to Harvey. You could have come home first."

"Yeah, but I didn't."

"But they don't know that."

"Yes they do. That's what I told the police."

"You talked to the police?"

"Just Chief Harper."

"Does Becky know?"

"It was off the record."

"You guys do know I'm sitting here?" Aaron said.

"You're not writing this, Aaron."

"Of course I'm not writing this. People would think I was a gibbering idiot. Let's nail down what I'm not writing. Cora, is it my understanding that you're trying to get Harvey to change his testimony about when you delivered the chairs because if he doesn't it's going to make you look guilty?"

"*Look* guilty? No. If he doesn't change his story, I *am* guilty. I have a little problem, Aaron. I told Chief Harper I picked up the chairs and took 'em straight to Harvey. I also told him the body wasn't there. Well, if the body wasn't there by four-thirty, I am out-and-out lying, because the guy was dead before four o'clock. And it's not like he could have been shot somewhere else and been brought to the motel, because the gun *was* there, and hadn't been fired yet."

"Did you tell *that* to Chief Harper?"

"Off the record. If those are the facts, I must have done it. It's even got me convinced."

"So Harvey must be wrong," Aaron said.

"Thank you!" Cora said. "Finally! Someone taking me at my word and stating the obvious. That's right. I! Didn't! Do it! So anyone *proving* I did it must be mistaken. I know I didn't do it, which is how I know Harvey is wrong, which is why I'm asking him to evaluate his statement to the police."

Cora flopped down on the couch, pulled out a cigarette, tapped it angrily on her lighter. "Besides, I'm not guilty of nearly enough things in this case. I'd sure hate to miss a chance at tampering with a witness."

Sherry said, "If what you say is true, between three-thirty and four Benny Southstreet returned to his motel room, most likely in the company of his killer. The killer got possession of Benny's gun, shot him, stuffed the body in the bathtub, left the gun on the floor, and got the hell out of there without being seen. All in the space of half an hour."

Cora shook her head. "It's not much, but it's all I got. You put it that way, it could have happened. You put it Harvey's way, it couldn't."

"Just as long as he changes his story before he talks to the press," Aaron said. "Public opinion's a tricky thing. People get something in their minds, it's hard to change it. It's important the first thing they hear is three-thirty. If you want, I can do a whole column based on that, get the idea out before anyone has a chance to hear what Harvey has to say. If he decides to stick to four-thirty, they'll have heard your story first."

"Good idea." Cora heaved herself off the couch, headed for the door.

"Where are you going?"

"To get my story out first."

Realization dawned. "Hey, it was my idea!" Aaron protested.

"So come along." Cora banged out the door with Aaron and Sherry on her heels. She strode down the driveway to where the news crews were waiting. "Okay, gang, fire 'em up. You're getting a statement."

Microphones were shoved in Cora's face, as camera crews jockeyed for position.

"Can we get your house in the background?"

"You can if you aim right. That's up to you. Okay, we're going in five, four, three, two, one." Cora turned on the Puzzle Lady charm. "Hi. I'm Cora Felton. I have a statement to make regarding the Benny Southstreet murder. I have helped the police in the past, and I am eager to assist them in this particular case. Here's what I know so far. At three-thirty yesterday afternoon, I inspected Benny Southstreet's motel room. Mr. Southstreet was not there. His body was not there. His gun was there, but it had not been fired. I left the motel room at three-thirty yesterday afternoon, and never went back. I never saw Mr. Southstreet yesterday, alive or dead, and I have no knowledge as to how or when he returned to his room. Thank you very much."

Cora strode back up the driveway as reporters shouted questions.

The phone was ringing when they came in the door. Sherry ran to answer it.

"If that's the media, she's not talking," Aaron said.

"Now you're my publicist?" Cora said.

"It's Becky," Sherry called from the kitchen.

"Uh-oh." Cora padded into the kitchen to take her medicine. "Hi, Becky. Been watching TV?"

"No. Why?"

"Oh. Never mind. Why'd you call?"

"It can wait. What did I miss on TV?"

"You first."

"Cora."

"You called me. What's up?"

"Autopsy report," Becky told her. "Doc narrowed down the time of death. He's now placing it between one and three."

Cora's mouth fell open. "One and *three!*"

"Yeah. Now, what did I miss on television?"

"Oops."

41

"Is there anything *else* you want to tell me?" Becky asked.

Becky and Cora were eating takeout in her office. Becky was picking at a chopped salad, and Cora was building her strength with a pastrami on rye.

"You mean like I killed Benny Southstreet?"

"Is that a confession?"

"Not so you could notice."

"Well, could you do me a favor and stop with the sardonic admissions? Someone's going to quote you out of context."

"It's just us girls together."

"Yeah, but one of these girls would be a lot happier if the other of these girls would keep her mouth shut."

"How was I to know the doctor was going to blow the time of death?"

"Are you sure he did?"

"Yeah, I'm sure. I had that gun in my

hand. It was after three o'clock and it hadn't been fired."

"Could you have made a mistake?"

"No, I could not have made a mistake. This is not some minor thing like picking up the dry cleaning. This is my murder alibi."

"It wasn't at the time."

"Huh?"

"When you saw the gun there hadn't been a murder. There was no reason to note the time."

"There was no reason to blow it by two hours either."

"*Two* hours?"

"Harvey Beerbaum says four-thirty. I say three-thirty. You say *two*-thirty. That's a hell of a stretch."

"It's gotta be two-thirty. At least, that's what I've gotta sell a jury. Which is a real kick in the head, now that you've said three-thirty. You know how hard it is to change a first impression."

"That's why I did it. To head off Harvey. How was I to know I was going to be undermined?"

"There's no way to know. Because you don't know what the police are doing. You don't know what the medical examiner is doing. You don't know what the facts of the case are. That is why your attorney told you to make no comment. Too bad you didn't listen to your attorney."

"Don't you find it pretentious talking about yourself in the third person?"

"I'm not interested in word games. Aside from the puzzle the guy had on him. You know anything about that?"

"Harvey solved it."

"I know he did. I understand Benny accuses you of the murder."

"That is *so* stupid. Benny realizes I'm about to kill him, so he writes a crossword puzzle telling the cops I did?"

"He really accuses you?"

"Of course not. It's just a stop-you're-killing-me wisecrack."

"Are you sure?"

"I got a copy of it here."

Becky took the puzzle, looked it over. "There's nothing to it."

"Right."

"What do you make of it?"

"I'm being framed. The killer left it by the body to implicate me."

"You really think you're being framed?"

"Well, it's either that or I killed him. And I happen to know I didn't."

"How did the killer frame you?"

"I have no idea. But, boy, is it working. I told a story that's contradicted by medical evidence, forensic evidence, fingerprint evidence. Plus I've got the motive, what with him claiming I ripped him off, and you helping him sue me for big bucks. Say, could you testify against me?"

"It would be my pleasure."

"I mean would you be allowed to? You being the defense attorney, and all."

"Believe it or not, it's never come up in the course of my practice. I'd have to look up some precedents."

Cora snorted in exasperation. "Couldn't you just say no?"

"Actually, I think there's some cases where an attorney can be called as a witness. But, don't worry, I won't testify against you, regardless of the situation."

"Much better. Now, what's our defense?"

"I was kind of hoping you didn't do it."

"Well, you got lucky. I didn't. How we going to establish that fact?"

"The frame is too good. We can't get around it. So we have to prove it's a frame."

Cora heaved herself to her feet.

"Okay. I'll rattle a few cages. See what I can scare up."

42

Mr. Wilbur was out on the lawn polishing a gnome. The gnome was filthy. The rag was filthy. The rubbing wasn't accomplishing much. Still, Cora was impressed by the effort. It was the first she'd seen of Wilbur taking any interest in any of his possessions. Except for his chairs.

Wilbur glinted up at Cora with an evil eye. "What do you want?"

"I was hoping we could have a little chat."

He snorted. "Yeah. Like I wanna talk to you. You killed Benny."

"Oh, Benny, is it? Good friend of yours?"

"I barely knew him. Don't make him any less dead."

"No, I suppose it doesn't. And you think I did it?"

"Police do."

"And they're always right. Has this been your experience?"

Wilbur said nothing, rubbed the nose of his gnome.

"Of course, if I didn't do it, you'd be suspect number one."

That got his attention. "What?"

"The way I understand it, Benny had your chairs. You're so nutzo about the damn things, you'd have popped him if he wouldn't give 'em back."

"Yeah, well, I didn't."

Wilbur moved across the path to a second gnome. Cora, looking back and forth, couldn't tell the difference between the one he'd polished and the one he hadn't.

"Sorry to disappoint you, lady. I went to see him the day after he got killed. The police were already there."

"You were supposed to see him the day of the murder. What happened then? Did you go?"

"I don't have to talk to you."

"No, you don't. But if the police think you've got information about the crime, they're gonna want to know what it is."

"The police don't know anything about it."

"They will when I tell 'em."

"You think they'll listen to you?"

"Of course they will. My lawyer's advised me not to talk. Under the circumstances, they'll listen to anything I have to say. Suppose I tell 'em you had an appointment with Benny Southstreet at two o'clock."

Wilbur peered at her suspiciously. "You're the one who broke into my house?"

Cora's eyes widened in mock surprise. "Someone broke into your house? Don't tell me, they took your chairs."

Cora could practically see Wilbur's mind calculating. "So," he said. "You broke into my house, you went to meet Benny Southstreet. Benny wasn't there. So you went back later and killed him."

Cora nodded approvingly. "Good. I can't tell if you really believe that, or if you're just trying to make me think you didn't do it. Either way, I admire your cool. So how come you didn't keep your two o'clock appointment?"

"Who says I didn't?"

"Are you saying you did? You were in there all the time with Benny? Or Benny's body?"

"I've given my statement to the police."

"And they bought it. I wonder what you told them. Let's see, did you tell them you had a two o'clock appointment? You had to. You had to explain why you showed up at the crime scene. What'd you tell 'em about the day of the murder? That you just didn't go? That wouldn't fly. So, you tell 'em you went and he wasn't there? You got a little problem with that. I was there at two o'clock and I didn't see you. When the police hear that, they may have a few more questions."

Wilbur folded the rag over. The other side was just as dirty. His eyes gleamed. "Suppose I got there *before* two o'clock? Suppose Benny wasn't there? Suppose I sat in my car across the street from the motel where I could see the door? To see if Benny returned?"

"Did he?"

"You know he didn't. You were there. You drove up, knocked on his door. Got no answer. You must have come back later."

"Did you see me?"

"I didn't stay. I got a business to run."

Cora kept a straight face, refrained from comment. "When'd you leave?"

"What's it to you?"

"Did you wait until Benny came back?"

"You know I didn't."

"How would I know that?"

"You're right," Wilbur said. "You don't know that. I could have seen him before you did. Then you could have showed up and killed him."

"I'm curious about when you left the motel."

"Why?"

"A schoolgirl whim."

"Lady, you're something else. I left at two-thirty. You hadn't come back yet. Benny hadn't come back yet. Nobody had come back yet. Nobody had been at the motel. At least while I was there."

"You left the motel at two-thirty?"

"At least nothing's wrong with your hearing. Yeah, I left at two-thirty. I don't care how smug and mysterious the guy is, a half hour's all I'm gonna wait."

"Why do you say smug and mysterious?"

"The guy said he had my chairs."

"Maybe he did."

"No, he didn't. He had chairs he ripped off from somewhere else."

"But you didn't know that."

"Says who?"

"You didn't know that. You hadn't seen the chairs. You had no idea where he got them. It could have been from anywhere. He could have been the guy who stole 'em from you."

"Sure, lady. And then he kept them for a year and then called and told me he had 'em."

Cora shook her finger. "Uh-uh. You don't get to call it unlikely. The whole thing's unlikely. Someone making such a big deal about a bunch of chairs is unlikely."

"Not such a big deal. They're stolen. I want 'em back."

"Yeah, but why are you so obsessed? The only explanation I can come up with is you think you know who stole 'em. You can't bear to see that person get away. But you can't prove it without the chairs. So you're desperate to find 'em. How about that? Am I close?"

"Not even in the ballpark." Wilbur snorted. "Women. They overthink everything. Something so simple, they make a big deal."

"I don't see what's so simple."

"You prove my point. And you wonder why I'm upset when Chief Harper palms me off on you?" Wilbur was in danger of rubbing the gnome's face off. He realized what he was doing, stopped, leveled his finger. "Lady, I don't need a killer telling me my business. Get the hell out of here before I call the cops."

Cora was tempted to call his bluff, but she didn't really feel like talking to Chief Harper at the moment.

She got the hell out of there.

43

Paul Fishman looked confused. It occurred to Cora a less handsome man couldn't have gotten away with it. He crinkled his nose, shrugged his shoulders with an aw-shucks expression. "Excuse me?"

"I want my pictures." Cora flopped her drawstring purse down on the counter, reached in, and pulled out her gun.

That wiped the goofy grin off his face. "Whoa!" Paul took a step back and nearly fell over. "Hey! Hey! Lady!"

"Oh. Sorry." Cora stuck the gun in her purse, fished out her wallet, and calmly produced the stub from the Photomat envelope. "Here you go."

Paul took the stub gingerly, read the number as if it were a valuable clue. "Oh." He put down the stub, placed his hands flat on the counter, took a breath. "I'm afraid I don't have them."

"I know you don't. Now, what are we going

to do about that?"

Paul exhaled sharply, blew the stub off the counter. It floated to the floor. Cora stooped down and retrieved it. "Let's hang on to this, shall we? Just in case there's any question about it." She stood up. "There's not going to be any question about it, is there?"

Paul was pawing through a box under the counter. He flinched and nearly banged his head. "No, of course not."

"What are you doing?"

"Checking for duplicates. There don't seem to be any."

"What a surprise."

Paul stood up, spread his hands. "Look, I know you're angry. But you gotta understand. It was my duty."

"Your duty? You run a Photomat. I don't recall any list of duties."

"My civic duty. In a police investigation, anyone with any information, it's their duty to come forward."

"Why? Do you think I did it?"

"Of course not."

"Of course not? That's generous of you. The police think I did it."

"I can't believe that."

"You believed it enough to give them my pictures."

"I didn't think they implicated you."

"They were *my* pictures! Who'd you think they implicated? Michael Freaking Jackson?"

"Sorry. I just didn't think."

Cora shook her head. "No, no, no, no, no. You're doing the dumb blonde bit on me. Just because you're young and good-looking, don't think you can get away with that crap. You can't have it both ways. Were you doing your civic duty, or did you have no idea what you were doing?"

"You're quick with words."

"You think so? Wait'll you hear my lawyer. When you get cross-examined on the stand."

"I'm not a witness against you."

"Well, you're sure not a witness *for* me."

"I swear I meant you no harm."

"Well, you wanna make it up to me, tell me what happened."

"What do you mean?"

"How'd you come to turn me in to the cops?"

"It wasn't like that at all. You gotta understand. I'm in the Photomat. It's a one-man operation. And business is slow. Oh, I'll have a run of customers. But in between I'm just making prints. With the equipment these days it's not hard. Lighter, darker, color correction. I can do it in my sleep." He lowered his voice conspiratorially. "I got a little TV under the counter. I keep the volume down, so no one sees it. Or some bozo would claim I wasn't paying attention and his pictures were the wrong tint.

"Anyway, Channel 8 is on, and Rick Reed's doing a remote from the motel. There's shots of the sign, and shots of the door to Unit 12, and it all seems damn familiar. Then I remember. Your prints. The ones you didn't come back to pick up."

"It's amazing you remembered. I'd have thought you'd be distracted by the cheesecake."

"Huh?"

"Photographer's word for sexy pictures. Probably before your time." Cora shook her head. "God, I'm getting old."

Paul Fishman had calmed down, gone back into his pretty boy, aw-shucks mode. "Lady, I'm really sorry. If there's anything I can do . . ."

Cora cocked her head, ironically. "Well, you might of contradicted me."

44

Cora got back to the house to find Brenda's car parked out front. She groaned. That couldn't be good.

It was even worse.

Dennis and Brenda were sitting on the couch. Dennis was dressed for work in a suit and tie. Cora wondered why he wasn't there.

Sherry, in sweater and blue jeans, sat opposite them in an easy chair. Sherry looked gorgeous and buffaloed. As if the world were spinning out of control, and there was nothing she could do about it.

Cora scowled. "All right, what's going on here?" she demanded.

Dennis had on his most earnest face. He might have been channeling Rudy Guiliani, post 9/11. He was a mensch, a healer, a helpmate, a pillar to lean on, a solid rock, a friend in time of need. "It's terrible. We came to help."

Cora snorted derisively.

Brenda said, "I told him you wouldn't want it, but he wouldn't listen."

Cora could imagine that conversation, a knock-down, drag-out fight that had wound up with Brenda tagging along. Dennis was doing a great job of pretending he didn't resent her.

"Then maybe he'll listen to me," Cora said. "Dennis, I don't want you here, I don't need you here, now get the hell out of here before I pick you up and throw you out. Is there any part of that you don't understand?"

Dennis nodded in perfect agreement. "I know just how you feel. If it happened to me, I'd feel that way too. And I would never think of intruding on you at this time. Except I have some information. Something important. And I want to bring it to you instead of the police, because the police obviously don't know what they're doing, or they never would have arrested you." He magnanimously included his wife with a gesture. "Brenda didn't want me to come, but I just had to tell you."

"And a phone call wouldn't have had the same dramatic umph," Cora said dryly.

"See, I *told* you you should have called," Brenda said.

"Well, we're here now, and we've gotta

make battle plans. Before the police make a tragic mistake."

"Sherry," Cora said, "why don't you go to your room. I don't want you to see me beat up your ex-husband and your best friend."

"Oh, stop it," Sherry said. "Let him have his say, and then throw him out. It's easier than arguing."

"What's his pitch?"

"He wouldn't say. He insisted on waiting for you."

"I'll bet he did." Cora dug her lighter and cigarettes out of her purse, fired one up. She stood facing Dennis Pride, puffing the glowing end red-hot, as if ready to torture him if he deviated from the truth. "All right, make it snappy."

Dennis smiled. He leaned back on the couch, perfectly at home. "The police got off on the wrong foot. They think you stole the guy's crossword puzzle and killed him when he made a fuss. That's a real joke, since you couldn't do a crossword puzzle to save your life."

Cora looked at Brenda.

"He's my husband," Brenda said. "Of course he told me. And Sherry's my best friend."

"And you're threatening her with exposure? Some friend."

"That isn't it at all," Dennis said. "I'm just pointing out how mistaken the police are. Too bad you can't afford to set them straight."

"You came here to tell me this?"

"No. I'm just explaining why I did. Anyway, that's the police theory, and it's stupid as all hell, but you're hard-pressed to deny it. So you gotta come up with another explanation. One that they can buy."

"That's brilliant! My God, why didn't I think of it?" Cora blew a perfect smoke ring.

"Yeah, but I got one. Benny Southstreet ripped off Chuck Dillinger. Chuck wanted his money back. This was the result."

Cora's eyes narrowed. She sat down on the couch next to Dennis, studied his face as if he were a World Series of Poker player who'd just gone all-in. "How do you know that?"

"So it's true?"

"I have no idea if it's true. I'm asking what makes you think so."

Dennis smiled. "I get around. I see a lot of people, know a lot of things. Chuck thinks I'm on his side. I could worm my way into his confidence, find out if he's guilty. Because *someone* is. We know it wasn't you."

"Worm your way. Now, there's an image that will haunt my dreams. Brenda, if you have any influence over this guy at all, get him out of here. I'm tired, and I'd like to rest."

"Yes, of course," Brenda said. "We're just concerned. What with your TV statement. And then the autopsy report came out. And then with the speculation about your column."

"What speculation about my column?"

"It was on the *Today Show.* The effect on the Puzzle Lady. They said half of the syndicated papers are standing by you. Of course, that means half of them aren't. If you lost that much business the first day, it's only going to get worse the more this thing drags on."

"Sherry? Did you know this?"

"It's all right."

"It's *not* all right. It's bad enough being in this position, without losing our livelihood. If the cereal company follows suit, we'll be in big trouble."

"Actually . . ." Brenda said.

"Actually what?" Cora demanded.

"Granville Grains issued a strong statement of support," Sherry said. "But they're pulling the TV ads while the matter is pending."

"In those words?"

"Cora —"

"While the matter is pending?"

"If there's anything we can do to help . . ." Dennis said.

"Go away, and don't come back. If you get any more bright ideas, take 'em straight to the police. If they're lies, I don't want to hear them. If they're the truth, they can't hurt me. Now, go, go, go!"

"But —" Dennis began.

Brenda was tugging at his arm. "Let's go, honey. You've done all you can here."

Between Brenda's urging and Cora's threats, they managed to get Dennis out the door.

Cora turned around, mopped her brow. "Good God, could it get any worse?"

"It'll be all right," Sherry told her.

"And you weren't going to mention I lost my job?"

"You didn't lose your job. You're just losing some residuals. While the ads are on hiatus."

"And if it goes on too long, they'll hire another spokesman."

"Spokesperson."

"I'm going to hurt you."

"How do you suppose Dennis found out about Chuck Dillinger?"

"I don't know, and I don't wanna know. That guy is living poison, Sherry. You keep him out of your life."

"You're charged with murder. If Dennis

307

knows anything that might help . . ."

Cora made a rather disparaging comment about what Dennis might know. "He's guessing, Sherry. The only way he'd know something useful would be if he bumped the guy off."

"You're not serious."

"About him killing the guy? No. About him not knowing anything useful? You can bet on it."

45

Chuck Dillinger stepped down onto the platform of the Bakerhaven train station, and looked around for his wife. He was surprised not to see her. The station was small. There was no crowd. She was usually standing right there.

Cora Felton stepped out of the shadows. "Need a ride?"

Chuck scowled. "What are you doing here?"

"I thought you might want a lift. You're miles from home, and the cab service here is so poor."

"Where's my wife?"

"She couldn't make it."

"She asked you to pick me up?"

"Not exactly. You want to take a ride? Standing here reminds me of one of Lady Bracknell's lines in *The Importance of Being Earnest.* Something about exposing us to comment on the platform. I think it had to do with missing trains, though."

Chuck shifted his briefcase from hand to hand. "Look, I'm trying to make allowances. I know you've been arrested. You must be very upset."

"You don't know the half of it."

"Maybe not, but it's none of my business. Why don't you run along?"

"And leave you stranded? That wouldn't be very neighborly."

"My wife's coming to pick me up."

"She's going to be delayed."

"What makes you think so?"

"I pounded a nail into her tire. Right rear. She won't get a block. Then she's gonna have to change it. And even if she does, it won't help, because these new cars have those tiny spares just good enough to get you to the gas station. Don't you hate them? Anyway, she'll have to get the tire fixed. By the time she does all that, we'll be long gone."

"You sabotaged her car?"

"It sounds so bad when you say it like that. But I had such short notice. I had to talk to you. It's important. Not just because I'm arrested for murder. That's annoying, but it will go away. Some things won't."

"What are you talking about?"

Cora gestured to her Toyota, parked in the

lot. "Come on, hop in, I'll give you a ride."

Chuck looked at her suspiciously.

"Hey, come on. If I were that crazed killer they're all talking about, you'd be dead by now. That was a joke. Come on, I won't bite you."

Chuck glanced around the parking lot. Aside from Cora's, there was only one car, presumably for the woman in the ticket booth. He weighed his options, climbed in.

Cora's purse was on the seat. "Just put that on the floor. Throw your briefcase in back. You might wanna fasten your seat belt. It's gonna be a bumpy ride."

He looked at her, baffled.

"Bette Davis, for Christ's sake. Does everyone have to remind me that I'm old?"

Cora started the engine, pulled out of the lot. "Okay, here's the deal. You know a guy named Dennis Pride?"

Chuck turned sideways in his seat. "What about him?"

"He's a psychotic wife-beater. And that's his good side. He's my niece Sherry's ex-husband. Totally obsessed with her. Won't leave her alone. Even though he's remarried, and she's about to be. Makes any excuse at all to see her."

"I don't understand."

"I don't want you to be that excuse. Dennis claims he knows something about you and Benny Southstreet. I don't think he does. I think he's just bluffing. But he's counting on the fact that I've been arrested, so Sherry will do anything to save me. I don't want that to happen. That's why I'm warning you about Dennis. He's pond scum. He's the Ebola virus. Am I getting through to you? This is not someone you want to have anything to do with."

"Miss Felton —"

"Dennis claims he knows something about you. So what does he know?"

"Nothing."

"That would be my first guess. The thing is, he had to get to you. So what did he say?"

"He claims he knows Benny Southstreet ripped me off."

"Really? How does he know that?"

"I have no idea."

"When did he tell you this?"

"I don't remember."

"Well, it was obviously after you were ripped off. Was it before the murder?"

"I don't know when the murder was."

"Good answer. That's the type of thing my lawyer wants me to say. But we're all agreed Benny bit the big one the day before his body was found. Was it before that?"

"Yes."

"I thought so."

"Hey, you missed the turn!"

"No I didn't. We're not finished talking."

"I don't know what else we have to say."

"Just this. You get anything, you give it to me, you stay forever in my good graces."

"I don't have anything."

Cora waggled her fingers, drove with one hand. "That's the iffy part. I think something was stolen from you. Maybe it was hundred-dollar bills. Maybe it wasn't. But it was something. I say that because I'm a seasoned investigator, a good judge of character. I got an opinion you can take to the bank. If Dennis says that, it's because he's a moron, and he's guessing. Tell him to run along, because he's got nothing to back it up, and if you call his bluff he's done.

"That's one thing. Here's another. If Dennis bothers you again, you tell me, and I will bitch-slap him so hard they'll have to scrape him off the sidewalk."

Cora put her blinker on, pulled into the garage at the far end of town. Mimi Dillinger, wailing babe in arms, was standing next to a grease-smeared mechanic who had her car up on a jack and was taking off the wheel.

"Tell your wife how lucky you were I happened along and gave you a ride."

313

Cora grinned as Chuck got out of the car. As she pulled into the street, she had to resist an overwhelming temptation to floor it and peel out.

46

Buddy was yapping hysterically when Cora got home. Sherry'd left him shut up in the house. Cora wondered how long her niece had been gone. To hear Buddy, it was days.

Cora opened the front door. Buddy went through it like a shot, and proceeded to run crazy circles on the front lawn. Any urgent purpose he might have had for going out was forgotten in the simple joy of being alive on a sunny country day in Connecticut.

"Come on, kid, you're making me dizzy." Cora sank down on the front step, pulled her cigarettes out of her purse, lit one up. She took a deep drag, thought about the case.

It was strange not to be able to solve it. No, that was arrogant. It was strange not to have the first clue. It was almost as if being personally involved made it impossible for her to think straight. If so, it was preferable to the onset of Alzheimer's. Early Alzheimer's. She wasn't *that* old. No, sir. There were a few more good years in the old gray mare.

Stop with the *old gray mare.*

"Sheesh!"

Buddy came trotting up, sniffed her legs.

"Hey, Buddy. Why don't you go find a clue. Do something to solve the crime. Like not bark in the nighttime."

Buddy studied Cora's face, as if considering the concept.

"Doesn't sound like much fun, does it? Okay, here's the bit. Somebody killed Benny Southstreet and made it look like I did. Either that was entirely fortuitous —" Cora groaned. "Oh, for God's sake, she's got me saying words like *fortuitous.* The killer's either lucky or good. If he's lucky, it doesn't help me. But if he's good, it helps me a lot. Because I can learn from him. His actions will be directed, they'll have a purpose. I can rely on cause and effect. The killer framed me because he wanted me framed. The question then is, why?

"The obvious answer is the chairs. The problem is the killer didn't take them, I did. Though, as Becky points out, he might have been killed for not having the chairs. Which makes no sense at all.

"The other possibility is, he was killed for ripping off hundred-dollar bills from Chuck Dillinger's study. The problem is, Dillinger

316

says he didn't. The saving grace is, murderers sometimes lie. If Dillinger killed him to get the hundred-dollar bills back, that works okay. Because I didn't steal the hundred-dollar bills. So if Southstreet stole them from Dillinger, Dillinger could have killed Southstreet for 'em just fine.

"Except I had the gun. It really doesn't work with me having the gun. With me having the gun, the only one who could have killed Benny Southstreet was me.

"Which is how it's gonna look to a jury."

Cora took a deep drag, blew it out. "Which is why I better start thinking straight in a hurry.

"For starters, why is Wilbur getting a free pass? He was supposed to be there at the time of the murder. According to his own statement, he *was* there at the time of the murder. We have only his own statement for the fact that he left without seeing Benny Southstreet.

"If he had seen Benny Southstreet, and killed him, why would he come back the next day and walk into the arms of the police? After he so neatly framed me. Why would he do that?

"Well, I have to assume he can reason too. So, he's gotta ask himself how I got a line on Benny Southstreet and knew he was at the motel. His shop was broken into, and there was a message from Benny on his answering machine. If I was the one who broke in, then I know he had a two o'clock appointment with Benny Southstreet. And I would be sure to tell the police. He heads that off by admitting it. He comes back to the motel the next day, and tells the police he's come to see Benny Southstreet because he tried to see him the day before, and Benny wasn't there.

"How does that sound?"

Buddy was looking up at her, wagging his tail.

"Oh, my God, I'm talking to a dog!"

Cora ground out her cigarette in the dirt. She got up, went in the kitchen, fixed Buddy's kibble. She opened a can of tuna fish, mixed some in.

"I know I'm not supposed to do this, but you've been a real good dog, waiting for Mommie all day long."

Cora set the bowl on the floor, watched the little poodle gobble it up.

"Now, how about a treat for Mommie."

Cora glanced around the kitchen. A *real* treat for Mommie, a belt of hooch, had been disposed of long ago. There was not a drop in the house. Second on the list — a distant second — was chocolate. A nice Whitman's Sampler. That would give her brain a workout, detecting which candies held the mother lode, the gooey caramel centers Cora preferred infinitely to the coconut or cherry.

Cora knew without looking there wasn't a candy in the house. She could always go out and buy some. As long as she was out . . .

There was a Starbucks in the mall. Cora didn't drink Starbucks coffee — she was loyal to Cushman's Bake Shop — but Starbucks had a caramel Frappuccino, a calorie-laden piece of heaven with whipped cream on top. Cora allowed herself one only on special occasions, or in times of dire stress.

Being a murder suspect, Cora decided, surely qualified as both.

47

The mall parking lot was jammed, and it took Cora a while to find a space. She circled the rows, working it out in her mind. Not the case. The Frappuccino.

The problem was the size. *Grande* sounded too big. *Large* sounded too small. *Venti* didn't sound as large as *Grande,* but was actually larger. So the dilemma was, was it more important for the Frappuccino to *sound* small when she ordered it, or *look* small when she picked it up?

Cora was still working on the problem when she finally found a parking space two rows down from Starbucks.

She heard it as soon as she got in the door. The unmistakable sound of a baby in distress. Or hungry. Or displeased. Or unhappy. Or desperately afraid the adults in the immediate vicinity might be enjoying a moment of peace and quiet. It sounded familiar. Which was not surprising. Any baby crying would sound familiar. But it sounded like a particular baby.

Sure enough, it was.

Mimi Dillinger stood, coffee in hand, Darlene on hip, talking to a young man in a gray suit and purple tie, who appeared smitten enough with her feminine wiles not to notice the spawn of the devil she held. Mimi ignored the baby, too, as completely as if it were someone else's child that was making all that racket, and listened intently to what the young man was telling her. Of course, it occurred to Cora, she would have to listen intently just to *hear* what the young man was telling her. Even so, she seemed to have more than just a casual interest.

Cora perked up. Had she uncovered the young mother's secret love life, after all?

Apparently not. Either that or it was rather kinky, because the guy sat down at a table with an attractive young lady in a nurse's uniform, who didn't look like she was up for a ménage à trois — but then, one never knew.

Mimi, left alone, descended on Cora. "You gave my husband a ride."

Cora braced for an accusation. Did Mimi suspect her of sabotaging the car?

No, she didn't. "I can't thank you enough. I got a nail in my tire. That's what I was doing at the garage."

"Oh. Do you have one of those teeny spares?"

Mimi looked blank. "Teeny spares? I don't know. I didn't try to change it. Just drove to the garage."

"Little hard on the rim."

"That's what the mechanic said. At least I think that's what he said. Darlene was in a mood."

"Hard to believe." Cora waggled her fingers at the baby, was glad she didn't bite them.

"Yes, well, I just wanted to say it's horrible, this whole thing. I know you didn't do it."

"Spread it around. I'm hoping to taint the jury pool."

Mimi wasn't sure whether to laugh. "Ah, yes. Well, I don't know if this helps, but about the break-in . . ."

"What about it?"

"You wanted to know why Chuck said the study. When nothing was missing. And it was the kitchen window that was broken."

"Yeah?"

"Well, something's missing."

"What?"

"An ice pick."

Cora's eyes narrowed. "You're kidding."

"I just noticed. Because it was in the

kitchen, not the study, and who notices an ice pick? But I opened the drawer to get a spatula, and it wasn't there. The ice pick, I mean. Which doesn't make any sense. Why would someone steal an ice pick?"

"You're sure you didn't misplace it?"

"How could I misplace it? I never use it. But it was in the drawer."

"When's the last time you remember seeing it?"

"I *don't* remember seeing it. Why would I? It was always there. But —"

Mimi's observations about the ice pick were preempted by a particularly loud wail from the baby, who needed to be either changed, fed, or strangled.

Cora pushed her way up to the counter, where she opted for a Venti Frappuccino, which could have passed for an intercontinental ballistic missile. She plunged an extra-long straw through the caramel and whipped cream, took a preliminary sip, and sighed happily. God was in his heaven and all was right with the world.

It was even quiet. Cora glanced around, saw that Mimi and Darlene had left. Cora didn't set much stock in the ice pick story, but it was nice Mimi didn't blame her for the car. Not that Cora would have minded Mimi's animosity; still, she hated to be accused of things she had actually done. Probably a carryover from her days of being named corespondent.

Cora came out the front door of Starbucks, to discover Paul Fishman bearing down on her from across the parking lot. Cora was momentarily embarrassed to be caught holding the huge coffee treat. Then she remembered the man was responsible for turning her in to the cops. She could drink whatever she wanted in front of him. No matter how handsome he was.

"Miss Felton," he called.

Cora turned, fixed him with a gaze as frosty as her Frappuccino. "Yes?"

"I thought I saw you drive in. I was with a customer. I had to finish up with him."

"What do you want?"

"Oh. I'm sorry." Paul held up a film packet. "I found them."

Cora frowned. "Found what?"

"I felt so bad about it. You not getting your pictures, and all. On top of everything else. And it being my fault. So I looked around the booth for the extra set of prints, and darned if I didn't find them. They weren't where I thought they were because it was the day before."

Cora blinked as she tried to untangle that verbal construction.

"I often run 'em. Because most people order two sets of prints because the second set is cheaper. Much cheaper. You didn't, so I only put in one set. Sometimes I don't notice, and leave the extra set in the envelope. But when I do notice, I take 'em out. Otherwise, no one would order 'em. Because they'd know they'd get 'em anyway." He pressed the packet into her hands. "I gotta get back to the booth. Anyway, I'm not a bad guy, really, and I wanted you to have the prints."

Cora frowned as she watched him hurry away. On the one hand, it was a nice gesture. On the other hand, he had a lot to make up for.

Cora wanted to look at the pictures. It was hard, holding her purse and a Venti Frappuccino.

Cora found her car, always a challenge in the mall lot, threw her purse on the passenger seat, stuck the Frappuccino in the drink holder, and pulled open the packet.

They were the same prints he'd given the police, again in reverse order, starting with the motel sign.

Cora flipped through them, looking for a clue. Not that she expected one. Still, the guy had gone out of his way to give them back. Surely they must mean something.

Yeah, Cora thought. In a book. Where the author wouldn't be talking about them unless they meant something. In real life, they were just a bunch of pictures. Of the motel room and some chairs. Not to mention a rather nice shot of Sherry. Cora wondered if Sherry was out with Aaron. Had patched things up. If only.

Cora went through the motel room shots again. There must be something. Was the gun in the picture? Surely the police would have mentioned that. Was the briefcase in the picture? Some article of Benny Southstreet's clothing. Some take-out food. Anything.

A dog that didn't bark.

Cora was losing it.

Cora tossed the pictures on the front seat, took a huge sip of Frappuccino. The mother of all ice-cream headaches ripped her brain apart. Oh, my God! What a wake-up call!

Cora took deep breaths, composing herself.

Ice cream?

Ice pick?

Yeah, sure.

Get a grip.

Cora leafed through the photos again. There must be something. But there wasn't. Nothing but a lousy roll of duplicate prints.

Cora shoved the photos back in the envelope, took a cautious sip from her Frappuccino, and started the car.

She frowned.

Someone had stuck a flyer on her windshield. Cora hated that. The practice, common enough in New York City, hardly ever happened here. It was almost fitting that it should on this day of all days.

Cora opened the door, got out, reached over, and pulled the flyer from under the windshield wiper blade.

Cora looked at the flyer. Not that she cared what it was, but she always made it a point not to patronize the businesses that littered the parking lot with advertising. She hoped it wasn't a store she liked.

It wasn't.

It was a crossword puzzle.

ACROSS

1 Numbered items in a user's guide
6 It covers the field
10 Laughingstock
14 Poisonous
15 Sorry sort
16 "Heads___, tails . . ."
17 In abeyance
18 "Bus Stop" dramatist
19 Hawk
20 Start of a message
23 Storable sleeper
24 BPOE member
25 Subj. at Juilliard
26 Worker with flowers
29 Message part 2
33 Mazda roadster
34 Taoism founder
35 Browning's "Rabbi Ben ___"
38 TV show with skits
40 "And . . . ?"
41 Propeller base?
44 Comb the "wrong" way
47 Message part 3

328

50 180° from NNW
51 ___ Lingus, Irish airline
52 Dundee denial
53 Civil War side: Abbr.
56 End of message
59 Overfill the bill
62 Scouting outing
63 "Rocky" actress Shire
64 Red ink
65 ___-Day vitamins
66 Vote in
67 Do as you're told
68 Just so
69 Watch again

DOWN
1 One who plays hurt
2 Scout master?
3 Lives
4 Type size
5 Whence "Beware the Ides of March"
6 Tchotchkes and knick-knacks
7 Rhody, of song
8 Ruling body
9 "The Godfather: Part II" to "The Godfather"
10 Jazzman's jargon
11 Have debts

12 All in the family
13 Conclusion
21 Edison's middle name
22 Annapolis initials
26 This and that?
27 Other than that
28 First lady's home
30 Muscat-eer?
31 Language including Zulu
32 Clan symbol
35 Drops in the ocean?
36 Olympian ruler
37 Award stars to
39 Unmarbled cut, say
42 "___ first you don't . . ."
43 Optical range
45 Without delay, initially
46 Helter-___
48 "Twelfth Night" duke
49 Places for professeurs
54 Salami unit
55 "It's ___!" ("I'll be there!")
56 Half a spider's description
57 Furniture brand
58 Lock in the store?
59 Day-___ paint
60 Tennis shot
61 "___ it or lose it"

48

Sherry and Aaron were at the movies. It was Aaron's idea, to which Sherry had readily agreed. They couldn't argue in the movies. They couldn't snipe in the movies. They couldn't air petty jealousies about ex-husbands and ex-girlfriends. They couldn't have misunderstandings in the movies. By and large, the movies were a hell of a safe place to be, a place to while away two hours in companionable silence. It occurred to Sherry if she and Aaron would just spend all their time in the movies, they'd get along great.

Someone slipped into the seat next to them. Sherry bristled. It was a big theater, it was only half-full, and there were a lot of empty seats a person could have chosen without intruding on a young couple obviously on a date.

Sherry felt a tug on her shoulder. That was the last straw. It was bad enough to come barging in late, but if the person wanted a plot summary, it was beyond all bounds. She and Aaron would have to move.

Sherry looked over, to find Cora sitting next to her.

"What the hell are you doing here?"

"Come on," Cora said, gesturing for Sherry to follow.

"Are you nuts? I'm on a date."

"What's going on?" Aaron demanded.

"Shhh!" someone hissed from behind.

"You stay. She'll be right back."

Cora grabbed Sherry's arm, dragged her out the door.

"Where are we going?" Sherry protested.

"To the bathroom."

"I don't have to go to the bathroom."

"Yes, you do." Cora dragged Sherry down the hall.

"How did you find me?"

"It wasn't easy. You know how many screens there are in this damn multiplex? I started with the chick-flicks first."

"Do I look like a chick-flick person?"

"They're date movies. The type of movies a guy takes a girl to."

"Aaron knows better."

"I'm happy for him. So he takes you to a thriller instead?"

"It got two thumbs up."

S	T	E	P	S		T	A	R	P		J	O	K	E
T	O	X	I	C		R	U	E	R		I	W	I	N
O	N	I	C	E		I	N	G	E		V	E	N	D
I	T	S	A	N	A	N	T	I	Q	U	E			
C	O	T		E	L	K		M	U	S		B	E	E
		S	O	I	V	E	B	E	E	N	T	O	L	D
		M	I	A	T	A			L	A	O	T	S	E
E	Z	R	A			S	N	L		T	H	E	N	
B	E	A	N	I	E		T	E	A	S	E			
B	U	T	I	F	Y	O	U	A	S	K	M	E		
S	S	E		A	E	R		N	A	E		C	S	A
		I	T	S	S	I	M	P	L	Y	O	L	D	
G	L	U	T		H	I	K	E		T	A	L	I	A
L	O	S	S		O	N	E	A		E	L	E	C	T
O	B	E	Y		T	O	A	T		R	E	S	E	E

ACROSS

1 Numbered items in a user's guide
6 It covers the field
10 Laughingstock
14 Poisonous
15 Sorry sort
16 "Heads___, tails . . ."
17 In abeyance
18 "Bus Stop" dramatist
19 Hawk
20 Start of a message
23 Storable sleeper
24 BPOE member
25 Subj. at Juilliard
26 Worker with flowers
29 Message part 2
33 Mazda roadster
34 Taoism founder
35 Browning's "Rabbi Ben ___"
38 TV show with skits
40 "And . . . ?"
41 Propeller base?
44 Comb the "wrong" way
47 Message part 3

50 180° from NNW
51 ___ Lingus, Irish airline
52 Dundee denial
53 Civil War side: Abbr.
56 End of message
59 Overfill the bill
62 Scouting outing
63 "Rocky" actress Shire
64 Red ink
65 ___-Day vitamins
66 Vote in
67 Do as you're told
68 Just so
69 Watch again

DOWN

1 One who plays hurt
2 Scout master?
3 Lives
4 Type size
5 Whence "Beware the Ides of March"
6 Tchotchkes and knick-knacks
7 Rhody, of song
8 Ruling body
9 "The Godfather: Part II" to "The Godfather"
10 Jazzman's jargon
11 Have debts
12 All in the family
13 Conclusion
21 Edison's middle name
22 Annapolis initials
26 This and that?
27 Other than that
28 First lady's home
30 Muscat-eer?
31 Language including Zulu
32 Clan symbol
35 Drops in the ocean?
36 Olympian ruler
37 Award stars to
39 Unmarbled cut, say
42 "___ first you don't . . ."
43 Optical range
45 Without delay, initially
46 Helter-___
48 "Twelfth Night" duke
49 Places for professeurs
54 Salami unit
55 "It's ___!" ("I'll be there!")
56 Half a spider's description
57 Furniture brand
58 Lock in the store?
59 Day-__ paint
60 Tennis shot
61 "___ it or lose it"

333

"Get in here."

Cora dragged Sherry through the swinging door into the ladies' room. It was empty. Cora glanced under the stall doors, but there were no feet. "Here. Solve it."

Sherry took the piece of paper Cora slapped into her hands. "What's this?"

"Someone stuck it on my car. It's either an ad for Victoria's Secret, or it's a clue. I could use a clue, since nothing's working out."

"I can't solve this."

"Why not?"

"I don't have a pencil."

Cora slapped one in her hand. "Yes you do. I'll be right outside. Hurry up, will you? I wouldn't want you to miss a two thumbs-up thriller."

Cora went out and waited in the hall. She hated intruding on Sherry and Aaron just when they'd patched things up, but she had no choice. There was no one else to solve the puzzle for her. Except Harvey Beerbaum, and she couldn't think what to tell him. Aside from the fact she wasn't the Puzzle Lady. Which might not be a bad idea, all things considered. Gradually ease herself out of the part, return to a life of . . . what? Questions from people who didn't like being duped?

Sherry came out the ladies' room door,

handed Cora a folded piece of paper and a pencil.

"Thanks," Cora said, but Sherry had already stalked off down the hall back to her movie.

Cora unfolded the paper, looked at the puzzle.

The only thing that mattered was the theme answer. So what was the theme answer? *20 Across: Start of a message.*

Never mind the clue numbers. It's the long entries.

Cora read:

It's an antique
So I've been told
But if you ask me
It's simply old.

49

Wilbur's Antiques was dark. The light upstairs was on. The light in his apartment. The light where he lived. There was a car parked outside. A car that by any rights belonged to him, indicating that he was home. And awake. At any rate, he'd be sure to hear her breaking into his shop.

Good thing she wasn't going to do that.

Cora had another objective in mind.

Wilbur had been entirely too glib when she'd asked to inspect the crime scene. What's to inspect? The four chairs were there, now they weren't. That was certainly true, and yet . . . It had kept her from inspecting the barn. The barn had been, to all intents and purposes, merely the repository for the ladder with which one reached the window of the antiques shop. One broke into the barn in order to break into the shop. The barn had never been broken into in its own right. Not since the disappearance of the chairs. The barn had been given short shrift. It deserved better.

Or so Cora thought as she crept through the dark, clutching the hammer and flashlight she'd brought along for the occasion. She kept the flashlight off, relying on the moonlight to guide her through the bushes and shrubs that bordered the back of Wilbur's property.

Cora tiptoed up to the front of the barn. She inserted the claw of the hammer under the edge of the three-quarter-inch plywood over the broken window in the door, and began prying.

It took a while. When she'd pried the board off before, she'd been working on a huge rush of adrenaline. And she'd had no need to keep quiet. She'd also been rather zealous in pounding it back on, never dreaming she might ever want it off again.

Cora stuck her hand through the broken window, and unlocked the door. She wondered why the man didn't invest in a simple hasp and padlock, rather than relying on the flimsy doorknob lock that had been breached before. Well, lucky that he hadn't.

Cora set the hammer down on the plywood board, opened the door, and crept inside.

She had to risk the light. Without it, she

couldn't see a damn thing, was liable to walk into a wall. The flashlight was long and thin, held three D batteries, an inconvenient number, since they were always sold in pairs. She kept one hand over the lens, let the light filter out between her fingers. It was most unwieldy. Cora had to sling her purse over her shoulder, use both hands to aim the light.

The crossword puzzle came to mind, about one man's antiques being another man's junk. That wasn't quite it, it was something about merely old, but the sentiment applied. The items in Wilbur's barn made the ones in his shop seem positively priceless.

There was an old-fashioned icebox, with no doors. On closer inspection, with no bottom either. An iron with one foot of electric cord and no plug, the wires neatly scraped clean, just in case one wanted to stick them into a wall outlet and electrocute oneself. A metal drawer full of bolts and washers but no nuts. An archery target with the straw coming out from the arrow holes that had all but demolished it. An oil painting, apparently intact, on stretched canvas but with no frame.

Cora stopped at that. Could it possibly be valuable? It was an abstract blob of color, looked like a kindergartener's finger painting. Still, one never knew.

Cora worked her way through the barn to the back wall. Discovered a convertible couch without cushions. It had a mattress, however, which presumably could be folded out for a bed. It occurred to Cora she'd need a bed soon, when Sherry got married and she had to move out. Not that Sherry'd said anything about her moving out, but still. She wasn't living with newlyweds. She wouldn't be able to stand it.

A little farther on was a rectangular table covered by a tarp. Cora lifted one corner, saw it was a picnic table. The wood was old, faded, eroded, half eaten away. What would possess a man to keep such a thing was beyond her, let alone protect it with a tarp.

Cora couldn't see what was underneath the table, but it was most likely rotted wooden picnic benches. Nonetheless, she figured she should check. She moved around the table to get a better grip on the tarp.

There came a bright flash, a sound like thunder, and a bullet whizzed by Cora's head and embedded itself in the wall.

Cora stumbled back and fell. She banged her head against the concrete floor, and went out like a light.

50

Chief Harper arrived at the antiques shop to find Mr. Wilbur serving Cora Felton a cup of hot tea. Cora was wrapped in a blanket, sitting in a plastic lawn chair at the side of the shop. Chief Harper drove over the grass to get there.

"Watch out for the gnomes," Cora muttered, as he walked up.

"What's going on?" Harper demanded.

Wilbur jerked his thumb. "The cop's out back. The big dumb one. I wouldn't expect much."

"Someone called the police."

"Yeah. I did."

"To report a break-in."

"That's right."

"Your shop was broken into?"

"No. The barn."

"What's Miss Felton doing here?"

"She broke in."

"What?"

"That's why I'm giving her tea. I always give tea to people who break into my barn."

"There was a report of shots fired."

"One shot. I was inside. I ran out to see what the hell was going on."

"With someone shooting a gun?"

"Sounded like a pistol." Wilbur jerked his thumb at the double-barreled shotgun leaning up against the side of the house. "I can handle a pistol. I went out, found her lying on the concrete floor."

"She'd been shot?"

"I'm right here," Cora said irritably.

"She'd been shot?" Harper repeated.

"No. Fainted from the shock."

"Hell I did!" Cora protested. "I tripped in the dark and bumped my head."

"Miss Felton, I'm trying to avoid asking you questions your lawyer wouldn't want you to answer. You have the right to remain silent. Why don't you exercise it?"

"There's a handy thing to tell a woman," Wilbur said. "Maybe I should have been a cop."

"Damn it," Cora said. "Would someone mind telling me what the hell happened here?"

"You don't know? I guess you really did hit your head." To Wilbur, Harper said, "Keep her here. I'll check in with Sam."

"I called for an ambulance. They're gonna wanna take her."

"You called for an ambulance?"

"She's got a pretty good gash in her head."

"From falling on the floor?"

"That's right."

"Any chance she was coshed?"

"Coshed. There's a word."

"Could it have happened?"

"Sure. I don't know where they could have got to. I grabbed my gun and ran out as soon as I heard the shot. The shooter might have got away, but not if he hung around to hit her on the head."

Chief Harper looked at Wilbur thoughtfully. "You're being damn nice to someone who broke into your barn."

"She's been working on my robbery. Which is a darn sight more than other people I could mention."

Chief Harper stomped off to look for Sam Brogan.

"Why *are* you being so nice?" Cora asked.

"Someone tried to shoot you. In my book, if they're shootin' at you, you must be doin' something right."

"That's no answer."

"How about I don't want you to sue me for gettin' hurt in my barn."

"That doesn't really fly. Particularly with

you making the suggestion."

"I suppose not." He paused a moment. "You put the chairs on eBay."

"And you bid on 'em."

"I didn't know it was you."

"I didn't know it was you either."

" 'Cause you didn't tell me you was doin' it."

"What would you have done if I had?"

"Told you not to. It was a stupid, dumb-ass, girly thing to do. But it means you were trying to help."

"Wanna know why I broke into your barn?"

"Don't give a damn. You're a murder suspect. You must be desperate. Can't count on you to think straight."

Chief Harper came back from the direction of the barn. He had a funny look on his face. "Miss Felton. You feel up to examining the scene of the crime?"

"No, she doesn't," Wilbur said. "She's waiting for the ambulance."

"Phooey on that." Cora lunged to her feet. "He's not asking me to dance, just to look at something. How can that possibly hurt?"

Nonetheless, her legs were a little wobbly. Chief Harper had to hold her up.

Wilbur took her other arm. "This is not a good idea. The paramedics will be mad."

"So you stay and explain it to them," Harper told him.

"Just a damn minute here. That's my barn."

"Then you've seen it before. Wait here. Don't make me waste a man detaining you."

The barn was lit by bare bulbs that hung from the rafters. Adequate lighting did nothing to improve the appearance of the merchandise. If anything, it exposed its flaws.

Sam Brogan was inspecting the side wall. He did not look happy. But then, he never did. He turned as they approached. "Good. You got her. Sure hope you're telling the truth. I'd hate to search the whole damn place."

"What are you talking about?" Cora asked.

"That's just Sam bein' Sam," Chief Harper said. "He's looking for the bullet in the wall. To corroborate your story."

"I haven't got a story. I was in the dark. Someone shot at me. That's all I remember."

"Do you remember where you were?"

Cora looked around. The picnic table was in the far corner of the barn. The tarp hung down the side. It was a green tarp, old, frayed, with eyeholes where ropes could be tied.

"I was standing right about here," Cora said, walking over to the table. "The bullet whizzed by my head."

"Where did it come from?"

"The direction of the door. But it seemed closer."

"How much closer?"

"I don't know. Halfway, maybe."

Chief Harper moved into position somewhere near the middle of the barn. "You got that, Sam?"

" 'Course I got that," Sam snorted. "It's not where she fell," he added grumpily. "Next time fall where you're shot."

"Where did I fall?"

"More to the left," Harper said.

"My left?" Sam asked.

"Not you. Her."

"Her left?"

"Sam, I'm talking to Cora. You fell more down here. Any luck yet, Sam?"

" 'Course not. You got me lookin' to the left. Wait a minute! Here we go! Lower than you thought. Closer to your heart than your head."

"Mark the spot and dig it out. Try not to scratch the bullet."

"Are you done with me?" Cora said. "I need a cigarette."

"Go ahead and have one."

"I'd love to. You find my purse?"

"Yeah."

"Well, could I have it?"

"Not just yet."

"Come on, Chief. Let me have my smokes."

"You've got a gun in your purse."

"So?"

"This is not kosher for a murder suspect."

"Hey. I'm innocent until proven guilty. I have a right to bear arms."

"That doesn't mean it's a smart thing to do."

"Chief, I just want a cigarette. Can I have my purse back?"

"Not right now. You weren't aware anyone was watching you until you heard the shot?"

"Or saw it. I'm not sure which came first."

"But you didn't know anyone was here?"

"If I did, it was subconscious."

"But you didn't shoot anyone? Perhaps wound your attacker?"

"Wound him? I barely had time to *resent* him. I tell you, the shot rang out and I went down."

"Okay, got the bullet," Sam Brogan called.

"Run it down to the lab."

"This time of night? The technician will be asleep."

"Wake him up, Sam." Chief Harper turned back to Cora. He didn't look happy. "Miss Felton. We're going down to the police station. The prosecutor has a few questions."

Wilbur came bubbling up. "Ambulance is here!"

"Sorry, Chief," Cora said. "That's my ride."

Harper shook his head. "You can take the ambulance if you want. But we're going down to the station."

51

Henry Firth twitched his nose and smiled.

Cora wasn't fooled. The prosecutor had always reminded her of a rat. Now he reminded her of a smiling rat. It was mostly his pencil-thin mustache. It occurred to her he must not be married. A wife with any artistic sense would have made him shave it off. Yet, here he was, once again, sticking his rat-like nose into everybody's business.

"What's this all about?" Cora demanded. It was not the first time she'd asked.

"Let's wait for your attorney."

"I don't need my attorney. I need a cigarette. You're not letting me have one. That's tantamount to torture. As I'm sure my attorney will point out."

"Let's leave that to her, shall we?"

"I don't know why Chief Harper called you in. We were having a perfectly nice discussion."

"You're the defendant in a murder case.

It's a delicate situation."

"It's not a delicate situation. It's a load of hogwash. It's got nothing to do with this."

"I'm glad you think so. You were shot at. That is a crime. It requires investigation. You are one of the people called upon to testify. It is crucial that none of the testimony you are to give should in any way compromise your position as a defendant."

Cora's eyes twinkled mischievously. "I can think of something that might compromise your position as a prosecutor."

"Be as rude as you want," Henry Firth said. "You're not provoking me. We're waiting for your lawyer."

Becky showed up ten minutes later. She looked like a million bucks in a casual cream-colored silk shirt that complemented her understated makeup. Cora figured she'd taken the extra time to achieve the effect.

Her attitude, however, was no-nonsense. "All right, what's the story?"

"Your client was apprehended breaking into Wilbur's barn."

Cora waved her hand. "Pffft!"

"There. As my client so correctly says, pffft! I'm not sure if that's an official legal pleading, but it ought to be. Do you have anything else?"

"There was a shot fired."

"By my client?"

"I'm not making any claims. I'm just presenting facts."

"You'd better present 'em in a way that accounts for your detaining my client. Otherwise, you are going to be one unhappy prosecutor."

"Nonsense. We have a case of breaking and entering and shots fired. It has to be investigated. Your client is at worst a principal and at best a witness. We need her story. Unfortunately, she is a defendant in a murder investigation. So we're being very scrupulous and dealing with her through her attorney, even though she herself feels there is no need."

"You tell him that?" Becky asked Cora.

"I saw no reason to ruin your evening."

"Blowing your defense would probably ruin it more," Becky said. "You mind if I confer with my client?"

"Go ahead. I'll be right outside."

Henry Firth went out and closed the door.

"All right, what have you done now?" Becky demanded.

Cora gave her a short rundown of the situation.

Becky was not pleased. "You broke into his barn?"

"It sounds bad when you say it like that.

You should try an amused inflection, like, 'You broke into his barn?' "

"I'm trying very hard to keep you out of jail. You're not helping much. Now I gotta defend you on a breaking and entering charge."

"No, you don't. I already admitted the breaking and entering. There's nothing to defend."

"You *admitted* it?"

"I told Chief Harper. It seemed the thing to do. Being caught red-handed, and all."

"What did I tell you about not making a statement except in my presence?"

"That was about the murder. This is just a break-in."

"Cora —"

"It's all right, dear. Since I've admitted it, we're in a nice position. I have nothing to hide, I can tell 'em what they want to know, and go home."

"I don't think so."

"Why not?"

"If that were going to work, they'd have done it already."

"They would have. But Ratface wouldn't let me talk without you present."

"You wanted to talk, but he made you wait for me?"

"Yeah."

"I don't like it."

"I hate it like hell, but that's what happened. So what's up?"

"I don't know. Let's get him back and ask him."

Becky went out and returned with Henry Firth. The prosecutor seated himself at the head of the table. Becky sat next to Cora.

"Miss Felton, you now have your attorney present, as I suggested. I am going to ask you some questions with regard to the break-in at Wilbur's Antiques."

"Alleged break-in," Becky amended.

Henry Firth smiled. "Well, I think the break-in is pretty much a fact."

"I thought Mr. Wilbur wasn't pressing charges."

"That doesn't mean there wasn't a break-in. Come on, now. No one's taking this down. Let's not be technical."

"You're not going to be technical and construe any of my client's answers as incriminating?"

"Only if she's done something wrong. You haven't done that, have you, Miss Felton?"

"No, but I'm about to. Talk to us like equals, not morons."

"I'd be glad to. We'd be on slightly more equal footing if *I'd* broken into someone's house in the middle of the night, but I'll let it pass. Since no one's pressing charges, let's say you were there legally. What happened then?"

"This is not binding on my client?"

"With regard to breaking and entering? No. That charge has been dropped."

"Are you implying there are other charges?"

"Are you implying your client's done something wrong?"

"No, I'm not," Becky said irritably. "She's been charged with murder and she didn't do that either. You want to speed things along? I'd like to get out of here and go home."

"I'd like nothing better myself. Which is why I'm here. To advise you on your legal limits. I'm telling you Miss Felton can discuss being in Wilbur's barn."

"Without incriminating herself?"

"If she stole something from the barn, that would be illegal. If she killed someone in the barn, that would be illegal. In either case, she would be liable for prosecution. But as far as *being* in the barn goes, you have nothing to fear."

"Good," Cora said. "That's all I did, and I'd like to go home."

"I have a few questions."

"With regard to the crime that didn't happen?" Cora inquired sweetly.

"You're forgetting the shooting. That's certainly a crime, and that certainly happened. What can you tell me about that?"

"Not a thing. I heard a shot. A bullet whizzed by my head. I took a step back, fell, and was knocked unconscious."

"A bullet whizzed by your head?"

"Yes."

"It was dark. How did you know?"

"I heard it. Right after the explosion. It was like nothing I've ever heard before. Like someone frying eggs in my ear."

"You heard that?"

"For a second. Before the thud of the bullet hitting the wall."

"The shot took you by surprise?"

"I'll say."

"No advance warning?"

"None at all. I didn't hear anything. I didn't see anything. Suddenly, bang!"

"No time to defend yourself?"

"How?"

"I believe you carry a gun."

"So?"

"Did you draw your gun? Aim it at your attacker? Try to shoot back?"

"She told you what she did," Becky interposed. "Move on."

"She told me what she *did*. I'd like her to tell me what she *didn't* do."

"She doesn't have to. Move on."

"I'd like an answer."

"Oh, stop haggling," Cora said. "The answer is no. I didn't go for my gun. I didn't even *think* of my gun. I thought, 'Oh, my God, I've been shot!' I started back and tripped."

"You thought you'd been shot?"

"I thought I'd been shot *at*. I didn't know whether I'd been hit. Whether any second a searing pain would go raging through my body. I wasn't, and it didn't. The point is, it all happened too fast for me to do anything."

"You didn't fire your gun?"

"Of *course* I didn't fire my gun," Cora said irritably. "Could you get on to something that matters?"

"Oh, these questions all matter. Some of them are preliminary, but, believe me, they matter. The gun was in your purse?"

"You should know. You've got it."

"Uh-huh." Henry Firth popped his briefcase open, pulled out a plastic bag. "This was also in your purse. A crossword puzzle. It's been solved, and the theme answer is suggestive. It suggests an antiques shop."

"If you say so."

"The puzzle has been solved in pencil. Is that your handwriting?"

"Actually, it's my niece's, Sherry's. She

solved the puzzle."

"Uh-huh. And where did you get it?"

"It was stuck on the windshield of my car."

"Where was your car?"

"In the mall parking lot."

"What were you doing in the mall?"

"I went to Starbucks for coffee." Cora saw no reason to volunteer the information that the coffee in question was actually a Frappuccino the size of Vermont. "When I got back to my car, the puzzle was on the windshield. I gave it to Sherry because she likes to solve puzzles. I don't. I find solving crossword puzzles profoundly boring. If it ever gets out I said that, I will find you and I will kill you."

"Never fear. The point is, this was on your windshield and it wound up in your purse. And it somewhat suggestively refers to antiques."

"So far, that suggestion has come from you."

"Do you deny that it was the puzzle that made you look in Wilbur's barn?"

Becky held up her hand. "Oooh. Bad word, *deny.* You really didn't want to use that word, did you? It suggests an adversarial relationship under which one needs to rely on the protection of one's counsel."

"I certainly wouldn't want to do that."

Henry Firth reached in his briefcase, brought out another plastic bag, slid it in front of Cora and Becky. "Here's a solution grid. Would you mind comparing it to the crossword puzzle in front of you?"

Cora looked. It was indeed a photocopy of a solution grid such as might appear in the newspaper. There were no clues, and the squares in the grid were not numbered. And the answers were typeset rather than printed by hand.

But the entries were identical. It was clearly the solution grid to the puzzle Cora found on the windshield of her car.

She frowned. "Where did you get this?"

"Be careful," Becky advised. She, too, was frowning.

"I'm not making a statement. I'm asking a question."

"And a very good question," Henry Firth said. "That solution sheet came from Benny Southstreet's briefcase. Which is rather interesting. The man accuses you of stealing his puzzle, and winds up dead. Then you show up with another of his puzzles, taken from the briefcase found at the scene of the crime."

The prosecutor's beady eyes gleamed and his rat nose twitched like he'd just smelled the cheese. "Which brings up a question the police probably should have asked before, but I feel impelled to ask now. Do you happen to have any *more* of Benny Southstreet's puzzles?"

52

Becky Baldwin summoned up what dignity she could muster, no small task considering how furiously she'd been blushing a moment before. "Are we agreed that was off the record?"

Henry Firth's satisfied smirk at having managed to provoke her client was somewhat blunted by the colorful characterizations with which Cora had managed to describe him. The fact that she had not referred to him as a rat was not a matter of restraint so much as a seeming reluctance to use any un-X-rated word. "Absolutely. Now, if you don't mind, let's go back *on* the record."

Henry Firth opened his briefcase again, took out another plastic bag. "Miss Felton, is this your gun?"

Becky opened her mouth to object, but Cora was in no mood to keep silent. "I have no idea."

"It was in your purse."

"If you say so."

"I do say so. I'd like to know if it's yours."

"And I'd like to know why you're asking the question," Becky said.

"He's asking the question because he's a noodge who dots his *i*'s and crosses his *t*'s and wears belts and suspenders. I can't tell you if that's my gun because I have no way of knowing without looking up the serial number. It certainly looks like my gun, and if I'd found it in my purse, I'd probably think it was my gun, but when you hand it to me in an evidence bag, then I am highly skeptical. I have only your word for it the gun was in my purse, and that is, of course, hearsay evidence. Look, I wouldn't want to imply that your questions are stupid, or anything, but why are we discussing this at all?"

"This gun has been fired, Miss Felton."

"Then it isn't mine."

"Cora —"

"My gun hasn't been fired in months. The last time was at a pistol range in Danbury. Won a fiver off a deputy sheriff named Claiborne. He wasn't pleased."

"Any chance you left a spent cartridge in the cylinder?"

"None. I clean and load my gun after I use it. Always have, always will. My ex, Melvin, taught me well. Son of a bitch."

"This gun's been fired recently. It smells of gunpowder, and has a spent shell under the hammer."

"Then it isn't mine."

"Are you sure?"

"Sure I'm sure. I haven't shot anyone lately. I'm sure I'd remember."

"Then how do you account for the fact that the gun was found in your purse?"

"Once again I am hearing language I don't believe you mean," Becky said. "*Account for* is a nasty little phrase. I assume that's not what you meant to say."

"Then you assume wrong. The gun was in her purse. It needs to be accounted for."

"Just a damn minute here," Cora said. "Are you telling me you found a gun that's been fired in my purse?"

"At last, a meeting of the minds. Yes, that's exactly what I'm telling you, Miss Felton. Now, before this goes any further, let me say I appreciate your position. You're charged with a murder. The case against you looks pretty grim. You don't have much of a defense."

"Hey!" Becky interjected.

"You'd like to build up some support. Sway public opinion. Perhaps even the jury pool. At least raise the inference the crime was committed by someone else. What better way than to make it look like someone's trying to kill you?"

"Now you're claiming I fired the shot myself?"

"I'm not claiming anything. I'm just presenting the facts. If you can explain them, I'd be delighted to listen."

"She's not explaining anything," Becky said. "She's had a traumatic experience. She's been knocked unconscious. She may have a concussion. Under the circumstances, when she was shot at it's entirely possible she pulled a gun and fired a shot at her attacker and doesn't remember it. I'm not saying she did. I'm just saying it's entirely possible."

"Mr. Wilbur only heard one shot."

"Mr. Wilbur may have *fired* one shot. I'm not saying he did. I'm just pointing out how much weight his statement is worth."

"Mr. Wilbur might have fired the shot that whizzed by your client's head and embedded itself in the wall?"

"We're not making any accusations," Cora told him. "We're just listening to yours and pointing out how stupid they are."

"Anytime you're through having fun," the prosecutor said.

"You call this fun? Trust me, I can think of

things more fun."

"I'm sure you can." Henry Firth opened his briefcase again, took out a piece of paper. "Miss Felton, we ran a trace on the gun found in your bag. According to the files, this gun was registered to a Mrs. Cora Crabtree, of 890 Park Avenue, New York City."

Cora nodded. "The best thing about Melvin was his Park Avenue address. I always hated being Cora Crabtree, though. Like I married him for the alliteration."

Henry ignored this, reached in his briefcase again. "This is a photograph taken of two bullets on a comparison microscope. The bullet on the top is a test bullet fired from the gun found in your purse, the gun registered to Cora Crabtree. The bullet on the bottom is the one dug out of the wall in Wilbur's barn. They are identical. There is no doubt about it. The bullet you claim whizzed by your head came from your gun."

53

"See?" Becky said, as they drove away from the police station. "This is why you listen to your lawyer and don't make any admissions until you know what the facts are."

"I didn't make any admissions," Cora protested.

"All right, what about lies? What about assertions that can be proven false?"

"I didn't lie."

"You made assertions that can be proven false."

"That sounds bad. Can I go to jail for that?"

"No, but you can go to jail for murder. And one of the quickest ways to get convicted is by telling lies to the police."

"I didn't lie."

"You said someone shot at you."

"Someone *did* shoot at me."

"With the gun in your purse?"

"I admit that *sounds* bad."

"It not only sounds bad, it cooks your goose."

"Do people still use that expression?"

"This isn't word games, Cora. I'm interested in keeping you out of jail. Just for the record, impugning the character of the prosecutor's mother is generally considered a poor legal strategy."

"I implied she was lithe and vigorous."

"Cora."

"That was before I realized they framed me with my gun."

"How did that happen?"

"You're asking me? I was unconscious."

"That was *after* you were shot with your gun. Now, how did that happen?"

"If I knew how that happened, I'd know who shot me."

"I mean how could it have *possibly* happened?"

"The easiest explanation is there were two shots. While I was unconscious someone took my gun and fired the second one."

"That would mean Wilbur did it."

"Of course. He's the most likely suspect anyway. The fact he had the chance to fire the second shot puts him way at the top of the list."

"Who else is on it?"

"It's a rather short list."

"You're not being very helpful."

"What do you want from me, Becky? I've been framed for murder. I don't know why. I'm trying to work things out."

"I'm trying to help. If there were two bullets, how come the police only found one?"

"Because they didn't know there were two bullets. They found one and stopped looking."

"You mean . . . ?"

Cora shrugged. "I never looked for a bullet hole before. Except in a target. But to find a bullet fired into a wooden wall with not the best of light . . . I couldn't really blame Sam Brogan for missing one."

The cars were gone from Wilbur's Antiques. The place was dark and quiet.

"Where's your car?" Becky said.

"Just around the next corner. By the side of the road."

There was no traffic that time of night. Becky pulled a U-turn, came up behind the car.

Cora opened the door. "Thanks a lot. You're what I call a full-service lawyer."

Cora slammed the car door, stood there, and waved good-bye.

Becky didn't move.

Cora banged on the window. Becky rolled it down.

"Thanks for the ride," Cora said. "I can find my way home."

"I know you can. I want to make sure you get home safe."

"I'm a big girl, Becky."

"Yeah, but the police have your gun. It's probably the first time you've been unarmed in forty years."

"Hey!"

"You count on your gun. It's how you think. You act like you have a gun. Well, you don't. And if you act like you do, you could get in trouble."

"Thanks for your concern. I won't talk to strangers."

Cora turned on her heel, marched to the Toyota, fished her keys out of her purse, and zapped the lock. She climbed in, started the car, pulled out, and headed home.

Becky followed right behind, all the way into town, and all the way out again.

Cora set her jaw. Becky *lived* in town. Was such babysitting really necessary?

Becky didn't turn back until Cora reached her house.

Cora immediately pulled off to the side of the road and cut her lights. She made a U-turn in the dark — a K-turn, actually, as she recalled from the driving test she took as a girl — snapped her lights on, and headed for town.

Becky Baldwin was waiting for her in front of the library. Becky stepped out into the street, forced Cora to bring her car to a stop.

"I just can't get you out of jail fast enough," Becky complained.

"That's hardly fair."

"Where are you headed, Cora?"

"Out for coffee."

Becky greeted this prevarication with an exclamation of disbelief apt to be heard on a cattle ranch.

"Well said. Look. Here's the deal. You're my lawyer. It's your job to keep me out of trouble. That's what you're trying to do now. The problem is, you have no real authority to compel the police to make a thorough investigation of Wilbur's barn for the purpose of determining if a second shot was fired. Even if you could get a court order, by the time you did, such evidence, if it existed, would be long gone."

"So?"

"So let's go get it."

54

"You realize we could go to jail?" Becky said.

"That's why I have a lawyer," Cora told her.

"That won't help much if your lawyer's in prison."

"You worry too much. Wilbur already said he wouldn't press charges."

"I don't think that was an open invitation to do it again."

"Couldn't you argue that it was?"

"I can argue anything."

"There you are."

Cora opened the passenger door. "If a car goes by, honk once. If it's a police car, honk twice."

Becky looked aghast. "Are you kidding?"

"Yes. Don't do anything. Just sit here and keep reminding yourself you have a duty to your client."

"I don't think that includes being an accomplice."

"Then we'd better not get caught."

Cora slipped out of the car and disappeared in the shadows.

The shop was dark. Of course, it should be that time of night, but one never knew. Cora couldn't help but remember Wilbur's shotgun. Not that she thought he'd use it on her. But he wouldn't know in the dark. And buckshot was probably pretty painful. If not fatal.

The phrase *give 'em both barrels* occurred to Cora.

It did not cheer her.

Cora crept around to the barn. Wilbur hadn't bothered to board up the window. There was a crime-scene ribbon across the door, and that was it. It was a piece of cake to reach through the broken glass and unlock the door. Of course, that would get her fingerprints on it, but they were already there. Having been found unconscious on the floor, it wasn't like no one knew she'd been in the barn.

There was nothing to worry about. Becky would probably take her seriously, blow the horn if anyone came. Even though Cora had assured her she was kidding. So if she didn't hear the horn, everything was fine. A false sense of security, built on a faulty premise. What could be better?

Cora pulled her flashlight out of her purse, played it along the floor. If Wilbur was looking out his back window, he might see it. But if Wilbur was looking out his back window, the game was up anyway.

Come on. Get on with it. If there is a second bullet, where is it?

Never mind *if* there was a second bullet. There *had* to be a second bullet. She hadn't shot herself. That much she knew.

All right. Where was Sam looking?

He was over there, working in this direction. He found the bullet here. So the second bullet wasn't between here and there, or he'd have found it.

Where was the bullet he found?

Cora had no problem locating that. There was the hole Sam had dug in the wall. Plus he'd drawn a circle around it in magic marker.

Okay. So any second bullet would have to be to the right of that.

Cora shined the light, searched along the wall.

She hadn't gone more than ten feet when something barred her path.

She shined the light again.

It was a table. Covered by a tarp. A tarp with enforced steel rings.

Of course. That was where she was standing when the shot was fired. She'd found that table, was examining the tarp. The bullet should be right there. Let's see, she was in the process of raising the tarp. So where would the bullet have gone?

It would depend on the angle from which it was fired. The bullet hole was the right height. But well to the left. Assuming the shooter was standing where Cora had imagined. If Cora was wrong, the shooter would have had to be standing farther to the right, to have missed her head and hit the wall farther to the left.

If it was Sam's bullet.

But in that case, she would have shot herself with her own gun. Which she knew she didn't do.

So she had to scour the wall to the right. Where a bullet would have gone if she was bent over picking up the tarp.

She took hold of the edge of the tarp.

All right, what the hell was underneath it? She hadn't seen last night, and she couldn't see now. She'd have to bend over farther, pull the tarp up more.

Why bother?

What if the bullet went there.

Then there'd be a hole in the tarp.

There *were* holes in the tarp. Enforced steel holes.

All right, the bullet went through one of those? *You're getting desperate.*

Cora threw back the tarp, shined the flashlight.

She gasped.

Underneath the table were four rattan chairs.

55

Sherry Carter blinked bleary eyes up at her aunt. "What time is it?"

"What's the difference?"

"Cora."

"Come on, Sherry, wake up."

"My God, it's four in the morning!"

"Technically, yes."

"What do you mean, technically?"

"Well, if you go by the clock."

"Cora."

"Come on, Sherry. I need your help."

"What help could you possibly need at four in the morning?"

"Help with the computer."

"What for?"

"I need to do a search."

"You know how to Google."

"It's not a Google search."

"What kind of search is it?"

"I'm not sure."

"That doesn't help much."

"No, but it woke you up. Come on, splash some water on your face and meet me in the study."

Minutes later Sherry padded down the hall, to find Cora sitting at the computer with Google open.

"You *are* Googling," Sherry said.

"No, I'm staring at the screen. It's not quite the same thing."

"What do you want to trace?"

"Wilbur's missing chairs."

"Why do you want to trace them?"

"I found them."

"Where?"

"In Wilbur's barn."

"You're kidding."

"No. They were never stolen."

"But Wilbur thought they were?"

"No, he knew they weren't."

"But he reported them stolen."

"Yeah. He's guilty of filing a false report. If I were a cop, I'd have to arrest him."

"I don't understand."

"Join the club. So, here's what I wanna do. I want to trace the stolen chairs."

"But you know where they are."

"Right. But I wanna pretend I don't, start over, and see where they are."

"And your search will lead you to Wilbur's barn?"

"I'm hoping it won't."

"I can see why Google won't help you."

"Yeah. So what will?"

"A therapist, an exorcist, and a psychic." Sherry yawned, stretched. "I'd better make coffee. You're making less sense than usual."

"I'm not quite awake."

Sherry went into the kitchen, measured coffee into the automatic drip machine.

Cora followed her, sat down, lit a cigarette.

"Are you going to smoke in the kitchen?"

"I figured you were too tired to argue."

Sherry put milk and sugar on the table, sat opposite Cora. "Okay, coffee's brewing. Fill me in on your Internet search."

"I broke into Wilbur's barn last night."

"That's how you know about the chairs?"

"No, that's how I got arrested and shot at."

"What!?"

"Or vice versa. I actually got shot at and arrested. The other way makes no sense."

"Nothing you're saying makes any sense. What the hell are you talking about?"

"It didn't make the late news? I'm crushed."

Cora gave Sherry a rundown of her escapade in Wilbur's barn.

"You broke into his barn *twice*?"

"Yeah, but it doesn't matter."

"What?"

"Well, the first time he's not pressing charges, and the second time he doesn't know."

"But the cops have your gun and think you shot yourself?"

"They think I fired a bullet into the wall and pretended someone shot at me."

"So you went back into the barn to look for the other bullet, but you quit when you found the chairs?"

"Are you kidding me? I went over those walls with a fine-tooth comb. If there's a bullet in the barn, I can't find it."

"Is there a place a bullet might have been dug out of?"

"Just mine."

"So where is it?"

"Maybe it went out the window. Maybe there were two guys, and one of them's wearing it. There's lots of possibilities, just none that I can prove."

"Great." Sherry got up, poured coffee.

Cora took hers, slopped in milk and sugar, took a gulp. "Where's Aaron?"

"He went home."

"On good terms?"

"Not really."

"How come?"

"We had another fight. We went to the movies to make up."

"Oh."

"Yeah. Me running out in the middle didn't help."

"I'm sure you blamed me."

"That was small consolation."

"I mean to Aaron."

"So do I."

Cora chugged the rest of her coffee, pushed the cup back, and got up. "Come on. Let's go Google."

Sherry took her coffee into the office and sat at the computer. "What do you want to Google? Oh, I forgot, you don't know, do you?"

"Not really. I gotta find out why Wilbur stole his own chairs."

"Why in the world would he?"

"I don't know. I'm beginning to think it has something to do with the Kleinsmidt diamonds."

"Wait a minute. I thought the Kleinsmidt diamonds don't exist."

"They don't."

Sherry cocked her head ironically. "I can see why this might be tough to Google."

56

Cora Felton drove down the driveway just as Dennis Pride turned in. She spun the wheel, hit the brake, and skidded sideways, blocking the drive.

Cora was out the door before her car even stopped moving. She descended on Dennis, leveled a finger, and suggested if he were to back up it would be better for all involved, though not exactly in those words.

Dennis hopped out of his car with his hands raised, just as if he'd been stopped for reckless driving and was eager to show the arresting officer that he was sober and unarmed.

"Don't get out of your car," Cora told him. "Get back in your car, turn around, drive off, and don't stop until you run out of gas."

"I didn't come to see Sherry. I came to see you."

"I don't date married men."

That tripped him up. Dennis couldn't

think of a single response that wouldn't get him in trouble. It was almost comical. After an awkward pause, he opted to ignore the remark completely. "I followed him last night."

"Who?"

"Chuck Dillinger. I followed him to see what he'd do."

"What did he do?"

"Left the house, got in his car, and drove to the nearest gas station."

"And got gas?" Cora said, lightly mocking him.

"Yeah, he got gas. But while he was filling up he went to the pay phone and made a call."

Cora frowned. "From the pay phone?"

"Yeah."

"He didn't have a cell phone?"

"If he did, he didn't use it. He went to the pay phone. It's a gas station convenience store, with the phone on the outside wall."

"On Elm Street?"

"I don't know the names of the streets. At the traffic light."

"That's the one. So he made a call?"

"Yeah. I got close enough to hear. And I thought you should know."

"Why?"

"It was a funny call. He said, 'It's me. We got trouble.' Then he listened and said, 'I have no idea.' He listened again and said, 'No, she hasn't got a clue.' He laughed and said, 'Thank God she wrecked the car.'"

"Then what?"

"Then I think he saw me, because he said, 'Gotta go,' and hung up the phone."

"What did he do then?"

"Paid for the gas and went home. I watched the house for a while, but he stayed put."

"You drove all the way up from New York to tell me this?"

"I came by last night. With Brenda. There was no one here."

"With Brenda?"

"Yeah. *She* thought it was important."

"Okay, you told me. Now get the hell out of here."

Dennis glared at her to show he couldn't be pushed around, then did what she said.

Cora watched him drive off and frowned.

What Dennis told her was fascinating.

She wondered if it was true.

57

Chief Harper pulled into the Four Seasons Motel parking lot, to find the young desk clerk in the baseball cap waiting for him outside.

"Where is she?" Harper demanded.

The kid jerked his thumb. "Out back."

Harper followed him behind the motel office, where a large, green Dumpster stood. The lid was open, and there was a scrabbling inside as if the garbage was being picked over by an enormous rat.

Harper walked up, banged on the side.

Cora Felton's head emerged from the Dumpster. Her hair was matted and stringy, and there was a banana peel on her shoulder. She was wearing her Wicked Witch of the West outfit. In New York City she could have passed for a bag lady.

"What do you think you're doing?" Harper growled.

Cora held up a Diet Pepsi can. "Would you

believe collecting deposit bottles?"

"Cora."

She smiled. "I *love* it when you use my first name. I wish I didn't have to dress in garbage to get you to do it."

"This isn't funny."

"No, it's not. I phoned the police station three times this morning. You wouldn't take my call."

Harper stared at her. "You did this to get my attention?"

"Don't be silly." Cora chuckled. "That's like that Carly Simon song. You know, you're so vain you probably think this Dumpster's about you."

"So what are you doing?"

"Looking for evidence you missed."

"Evidence I . . . missed!" Harper could barely get the words out. He wheeled on the desk clerk. "When was this thing dumped?"

"Yesterday."

"See?" Harper said. "It's been dumped since the murder."

"That will make it harder," Cora said complacently. She climbed out of the Dumpster, led him aside. "Anyway, I'm glad you're here, Chief."

"Try not to touch me."

"Sorry. I need help with the case. That's why I called. I need your help."

"I might be more inclined to give it if you hadn't compared the prosecutor to a tree slug."

"I'm sure I never did that."

"I'm sure you did. From what I hear, it was one of your milder epithets."

"You know what he accused me of?"

"Yeah. A lot of things you probably did. Considering you're getting a pass on breaking and entering, I would think you'd be a little tolerant."

"He thinks I faked my own shooting."

"He's going by the evidence."

"The evidence is wrong."

"Evidence is evidence. You wanna come up with another explanation for it, fine. But the facts are the facts."

"It's not my fault I was framed."

"Well, it's not my fault either. I didn't shoot you with your own gun."

"No, you didn't. So you owe me a favor."

Chief Harper frowned. "I beg your pardon?"

"If you shot me with my gun, I'd be innocent, and I could prove it. The fact you didn't leaves me in a bind."

"That's looney logic, even for you."

"So I need a favor. Two, actually. Well, maybe three. But let's start with two."

"God save me."

"Barney Nathan listens to you. You have a working relationship. You can call him, say, 'What's up, Doc?' "

"You want me to ask the medical examiner about the autopsy?"

"Well, it's his job, isn't it?"

"It's not his job to make a case for the defense."

"No, but you could ask him to check for contributing factors. I mean, it's real nice you got the gunshot wound to the head from the gun with my fingerprints on it. But was there anything else? Like drugs, for instance."

Chief Harper sighed. "I've seen the autopsy report. Drugs didn't kill him. He was killed by a single shot to the back of the head. At an angle from which he'd have to be a contortionist to have fired himself."

"I know. But did he have any other problems?"

Chief Harper gave her a look. "I am not inclined to bother the medical examiner."

Cora shrugged. "I had a feeling you wouldn't be. All right, you can do me the easy favor."

"*Easy* favor?" Harper looked at her suspiciously. "All this talk about the autopsy report was just a ploy to get me to do something else?"

"Don't be silly, Chief. I *want* you to talk to the doctor."

"Yeah? So what's this 'easy' favor?"

"It really is easy, Chief. The type of thing you can do in your sleep."

"Oh, yeah? What?"

"I need you to trace a call."

58

Sherry Carter's mouth fell open. "My God, you're a mess! Where have you been?"

"In a Dumpster."

"That's what you look like. Where were you really?"

"Don't start with me."

Sherry spun away from the computer, picked a piece of romaine lettuce out of Cora's hair. "My God, you *were* in a Dumpster. What were you doing?"

"Going through the garbage."

"What for?"

"To attract Chief Harper's attention."

"Just because he wouldn't take your call?"

"No. But that's what he thought. I was out at the crime scene, looking for evidence."

"Find any?"

"None to find. The Dumpster was dumped yesterday."

"So it was a waste of time."

"No. The killer doesn't know it was dumped."

"You're setting a trap?"

"God, I hope so."

Buddy came skittering in the door, took one look at Cora, and skittered out again.

"Now, there's a vote of confidence," Cora said dryly.

"Do you have any idea what you're doing?"

"None at all," Cora admitted. "I'm just trying to stir things up."

"Why?"

Cora brushed cigarette ash off her outfit and frowned. She wasn't smoking. "The killer made a big mistake, trying to frame me with my own gun. There are only a few ways that could have happened. Just like there are only a few ways Benny Southstreet could have been killed. You put it all together and it's not a pretty picture."

Sherry looked at Cora closely. "Are you saying you know who did it?"

"If I did, do you think I'd be crawling around in the garbage?"

"Good point." Sherry's eyes twinkled. "Well, while you were doing that, guess what I found."

"What?"

"The Daniel Farnsworth Cane Company."

"They make canes?"

"No, that's just their name. I'm not sure why. Maybe they use cane in the manufacturing. Maybe one of the partners was named Cane."

"What the hell is the Daniel Farnsworth Cane Company?" Cora said irritably.

Sherry smiled. "See? This is what you do to me all the time. See what it feels like?"

Cora characterized Sherry as a particular body part of limited intelligence.

"That's no way to talk about the person who penetrated the records of the Daniel Farnsworth Cane Company."

"I don't give a damn about the Daniel What's-it's-name — Wait a minute. Does this company manufacture *chairs?*"

"Only for the last hundred years. Give or take a decade. The point is, they're still in business."

"I take it back. You're an absolute genius. You should have your brain bronzed. Or your mouse."

"Don't thank me. Thank Philip T. Crickstein. Bookkeeper for the Daniel Farnsworth Cane Company from 1935 to 1962. Mr. Crickstein kept such meticulous records that it is possible to trace purchases made over fifty years ago."

"You're way too pleased with yourself.

What did you find?"

"I found the record of Wilbur purchasing the chairs."

"He didn't buy them from the manufacturer. He bought them at auction."

"When?"

"Two years ago."

Sherry smiled, shook her head. "Not quite. He bought them from the Daniel Farnsworth Cane Company on June 6, 1952."

"What!?"

"That's right. And he didn't buy *four* chairs. He bought *eight*."

"Eight?"

"Yeah. And that's not the best part. He didn't have them shipped to himself. He had them shipped to a private home in Mount Vernon, New York."

"Please tell me you traced the address."

"I did, but that's where the trail gets cold. The records indicate a family named Austin lived there in the early '50s. Where they went after that is anybody's guess."

"Find them."

"That may take a while."

"I haven't got a while." Cora pointed to the computer screen. "Go on-line and find them. I don't care if you Google 'em or use MapQuest, or a computer dating service, just find them, for Christ's sake."

"I'll give it my best shot."

"Please do." Cora sighed grimly. "I gotta solve this damn case before I get framed for anything else."

59

"Tell me about the money."

Mimi Dillinger was blocking the doorway, so Cora couldn't get in. "I don't know what you're talking about."

"Yes you do," Cora assured her. "The first time I mentioned it you acted like every small-time punk who ever got picked up for questioning. Right down to the shifty eyes."

Darlene was crying. Mimi glanced over her shoulder. "This isn't a good time."

"It's the best time you got. It may be the *last* time you've got. If I were you, I'd take advantage of it."

"The baby's upset."

"So, what else is new? I don't care if you change it, nurse it, or spank it. Just so long as you talk."

"Can't you leave me alone?"

"Not anymore. I got shot at last night."

Mimi was horrified. "What!?"

"Yeah. As if I didn't have enough problems. And that's just part of it. Well, I'm tired of being a punching bag. I'm hitting back, and I'm hitting hard. And if you stand in my way, I'm hitting you."

"I don't know what you're talking about."

"You know *exactly* what I'm talking about. And you want to tell me. I know you do. You told me about the ice pick. That was kind of a test run. If that had gone well, you might have brought up the cash."

"What cash?"

"Don't be dumb. The money under the blotter. The hundred-dollar bills. That might have been two, or might have been more. That Benny Southstreet might have stolen, or your husband might have spent. That might be real, or might not, but you think the police ought to test. *That* cash."

"Oh."

"Good answer. Not enlightening, but beats a denial. Come on, help me out here. I need to know if I got shot at for finding that piece of hundred-dollar bill under your blotter."

Mimi's eyes were wide. "*You* found that?"

"Let's not get sidetracked. I want answers, and I want 'em now. After tonight, all bets are off."

"Why? What's happening tonight?"

"I'm wrapping up the case."

It was a stone-cold bluff. Cora would have

put the odds of her cracking the case as a slightly longer shot than her winning the Kentucky Derby.

Mimi bit her lip.

Cora whipped out a paper, waved it in Mimi's face. "I got the goods. It's all going down. The only question now is who's going down with it. I'm hoping it's not you."

"What's that?"

Cora glanced at the paper. It was an old cable TV bill from her Manhattan apartment. She quickly shoved it back in her purse. "Last chance. In or out. What's it gonna be?"

The kid was shrieking a blue streak, but Mimi didn't seem to notice. Her voice trembled. "What do you want?"

Cora's voice was hard as nails. "Tell me about the money."

60

Rick Reed couldn't have been prouder. "This is Rick Reed, Channel 8 News, bringing you an *exclusive* interview with Cora Felton, the world-famous Puzzle Lady, who has been arrested and charged with murder in the shooting death of Benny Southstreet. Miss Felton, why are you making a statement at this time?"

Cora, all decked out in her favorite Miss Marple wear, beamed at the camera. "Because the public has a right to know, and I want to tell them."

"And you're telling them *exclusively* on Channel 8 News."

"No, I'm telling them live, in person, at eight o'clock tonight at the Bakerhaven town hall."

Rick Reed looked crestfallen. "You're not telling us now?"

"No, I'm making my announcement tonight. I'd be delighted to have you there, just as I'd be delighted to have all of Baker-haven."

"You're going to address the town meeting?"

"That's right."

"Are you going to tell us who murdered Benny Southstreet?"

"I don't know who murdered Benny Southstreet. I'm hoping someone will tell me."

"You think the killer will be there?"

"I hope not."

Rick Reed frowned. "Why?"

"Because everybody else will." Cora smiled. "And then I'll know who the killer is. The killer will be the person who doesn't have the guts to show up."

"You think the killer will be afraid to come to the meeting?"

"Oh, yes. If he does, I'll expose him. Or her. But if he doesn't, I won't have to, because we'll all know who he is. The spineless wimp who didn't dare to come."

"And there you have it," Rick Reed concluded. "An open challenge to the killer, to show up at the town hall tonight at eight o'clock, to meet the Puzzle Lady, face-to-face. We'll be there, live, to see if the killer shows up, or wimps out. This is Rick Reed, Channel 8 News."

Cora smiled. "I know who you are, Rick."

"I was doing the wrap-up."

"That's fine, but I'm not done."

"No?"

"Wouldn't you like a little preview?"

"And how!" Rick preened for the camera. "And now, with an *exclusive* preview of tonight's town meeting, here is the Puzzle Lady, Cora Felton. What are you going to be talking about tonight, Miss Felton?"

"The autopsy report."

"What about the autopsy report?"

"The doctor only found one bullet. Which was a big break for the killer. There were two bullets. The doc only found one."

Rick Reed looked incredulous. "Wait a minute. You're saying there were *two* bullets?"

Cora smiled. "Can't put anything past you, Rick. Yes, that's exactly what I'm saying."

"You mean the autopsy report was wrong?"

"How many bullets were there in the autopsy report?"

"One."

"You do the math."

"And there you have it," Rick concluded. "A shocking accusation from the defendant, challenging the findings of the medical examiner. This is Rick Reed, Channel 8

News." He shot a glance at Cora Felton, mouthed, "Are you done?"

Cora smiled sardonically. "Am I ever."

61

Barney Nathan was right up front. Cora wasn't surprised. She'd been ducking the doctor's phone calls ever since the broadcast. Her answering machine was nearly fried from the volume and the language. She'd also refused to talk to him at the town hall. Through intermediary Iris Cooper, Barney had been promised he'd have his say as long as he held his tongue until called on, a condition to which he had agreed with great gnashing of teeth. Now the good doctor sat red-faced on the edge of his seat, ready to leap up at any minute.

Iris Cooper side-spied at him over the lectern. "Think he'll keep quiet?"

"Or explode," Cora whispered back. "I would say it's a fifty-fifty bet."

Rick Reed pushed his way through the crowd. "Okay, we got monitors in the back to carry the live feed. We're setting up some more outside."

"Outside?"

Rick grinned. "Yeah. Our little interview really packed 'em in. We've got almost as many people out there as in here."

"Just so long as the principals are in here," Cora said.

"You mean like Chief Harper and the prosecutor?"

"I'm sure they got in. I mean like Chuck and Mimi Dillinger. And Veronica Martindale."

"Who's that?"

"My surprise witness."

"You have a surprise witness?"

"Yes."

"But you told me who it is."

"So?"

"So it's not a surprise."

"I wasn't trying to surprise *you*. Aim your camera at her when the time comes."

"When will that be?"

"When I say so. Is it eight o'clock yet?"

"Just about," Iris said.

"It doesn't matter," Rick said. "We're not live."

"How come?"

"It's prime time. I can't go live in prime time. Not unless you plan to shoot someone."

"I'll see what I can do."

Cora took the microphone, addressed the crowd. "Good evening. I've asked for this special town meeting because I've been arrested for murder. When you get arrested for murder they tell you you have the right to remain silent. But they never tell you you have the right to talk. In fact, they warn you if you do, what you say may be taken down and used against you. I see the police are here, as well as the prosecutor and the judge, so if anybody'd like to take down what I say and use it against me, feel free.

"I challenged the killer to be here. I don't know if the killer took that challenge, because I don't know who the killer is. But everybody and his brother seems to be here, so let's assume the killer took the bait. Who could it possibly be?"

Barney Nathan shot to his feet. "Miss Felton!"

"Ah. Dr. Barney Nathan. You would have been my last choice. But if you want to confess, go right ahead."

"I want to object to you saying I botched the autopsy."

"I didn't say you botched it. I just said there were two bullets and you only found one. It's a math problem. You probably miscounted."

"There was only one bullet."

401

"You say that now, but wait till I get you on the stand. Sit down, Doc. I'll be right with you."

Cora waited patiently until the doctor subsided, then clapped her hands together. "All right, if we can table the doctor's ruffled feathers for a minute, let's see who else is here.

"Benny Southstreet couldn't be here tonight because I killed him. At least, that's the police theory. I can't say as I buy into it. It leaves a lot to be desired.

"Who was Benny Southstreet? He wasn't from around here. He was from New York City. I am originally from New York City, so one might suspect a connection. One would be wrong. I never met the man in my life, until he showed up to accuse me of stealing his puzzle.

"With regard to the theft of the puzzle, I can only say I was set up. Unintentionally, to be sure, but set up nonetheless. Mimi Dillinger wanted a crossword puzzle to help her break the news to her husband about her smashing his car. That's Mimi sitting there in the third row with her husband, Chuck. Got a babysitter, did you, Mimi? Believe me, I can't thank you enough.

"I gave her a puzzle of Benny Southstreet's, slightly altered to fit the occasion. I did not intend to steal from Mr. Southstreet, nor did I represent the puzzle as my own. It was a private matter, no one could possibly care.

"Except Mimi put the puzzle in the newspaper. Benny Southstreet saw it there, and flipped out. He came here, and accused me of plagiarism. Anyone who thinks I killed him because of that is a moron."

Cora nodded in the direction of Chief Harper and Henry Firth. "Begging the police and prosecutor's pardon. I should say in their defense, it's not really their fault. I've been quite adroitly framed. Benny Southstreet was killed at a time I was seen at his motel room, and at a time when I was the *only* person seen at his motel room. If I were a cop, I'd start looking pretty good to me too.

"Well, assuming I didn't kill Benny Southstreet, what really happened?

"Here's what I know so far.

"Benny Southstreet was a two-bit hustler, eager to embarrass me with a plagiarism charge in the hope of extorting some money. It wasn't going to fly, but Benny didn't know that. Hoping to support a suit, he breaks into Mimi Dillinger's house and ransacks the study, looking for evidence of my having given her his puzzle. Then he breaks into my house, to check out my computer. He wants to find the crossword puzzle in Crossword Compiler to clinch his case.

"Benny is a bit of a computer whiz, much more skilled than I am, and while he's there he checks me out. Discovers I'm bidding on eBay on a set of chairs. And the person I'm bidding against is none other than Mr. Wilbur here, of Wilbur's Antiques.

"This, I regret to say, is your basic comedy of errors. Mr. Wilbur had some chairs stolen. To trap the thief, I had Harvey Beerbaum offer an identical set of chairs for sale on eBay, hoping people would bid on them. Unfortunately, the only one who bids is Wilbur. I don't know it's Wilbur, so I bid against him, trying to judge his interest. And he continues to bid, not knowing it's me.

"Benny Southstreet has no idea why we're interested, but if the chairs are valuable, he wants 'em. He checks out Harvey Beerbaum's residence, finds security minimal."

Harvey lunged to his feet.

Cora added quickly, "Yes, yes, Harvey, that's no longer true, anyone attempting entrance now will be immediately electrocuted. Anyway, he breaks in, steals Harvey's dining room chairs, and offers to sell them to Mr. Wilbur, who actually had an appointment with him at the motel, right around the time

Benny was killed."

Wilbur sputtered angrily.

"Hang on, Mr. Wilbur. You'll get an opportunity to deny you killed him. So will anyone else who takes exception to what I'm about to say."

Cora spread her hands. "I'm laying out what happened here. To do that, I'm going to ask questions of some of the people involved. Please understand you are under no obligation to answer them. On the other hand, if you do, no one's going to cross-examine you, because this isn't a trial."

"Now, just a minute," prosecutor Henry Firth said.

"And that goes for you, too, Mr. Firth. If I ask you questions, you have every right not to answer."

"*I* may have some questions."

"Then you can call your own town meeting. But you can't ask 'em here."

"Wait a minute. You can't do that."

"Why?"

"Well . . . I don't like it."

"I don't believe that's a legal reason. Let's ask Judge Hobbs. Judge, do we care what the prosecutor likes?"

The elderly jurist smiled. "You're asking my opinion? I thought I had no jurisdiction here."

"See?" Cora said. "He has the right attitude. Okay, I'm going to make my presentation. Unless, of course, the prosecution insists on taking part. In which case we can all go home."

There were rumblings, and shouts of "No!" from the crowd.

Rick Reed pushed forward. "This is Rick Reed, Channel 8 News, coming to you live from the Bakerhaven town hall. On behalf of the Channel 8 News team, I certainly hope we continue with this groundbreaking news story."

"Excellent," Cora said. "My first witness is Rick Reed, of Channel 8 News."

The reporter's expression was priceless. "Me?"

"Relax, Rick. I'm not accusing you of the crime. But you were at the motel the afternoon it was discovered. Channel 8 carried live pictures of the body being taken away."

Rick glowed with pride. "That's right. We did."

"How did it happen you got there so fast?"

"I think you'll find Channel 8 News is often first on the scene."

"This particular instance. How did you get the lead?"

"Someone phoned in a tip."

"To you?"

"No. To the station."

"Are you sure of that?"

"Yes, because there was some discussion over whether it was legit, and whether we should go. Sometimes these things are pranks."

"But this one wasn't?"

"It sure wasn't."

"So that's why Channel 8 had live coverage from the motel?"

"That's right."

"Thank you very much." Cora looked out over the audience. "I'd like to ask a few questions of Miss Veronica Martindale. Miss Martindale, if you would come up here, please."

A rather distinguished-looking elderly woman in the back of the room got up and made her way down the center aisle. Her face was lean and unlined as if from a dozen face-lifts, though it was obvious she had never had a single one. She was slender, walked with a slight limp.

Cora Felton gave way, shared the stage with her for the camera. "You are Veronica Martindale?"

"That's right." Her voice was full, not at all reedy and old.

"Is that your married name?"

"Yes, it is."

"You're married?"

"Divorced."

"What is your maiden name?"

"Austin. Veronica Austin."

In the back of the room, Mr. Wilbur struggled to his feet. "Ronnie?" he croaked. He cleared his throat, gawked. "Ronnie!"

"That's right. Mr. Wilbur. Miss Ronnie *Austin.*" Cora beamed. "I think she can help you out with those chairs."

62

Cora Felton leaned on the lectern, smiled like a benevolent matchmaker. In the back of the room, Wilbur and Ronnie were huddled together, thick as thieves.

"So," Cora said, "that's that. I'm sure those kids have a lot to talk over, but we do have this little murder. Fortunately, Mr. Wilbur has nothing to do with it, so we can excuse him if he doesn't pay attention.

"The problem with this crime is it has no obvious solution. All the promising leads are dead ends. Like Mr. Wilbur's stolen chairs. And Harvey Beerbaum's stolen chairs. And Veronica Martindale's chairs, which were neither sold nor stolen. But that's beside the point. The fact is, the stolen chairs in Benny Southstreet's motel room had *absolutely nothing* to do with his murder.

"The problem was, neither did anything else. The crossword puzzles. The fingerprints on the gun. They meant nothing. And I should know. They're my fingerprints. So I knew they were meaningless.

"But I couldn't prove it. I needed a clue. And I couldn't get one. Nothing helped."

Cora smiled. "What I needed was a dog that didn't bark in the nighttime. You know what I mean? Since there was no clue there, I had to find a clue in something that *wasn't* there. Like a dog *not* barking. The dog knows the killer so he doesn't bark. So the killer is someone the dog knows.

"That was my problem. I needed a dog that didn't bark."

Cora looked out over a sea of faces regarding her as if she'd just taken leave of her senses. "Let's move on. Next up, I'd like to ask a few questions of Mr. Paul Fishman."

In the back of the room, the Photomat operator shifted uncomfortably in his seat.

"That's him right there," Cora said, for the benefit of the TV camera. "If he looks a little reluctant, it's because he thinks I'm going to bawl him out. That's not why I'm asking him up here. I'm asking him up here because he's absolutely dreamy-looking, and I have a question or two. Come on up. I bet you look great on TV."

Paul Fishman made his way forward.

Cora beamed. "What do you think, girls? Isn't he something? I'd marry him myself, if

I weren't up for murder."

Henry Firth strode to the front of the room. "Now, just a minute here! Paul Fishman happens to be a witness for the prosecution!"

"And I'm sure he'll make an excellent one," Cora said sweetly. "In the meantime, I'd like to ask him some questions."

"I don't want you tampering with a prosecution witness!"

"What's the matter? Are you afraid I'll get him to lie?"

"Of course not!"

"Then you must be afraid I'll get him to tell the truth."

Henry Firth opened his mouth, closed it again. The Channel 8 News crew filmed him gleefully as he sat back down.

"Mr. Fishman, you have no problem answering a few questions, do you? Before you send me up the river, I mean."

"I'm sure I won't do that."

"I am too. Let's get right to it. You gave the police some photographs I took of the murder scene?"

"I explained that."

"Yes, you did. And very nicely too. It was your civic duty. Ladies and gentlemen, this man is not only handsome, he is a patriot. Or a Good Samaritan. Or whatever. At any rate, he had noble reasons for ratting me out."

Paul opened his mouth to speak.

Cora held up her hand. "Relax. We won't get into that. Here's the point. Paul was in the Photomat. He has a little TV under the counter he watches when business is slow, and he happened to see Rick Reed, of Channel 8 News, bringing live coverage of the motel.

"Well, that caught his attention, because he'd just developed a roll of film with the very same pictures. He grabbed the film, hopped in his car, drove out to the motel, and gave the photos to the police. They were my pictures, and that's why he thinks I hold a grudge. Since then, he has gone out of his way to make it up to me. He even supplied me with a duplicate set of snaps."

Cora reached in her purse. "I have those pictures here. I'd like to show them to you now." Cora held them up. "It's going to be a little tough for you in the back row. Perhaps the camera can zoom in. Just watch the monitors."

On the TV monitors, Cora's finger pointed to a photo. "See, here's what caught his eye. Here's the motel sign." She flipped to the next photo. "Here's the motel room door. With the number on it. That's the number of

Benny Southstreet's unit. That's the same number Paul Fishman saw on TV."

Cora shuffled through the photos, held another up to the camera. "Here's a picture taken inside the room. It's not of a dead body. It's a bunch of chairs. The chairs belong to Harvey Beerbaum. Benny Southstreet stole them, in the hope of selling them to Mr. Wilbur, of Wilbur's Antiques. If you follow all of that, fine. If you don't, it's kind of incidental."

Cora grimaced. "That's the problem with this crime. Everything is kind of incidental. Anyway, these are the pictures. Here's another angle, and — Oh!"

A shot of Sherry Carter in a string bikini filled the screen.

"I'm sorry. That's not a crime scene. Though a figure like that ought to be a crime. That's my niece, Sherry. It's a picture I snapped of her sunbathing when she wasn't looking."

Sherry leaped to her feet, cried, "Aunt Cora!"

"You see my niece's distress. Clearly that's a picture she never expected to see on TV. Or in the town hall in front of a couple of hundred people. But I think we can agree it's a photo that immediately grabs your attention."

Cora turned, pointed her finger. "And yet Paul Fishman didn't see it. Isn't that amazing? This picture was on the roll he gave to the police. Paul developed the film, Paul printed the negatives, Paul put the photos in the envelope, and he didn't see the shot of my nearly nude niece." Cora smiled. "Nice alliteration. Why didn't he see that photo? Is he blind? Is he gay? Not at all. He's seen my niece before, even mentioned to me how attractive she is. Which means he's young, insensitive, and tactless, but not blind. And he's sure as hell the type of guy who'd notice a photo like that. And he didn't, because I asked him about it when he gave me the photos. So, my question, Mr. Fishman, is, *how'd you miss a shot like this?*"

"Are you serious?"

"Absolutely. It's been bothering me. It's one of the things I'd like to know."

"These are pictures of a murder scene. Why would I notice anything else?"

"Yeah, but when you developed the film, there hadn't been a murder."

"I wasn't paying particular attention."

"Yeah, but you saw the motel."

Paul frowned, said nothing.

"Well, you think about it, I'll give you another chance."

To Sherry's great relief, Cora put the photos away. Cora watched as Sherry sat down again. Aaron put his arm around her protectively.

Across the aisle, Dennis and Brenda were engaged in a rather animated whispered discussion.

Cora smiled, gestured to Barney Nathan. "Okay, Doc, your turn. Here's your chance to bawl me out. I understand you're upset about something?"

"That's putting it mildly." Barney Nathan stood up, adjusted his scarlet bow tie, and sniffed disdainfully. "You said on TV I botched the autopsy. That's slander. We're on TV now, and I'd like you to take it back."

"I said there were two shots, and there were two shots."

"There was *one.*"

"I'm glad to hear it. Did you confirm that by reexamining the body after I made that statement on TV?"

"Yes, I did. And it was absolutely false. There was only one bullet."

"Uh-huh. And did you discover anything *else* that you hadn't in your original autopsy?"

Henry Firth was on his feet. "I'm not going to let the doctor answer that! You said there were two shots. There *weren't* two shots. That's all that's important here. Anything else the doctor can testify to in court."

"You're not going to let him tell us what he found?"

"No, I'm not."

"Well, it doesn't matter. I'll get at it another way." Cora reached in her purse, pulled out a plastic evidence bag. "Mimi, here's a question you can answer from right where you are." She held up the bag. "Is this your ice pick?"

Mimi's mouth fell open. "Oh! You found it. Where did you find it?"

"Where did I find it, Mr. Fishman?" Cora asked cheerfully.

Paul Fishman's eyes were wide. "I don't know what you're talking about."

"Yes you do. I told you I'd ask you one more question. This is it. Answer it, and you can go." Cora's eyes burned into him. "Where did I get this ice pick?"

Paul Fishman turned, bolted up the aisle.

63

"Suppose your marriage went sour." Cora put up her hand. "No, not yours, kids. Yours is the perfect union, and if you don't get married straightaway I'm going to line you up and shoot you. Aaron, I'm only giving you this exclusive on the condition that you stop arguing with Sherry at once and get married immediately."

"What do you mean, exclusive?" Aaron said. "Chief Harper knows."

"Wrong answer!" Sherry cried in exasperation. "The right answer is, I don't need inducements, I'm marrying for love."

"Exactly," Aaron said. "Couldn't have put it better. Now, what is it that the police aren't talking about?"

"They're not talking about a thing, because they don't know anything, and they won't until the boys start ratting each other out. But I'll tell you what happened and you can quote me on it, and then if I'm wrong they can sue me for slander. At least they won't sue me for plagiarism."

Cora settled back in her chair, lit a cigarette. Sherry didn't even bother with a token protest.

"We start with the marriage going bad. Mimi and Chuck's marriage. I should have had a huge hint to begin with when she asked me for that puzzle. When a wife needs a crossword puzzle to tell her husband she wrecked the car, this is not a marriage made in heaven. You gotta believe things were on the skids way before she drove into that pole.

"So what's the problem? Well, they're newlyweds, her husband's a young lawyer, he's not making too much money, they recently got married and had a kid, or vice versa, and moved to town. What happens but Chuck falls in with Paul Fishman, a rather unscrupulous young man with access to people's photos. Paul comes across vacation photos every now and then where the husbands don't match up with the wives. It's easy to run a simple con game. Chuck approaches the victim with photos a client has given him that he'd very much like to suppress. He's so apologetic, sweet, and sincere, the victims are actually grateful to him."

"How do you know that?" Aaron asked.

"I don't, but it's a good guess. And it accounts for the money."

"What money?"

"The hundred-dollar bills under the blotter. The way I see it, that loot is what got Benny Southstreet killed."

Aaron frowned. "You wanna back that up a little?"

"Sure. When Benny Southstreet breaks into the study looking to nail me for plagiarism, Chuck Dillinger has a small fortune in hundred-dollar bills under his blotter. Which, of course, is blackmail money he was hiding from his wife."

"And Benny Southstreet stole this money?"

"If only he had."

"What do you mean by that?"

"If he stole it, they'd have made him give it back, and none of this would have happened. But Benny didn't steal the money. He stole Harvey Beerbaum's chairs."

"Cora."

"I'm sorry, but that's what happened. Benny ripped off Harvey Beerbaum's chairs, he left a message for Wilbur saying he had 'em, and he's waiting for him in the motel. Who shows up instead but Paul Fishman, who wants his money back. Benny claims he doesn't have it, and Paul takes him for a ride. They go to Paul's place, where Benny is given another opportunity to recall where the money is. Benny can't, so Paul brings Chuck into the picture.

"Chuck is horrified at the turn things have taken. Blackmail is one thing. Kidnapping is another. And it's clear Fishman is intending murder."

"Why?"

Cora smiled. "If Benny says, 'Here's your money, sorry I ripped you off,' he's a thief, and he isn't going to talk. If he says he didn't do it, he's an innocent man. He'll go straight to the cops.

"So they have to kill him. If they're going to do that, they need a fall guy. Luckily, they have one. Mr. Wilbur has an appointment at two o'clock to buy his chairs. Easy enough to frame him. Paul and Chuck leave the motel room door open. They leave the gun in plain sight. Wilbur shows up, knocks on the door, gets no answer. Tries the knob and goes in.

"The first thing he sees is the chairs. The next thing he sees is the gun. He picks it up, checks out the unit. Finds it unoccupied. He leaves the gun, takes the chairs.

"They bring Benny Southstreet back, stick him in the bathtub, shoot him in the head with the gun Wilbur touched."

Aaron put up his hands. "Wait a minute. That didn't happen."

"Right. Because Wilbur didn't go in. If he had, he wouldn't have taken the chairs, because they were Harvey's, and not what he wanted at all. But he didn't go in. I did. I was the one who touched the gun, took the chairs, and got framed."

"But the gun hadn't been fired."

"That's right. It hadn't."

"How can that be?"

"Perfectly simple. When I went in that motel room, Fishman was outside in his car, waiting for someone to go in and leave fingerprints on the gun."

"What time was that?"

"Around three."

"Then Barney Nathan blew the time of death."

"Not at all. That's where the ice pick comes in."

Aaron's eyes widened. "You mean . . . ?"

"Benny Southstreet was killed by an ice pick shoved through the back of his neck into his brain. Right about the time the doc says he was. Only not in the motel. Benny was lying dead in the trunk of Paul Fishman's car while I was in his motel room playing with his gun. After I left, Fishman stuck him in the bathtub and shot him in the head. Which is why the body didn't bleed much. The guy was already dead.

"Anyway, the gun with my fingerprints was fired into the back of his head in just the same spot as the ice pick. That's why I made a fuss about two bullets. I was hoping Barney Nathan would make a pass at the bullet and discover the other wound."

"But he didn't?"

"No, he didn't. But Paul Fishman didn't know that. When I asked Barney if he found anything else besides the bullet wound, he acted uncomfortable and the prosecutor wouldn't let the doc answer. That was because Barney had found drugs in the body, and Ratface didn't want him to talk about it. But Paul was sure we'd discovered the other wound. That's why he freaked out when I produced the ice pick."

"Where did you find it?"

"Are you kidding? I *bought* it. I was waving it around in a plastic bag. You think Paul Fishman's gonna look close and say, 'Hey, that's not mine'?"

"He thought you found it in the motel trash?"

Cora shrugged. "I doubt if he threw it there. I have no idea what he did with it. But just the fact I was searching the trash was enough to make him think I was looking for it."

"So that was all a bluff?"

"Big-time. I was holding a pair of deuces."

Aaron scribbled furiously on his pad. "Okay, I'm with you so far. But how'd you figure all this out?"

Cora gestured to her niece. "It helped enormously when Sherry solved the mystery of the chairs. Veronica Austin was Wilbur's childhood sweetheart. He had a tremendous crush on her. Being socially gauche, he gave her chairs."

"That's a kind of strange present," Aaron said.

"Wilbur? Strange? Surely you jest. Anyway, in spite of this awesome love token, she went off and married someone else. And proceeded to drop clean off the face of the earth. At least as far as Wilbur was concerned. Until a couple of years ago, when he had an epiphany."

"How come?"

"He saw the chairs in an auction catalogue. So he bought them, hoping they were hers. Only they weren't, they were her ex-husband's. Who got four of the chairs when they divorced. And the gentleman in question was no help in finding her. The chairs were being auctioned off as part of his estate."

"He died?"

"Yeah. Like an A. A. Fair title: *Dead Men Can't Sell Chairs.* Anyway, Wilbur tried to find her, but he had no luck. So he hid the chairs, and reported them stolen. Hoping the police would look for his, and find hers."

"That's a stupid idea."

"What's your point?"

"Why in the world would someone do that?"

"Men are not entirely rational where women are involved."

"No kidding," Sherry said.

"Guys'll do anything not to let on they care. Remember that *West Wing* episode where Josh has the hots for Mary-Louise Parker, so he's trying to invent some business excuse to call her? I think he finally came up with the funding for some project she was advocating that was going to be half a million short."

"That's really stupid."

"I rest my case. Anyway, Wilbur couldn't find Veronica by himself, but he had infinite faith in the police. If only they'd get off their duffs and do something. Which he wasn't shy about pointing out.

"And it finally worked. I don't know if that makes it any less stupid. Ironically, it took me finding the chairs that weren't really stolen to do it. I put Little Miss Internet on the case, and she was able to do what Wilbur couldn't."

"How *did* you do it?" Aaron asked Sherry.

"I made a few phone calls. Not to pooh-pooh my own abilities, but I probably got further sounding like a girl than a dirty old man. People were glad to help me."

"Sherry, sweetheart. Best not to reveal all your feminine wiles until after the wedding." Cora smiled. "Anyhow, getting all that out of the way helped. Once you realize Mr. Wilbur's a big red herring, the rest falls into place."

"I don't see how. You didn't have much to go on."

"Oh, I had a lot of clues. Mimi Dillinger told me about the missing ice pick. That started me thinking in the right direction. Mimi didn't report it at the time of the theft. She didn't even notice it was missing until after the murder. The ice pick was missing because Chuck brought it for Paul to use. Paul didn't have one — what guy who lives alone in a one-room apartment has an ice pick? He couldn't go out and buy one, because you don't want to be seen purchasing the murder weapon on the day of the crime. So he asked Chuck to bring him one. Chuck may not have known what Paul had in mind, but he sure as hell's an accomplice."

"That stuff you asked Paul to begin with — about seeing the motel on TV and bringing the police your photographs — that was just to lull him into a false sense of security?"

"No. That was to put him on edge. It scared the hell out of him when I walked into the Photomat with that roll of film. He's got Benny Southstreet bound and gagged in his apartment. I've got pictures of the scene of the crime. The film really shook him up. Which is why he made his big mistake."

"What big mistake?"

"Not barking in the nighttime."

"What?"

"I was looking for that type of Sherlock Holmes clue. Something that should be there, but wasn't. And there it was, right in front of my face." Cora gestured to her niece. "Sherry's bikini shot. The guy didn't even see it. *This* guy missed *that?* I don't think so. Not unless he was really stressed."

"When did she take that picture?" Aaron asked Sherry.

"Salesman's convention, Aaron," Sherry said sarcastically. "I was parading around in my bathing suit."

"Anyway, after I blunder into the frame-up, Paul can't believe he's lucky enough to have those photos. He wants to get 'em in the hands of the cops. He's watching the motel. As soon as the body is discovered, he phones in a tip to Channel 8."

Aaron snapped his fingers. "So Rick Reed will show up so Fishman can claim he saw the motel on TV."

"Exactly. As soon as they start broadcasting he drives up and turns over the photos. So the cops will get a line on me right away. And be sure to match my fingerprints with the gun."

"I'll be damned."

"Bad luck for Paul Fishman, I'm no patsy. Next thing he knows, I come walking into his Photomat demanding my pictures. He is not pleased to see me. He's just framed me for murder, and here I am asking him for the evidence. So, while I was there, he stole my gun."

"What!" Aaron exclaimed.

"Clearly he is not a nice man."

"How did he steal your gun? How did he even know you *had* a gun?"

"I may have flashed it just for the effect. . . ."

"Cora."

"Well, he gave my pictures to the cops. Anyway, he slipped the gun out of my purse while I was picking up my film receipt he conveniently knocked on the floor. I'm sure he didn't know what he was going to use it for at the time. But he wasn't happy at the way things were working out. He thinks he's framed me big-time for Benny Southstreet's murder, and I'm out walking around like nothing happened. So he tried to gild the lily with my gun."

"By shooting you with it?"

"By *missing* me with it. By making me *think* someone tried to shoot me with it, so that's what I'll claim. He probably intended to just throw the gun on the floor, but when I fell down and knocked myself out, he took the opportunity to plant it in my purse. Which was a risky thing to do. He's lucky Wilbur didn't catch him."

"How'd he know you'd be searching Wilbur's barn?"

"He sent me there. With the crossword puzzle about antiques. He's been waiting for me to show up. When I pull into the mall, he grabs a duplicate set of photos and follows me to see where I park. While I'm in Starbucks, he slaps the crossword puzzle on my windshield, then waits in the distance until he sees me come out. Then he walks across the parking lot from the direction of his booth."

"Where'd he get the puzzle?"

"Same place he got the one he planted by the body. From Benny Southstreet's briefcase. He went through it looking for the money Benny didn't steal. When he decided to frame me, he kept a few puzzles that might come in handy."

"Can you prove all this?"

"Practically none of it. I'm hoping Chuck Dillinger rolls over on him. Be a good move. Guy's got a wife and kid, not to mention a law degree. I'm sure the killing wasn't his idea. Even if he did supply the ice pick."

"Oh. Right. That was his."

"Paul didn't have to tell him what it was for. Chuck's not the moving factor. I bet a good attorney could cut a deal."

"Is Chuck representing himself?"

"Chuck's not a good attorney. Even if he was, you know the old saying: A lawyer who represents himself has a fool for a client. I steered Becky Baldwin in his direction."

"You didn't."

"She needs the work. And I gotta be a huge disappointment, not getting tried for murder, and all. Besides, it's a good time for her to keep busy."

"What do you mean?"

"Take her mind off the fact she's not getting married."

Aaron's laugh was forced.

"What about the money?" Sherry asked, changing the subject.

"Remember what I said in the beginning? About a marriage that went sour?"

"You mean . . . ?"

"Mimi stole the money. After the office was broken into. She took it to see what her husband would say. And it's the worst-case scenario. Because her husband says nothing. Absolutely nothing. The cops ask him what was taken, he tells them not a thing.

"That's bad enough, but it gets worse. I find the torn corner of a hundred-dollar bill under the blotter. Sam Brogan asks her husband about it, and Chuck claims he kept a few hundreds under the blotter for emergencies, and it must be from one of them. I mention this to Mimi, and it confirms her worst fears. Chuck said there were *two* bills? And they were *real*? And he *spent* them?

"Mimi's trying to work up the nerve to confront her husband when the roof falls in. Benny Southstreet's murdered. And the puzzle she gave her husband is tied in to the motive. And Benny's the odds-on favorite for the prowler who broke into her house.

"Mimi can't believe her husband's involved in Benny's murder, but she doesn't know what to think. When she finds her ice pick is missing, she's really confused. Why would anyone steal an ice pick?

"Mimi's freaking out. She's sitting on five grand of illicit money that her husband won't even acknowledge, but thinks the dead man stole. She tried to tell me about it, got cold feet. So I ran a bluff on her, and she caved right in. Once she confessed to taking the money, things fell into place."

"How'd you get a line on Paul Fishman?"

"I have Chief Harper to thank. The chief traced the phone call Chuck Dillinger made from the service station pay phone to Fishman's apartment."

"How did you know about that?"

"Dennis, playing detective. He followed Chuck to the gas station, told me about the call. Actually, the jerk wanted to tell Sherry, but I headed him off at the pass."

"You didn't mention that," Sherry said.

"It was on a need-to-know basis. Anyway, it was fine work on his part, and I made sure Chief Harper knew Dennis deserved the credit." Cora shrugged her shoulders. "Of course, that meant letting the chief know Dennis was violating his restraining order, but what can I say? It was a moral dilemma."

"Cora! You're a wicked woman."

"I prefer to think of myself as a wedding planner. Look how things worked out: I got that handsome Photomat guy arrested for homicide. That takes him out of the picture. I got Becky Baldwin busy defending his accomplice. And I got Dennis legally restrained. So you two can go ahead and get married."

"Sounds like the perfect wedding," Aaron observed.

"Trust me." Cora smiled. "It always is."

ABOUT THE AUTHOR

Nominated for the prestigious Edgar, Shamus, and Lefty awards, **Parnell Hall** is the author of seven previous Puzzle Lady mysteries. He lives in New York City, where he is at work on his next Puzzle Lady mystery.